A Handy Duo

Also by Sarah Madeline

A Fowl Match
A Merry Pair

A Handy Duo

SARAH MADELINE

For those who feel anxious in a crowded room. I hope you find a nice quiet place and a good book to keep you company.

Thornwood Valley

Valley Pond
Chicken Coop
nie's Diner
The String Cheese
Chloe's Closet
Roosters
The Cozy Cabin Inn
nie's Diner
The String Cheese
Chloe's Closet
Rooster's
The Cozy Cabin Inn
OPEN
Fix-Its
Dan's Auto
Stop and Fill
Suds in the Bucket
The Rhett Family Farm

Author's Note

While this book is mostly sweet and full of laughter, there are mentions of the following: grief, loss of parent, and divorce. Please continue reading with these in mind. If you have any questions, my email inbox is always open.

Chapter 1

MARIGOLD

My car just shut off in the middle of the road.

Please... no.

Hopeful thoughts do nothing to help my less-than-ideal reality, so I coast to the shoulder and shift into park. I stare out the windshield, racking my brain for a reason as to why it would die on me.

I filled up at a gas station twenty miles ago. Therefore, I'm positive whatever's going on has nothing to do with a lack of fuel.

My gaze wanders to the dashboard. It's void of color and warnings. I was expecting an array of red and yellow symbols signaling *disaster*. This somehow seems worse. Nothing happens when I click the hazard button, nor does the engine roar to life when I turn over the key.

There is only one logical explanation for my car's sudden meltdown: it has had enough of the summer heat.

I, for one, thought the hot breeze felt great against my sun-tanned skin while I was going forty miles an hour. I popped a cassette into the slot below the radio and sang along as "Margaritaville" by Jimmy Buffet played through the speakers. My hair blew out the window, and I tipped my sunglasses over my eyes, basking in the beautiful summer day.

That was *before* my car died.

I grab an envelope, which is actually a long-forgotten bill, from the sun visor to fan myself. I roll the window down the rest of the way with a cranking motion and reach over the center console to wind down the passenger window.

I don't want my passenger princess, Buttercup, to get overheated. She gives me a sweet, wet-snout smile from her spot in a polka-dot bed. I pet her head and tell her, "It won't be long. You're almost at your new home." She snorts in acknowledgement or approval. I'm not sure which one it is. I'm new to being a pig mom.

I put the bill in my mouth while twisting my hair into a braid, and I grab a pink scrunchie from the gear shifter to keep it in place. I continue fanning myself with the bill, trying to cool off.

I'm not ready to face my I-have-to-walk-because-my-car-is-dead fate yet. I should, though.

I look to the back seat. The giant cake and a bag filled with decorations I picked up for Dad's birthday are still safely tucked underneath the seat belts. Both are the reasons for my midday trip out of town. Also, there may or may not be a bag filled with a dozen packages of sour gummy worms on the floor behind my seat. I could have worse addictions, and Valley Harvest never has them in stock.

Everything is in order except for my car.

Plus, there was the whole Buttercup side quest I took. I saw a sign that said "Pigs for Sale" and an arrow pointing to a quaint one-story home. I couldn't stop myself from making an impulse decision. A woman with red glasses and a warm smile greeted me at the front door. A dozen piglets ran between her legs to jump on me. The price was irrelevant. I was sold the second their adorable little faces looked at me. Each pig had unique patterning with a palette of colors: white, brown, white with black spots, brown with black spots, etc.

The woman and I swapped pleasantries, and I learned her name was Penny. I pointed to the pig that stole my heart when she asked which one I was interested in taking home. Penny's voice was grainy when she said, "That one's Buttercup."

Buttercup was clearly the runt, but she was the one with the most energy. She ran circles around me and brushed her pink snout against my hand, begging for me to pet her. So what if I'm out a couple hundred dollars that I had to leave and withdraw from the bank? Then there was possibly another hundred that I bought her bed, toys, leash, and other things with. That money may have helped fix my car, but it's okay. Buttercup is irreplaceable!

I turn over the key in the ignition, giving it one more shot. Nothing happens, which is very on-theme for me. The familiar rumble of the engine is a fragment of my over-heated imagination.

I open the door and swing my Converse-clad feet onto gravel. Stretching my arms, I examine my surroundings. No one seems to be around. The one-lane road is deserted. My eyes track the shimmer of a heat haze hovering over the gravel up ahead.

To be fair, there are many trees to keep Buttercup and I company. There is also a single hawk, gliding effortlessly through the cloudy sky in the distance. It must be a sign that could mean one of two things. One: I'm currently on the right path. I can overcome any roadblocks in my way. Two: It's a bad omen. The hawk is going to attack me and pluck me right off the ground. I like the idea of the former. It's reassuring and less far-fetched.

I fiddle with my necklace while lost in my thoughts. I shouldn't be surprised that there's nothing but nature surrounding me. I know this road like the back of my hand. Thornwood Valley has been my home for my entire life, and there's only one way to and from town: Maple Ridge Road.

I'm not going to make it out of here any time soon by staring at a hawk that looks completely unbothered.

I put a harness and leash on Buttercup and set her on the road in the shade from my car. The trunk of my car creaks in protest as I open it to retrieve a rag and an adjustable wrench. Buttercup follows me as I walk around to the front of the car. When I find the release latch, the front hood pops open with a swoosh, and I secure it with the metal hood prop. I pull the dipstick, wipe it clean with the rag, and re-insert it to get an accurate read on the oil level.

Why not?

The oil is a little low but nothing concerning. I look at all the other fluids: coolant, power steering, and transmission. They're full. I peek at the belts; they look like they're on as well. I check the battery connections with the wrench. They're tight and clean. Besides, I cleaned them a month ago. I'm normally pretty good at troubleshooting. Apparently, whatever is going on is way out of my wheelhouse and into expert, mechanic-level territory.

I close the hood, put the tools away, and pick up Buttercup so that her feet don't get too hot. I stand on my tiptoes, reaching as tall as I can with my phone to check for a bar.

Please have service.

There's none. Not even a half-bar or a glimmer of hope is found.

"Oh well," I mumble to Buttercup. "According to the hawk, we're on the right path."

Unfortunately, walking is looking like my best chance at finding a signal. By some miracle, perhaps a good Samaritan will stop and give us a ride instead. Either needs to happen soon before the icing on the cake melts. Otherwise, the trip out of town and my grand surprise will be all for nothing. Well, at least I got Buttercup, some decorations, and gummy worms out of my road trip.

I'm a forty-five-minute drive from town. Once I get there, I have to drop off the cake and decorations at Annie's Diner. Then I'll go back to Fix-Its Hardware—my home away from home—to make sure Dad doesn't suspect his surprise party. I have a total of four hours to do all of that.

Impossible.

I can almost hear Mom's voice next to me. *Life's all about adventures, Marigold. You must take the brush and paint your own way. No one else can place the strokes on your canvas. Only you have the power to do so. There'll always be good and bad days. Many times, there'll be hiccups along the way. If you learn to embrace each one, then you'll truly understand how to create a masterpiece.*

"You were right," I whisper as I look at the field beside the road. "Today's only a hiccup." I know my mom's not there, but I can almost feel her presence with me.

I continue to walk, carrying Buttercup. With every step I take, the gravel crunches. A little dust fills the air too. An earthy scent prickles my nose as I take in a deep breath. The long stretches of road in front of me are daunting, but I keep my chin tilted upward and a smile on my face.

After a little while, I check my phone, holding it as high as I can to find service. One bar appears on my screen. I don't waste any time dialing the auto shop.

"Dan's Auto." I recognize Charlotte's (Char's) chipper voice right away as it plays through the speaker of my phone.

"Hey, Char. It's Marigold. I'm stuck on Maple Ridge Road right before the sharp bend. About forty-five minutes out. Could I get a tow? My car broke down. I'm so sorry if I'm inconveniencing you. I tried to see if I could fix it, but I don't know what's going on," I say quickly.

The shop is busy right now with the summer influx of customers. I don't want to make them go out of their way. The thought makes my stomach churn.

The clicks from her keyboard play through the speaker. "You're not an inconvenience. Dan and Mateo are working on some cars. One of them will be out to tow you right away. Which sharp bend? The one after the giant magnolia tree? Or is it the one before the abandoned cabin? There's also the bend by The Rhett Farm. Am I missing any? Hmm..."

"I can see the magnolia tree ahead. I walked pretty far from my car, though."

"I'll tell them now. Try to stay out of the heat and in some shade, will you?"

I nod, although I feel silly as I realize she can't see me. "I'll try. Thanks, Char."

"You got it! I'm gonna talk to the guys right now. Don't go anywhere. I'll be back in a jiffy. If I lose you, one of them will be out to get you regardless. I'll pick you up myself if needed. We gotta get you to that surprise party."

"Thank you." My heart warms in my chest because I know the lengths the people in our little town will go to for one another. This is nothing short of that miracle I was hoping for a few minutes ago.

The squeaking noise from the wheels of her chair rolling along the floor and country tunes play through the speaker of my phone as I wait.

After a minute Char says, "Marigold? Do I still have you?"

"Yes, I'm here."

"Dan just pulled out. He's on his way. Hang tight. He'll be there in no time." Her voice is calm and reassuring.

Thank goodness.

I don't want to pile more work on their shoulders during the busiest time of the year, but it wouldn't be very nice having to walk all the way into town or miss the surprise party that I had planned.

"Thank you. I appreciate it."

"That's what we're here for. I'll see you tonight at the party." She hangs up.

My arm strains as I hold my phone mid-air on my tip toes, trying to keep the one bar I found. I call my best friend, Daisy. She answers on the first ring. "Did you get the cake?"

"Yeah, I did," I say. "I also got a piglet."

"No way! Oh my God! I'm so excited! I'm going to spoil my new best friend! Did you name the piglet yet? Because if not, I would love to help you come up with one. I mean, Daisy Jr. has a nice ring to it."

I laugh. "Her previous owner, Penny, named her Buttercup, and I think it suits her. Did I mention she's currently shaking with excitement to meet you?"

"Ahh! I love it! How do you expect me to work after that news? There's no way I'm going to be thinking about anything but squeezing Buttercup in a giant hug." The phone quiets briefly. "Wait a minute. Did something go wrong? You sound... I don't know... different. Are you upset? Did you get the decorations?"

My best friend knows me too well. I don't have to say anything, and she can tell something is wrong.

"The decorations are secured." I can acknowledge that I got it accomplished without any hiccups.

"So, what wasn't—" Daisy's boss cuts her off, mumbling something I can't decipher. She yells, "Joe! I'll be out in a moment! I'm on the phone with Marigold! Give me five, no, make it seven! I'm still on my twenty-minute break! They can wait a little bit for their pizza!" She sighs dramatically. "I'm about to quit again. Joe is getting on my last nerve. Anyway, so what wasn't secured?"

"Umm. My car," I say, toneless.

She stammers, "What? Are you okay? Is your car okay? Is Buttercup okay?"

I nod my head as if to answer, *yes*, like she can see me.

Newsflash, Marigold: she can't!

I lighten my voice. "I'm great... We're great. I'm waiting for Dan to tow me back into town. He left a few minutes ago. My car's okay. Well, I think it is. It shut off randomly in the middle of the road, and I tried everything under the sun to fix it."

"Your poor go-kart." Her tone lilts in a teasing manner. "I've been waiting for this call. The day the ol' mobile took a crap has arrived. It's long overdue. Though, it's a bummer you're stuck so far out, girly."

I sigh melodramatically. *This again.* "I know you think that it's a *glorified go-kart*! I intend on getting it fixed. It's not retired yet."

"*Glorified* is what *you'd* call it. *I'd* call it a beater."

I dismiss her jokingly. "Whatever."

"Whatever!" She mocks me.

We burst into laughter for a minute or so. After a few beats of silence that have me almost wondering if the call dropped, I hear the clatter of what I assume is dishes in the background. "Can you keep an eye on Fix-Its and make sure my dad doesn't try to sneak out to go to Annie's? I don't want him to find out about his party. With my luck, he'd show up and ruin his own surprise. That would really take the fun out of the whole 'surprise' concept. You know what I mean?"

"I have it handled. I'll race out and distract him if I need to. It'll give me the perfect excuse to quit," Daisy says, a little too eagerly.

"Please don't quit because of me. You've been there for what, a week this time?"

"You'll be doing me a favor."

This is exactly why my dad won't let me hire her at the hardware store. I've begged him countless times. His answer is always a firm *no.*

I don't blame Daisy one bit. It can get boring doing the same monotonous thing every day. She likes adventure, while Thornwood Valley sticks to its quirky traditions and old-fashioned ways. As of late, the town has started to warm up to the idea of change; I'm glad because I have a few ideas of my own.

"Daisy! A party of eight just walked in. Could you seat them? I gotta pull these pizzas out," Joe calls out.

"I'm coming!" Daisy yells in reply to Joe. "Ughhhh," she grumbles, drawing out the word. "I gotta go. I'll keep an eye on Harvey. I won't let him leave. And give Buttercup all the snuggles and kisses for me. See you later, Marigoldie."

"Goodbye, Daisy Dollop," I say before hanging up.

I lower my arm and sink back on the heels of my feet. My Converse now have an indent line from the previous position.

I'm craving a sip of cool water. I should've asked Char to send some for Buttercup and me with Dan. Pennsylvania (PA) July heat is unforgiving. The sun scorches against my arms as beads of sweat trickle down my back.

It takes me half an hour to make it back to my car. When I reach it, I open the back door to check on the cake. It won't be long before the icing melts.

I sit in the front seat of my car, leaning back in the shade while Buttercup nuzzles on my lap. Eventually, my eyes flutter shut, listening to the sound of chirping birds.

I daydream about my big plans for Fix-Its. If only my dad would let me have a chance to do something on my own, it would have so much potential. I know it was his and Mom's place. That's why he hasn't wanted to change a thing. However, it desperately needs some upgrades. The building needs a fresh coat of paint. The shelves of products need some type of organization to benefit the customer experience. It would mean the world to me to keep Fix-Its going for years to come. I need to find the courage to speak up about these things, but I haven't yet. My head slowly bobs as I drift asleep, thinking about the long list of ideas.

Chapter 2

DAN

I turn the dial as the song "Fast Car," covered by Luke Combs, comes on the radio. I tilt my rearview mirror, and a dust cloud follows my path. In no time, I'll reach Marigold Evan's sedan. It's the only car I've had to tow today—so far at least. I grip the steering wheel with one hand while resting the other on the gear shifter. As I reach a sharp bend, I slow down, spinning my hands around the wheel to follow the curve of the road.

I keep an eye out for Marigold, remembering Char mentioned that she might be walking. There's no sign of her as I pass the magnolia tree. Its petals surround the trunk in a blanket of pink.

Marigold's Dodge Neon comes into view, parked on the left side of the road exactly where Char said it would be.

I line up my truck to the front of her car and push the clutch to engage the PTO. The door creaks as I step out and adjust the levers on the bed to tilt it toward the front bumper of her car. I grab the winch and pull it to the end of the bed. I do a double take as I look through the windshield to see Marigold's head tipped back against the head rest.

My heart thumps loudly in my chest as I run toward the driver's side to check if she's alright. As I get closer, I hear soft snoring, and I see with my own two eyes that her chest is rising and falling.

Thank God.

I let out a relieved breath to calm my racing heart.

I unhook the winch and connect it to the car's undercarriage, knocking off a few rust chips in the process. Using the hydraulic lever, I tighten the cable until there's no slack.

All that's left to do is wake Marigold up so we can get out of here.

I stand beside her car, resting one arm against the roof and leaning down toward the window. Marigold's still snoring. It's alarmingly hot today, and I don't like the idea of her sitting in there much longer.

"Marigold?" I knock on the door frame with my free fist, and that's when my eyes lock on a *pig* in the passenger seat.

Where the hell did this pig come from?

I didn't know Marigold had a pet pig. I could've missed it before, but I doubt that's something I'd forget.

The pigs' eyes snap open and lock with mine.

Umm... What should I do?

I give the piglet a shaky smile to show it that I'm friendly.

"Be a good pig. Stay there... I come in peace," I say as I hold up my hands slowly. It's as if I gave the pig a target to zero in on.

It scurries over Marigold's lap and lets out a little squealing noise that almost resembles a battle cry. It launches itself through the open window, aiming straight for my face.

Holy shit!

I wrap my arms around the pig in an attempt to catch it because, well, I don't want Marigold's pig to fall or possibly get hurt.

Since when did pigs jump so high? Apparently, I know less than I thought I did about them. That much is evident. The saying *when pigs fly* might need to be changed. It's an accurate representation and shouldn't be an idiom.

I stumble backward as the pig pulls its tongue out of its mouth and licks my face in greeting.

Nope. No, thank you.

I never considered myself a pig person. I like pigs... I guess? I've been around them from a distance. This pig seems kind of likeable—if that's the word for it. However, I would've been more content without the slobbery-face kisses. Now, those beady eyes are staring straight into my soul.

I hold the pig away from my face, and it squirms excitedly as if it wants to continue savoring me.

I scrunch my eyebrows.

No, buddy. You are not allowed anywhere near my face again. Thanks.

I knock on the door frame again while holding the face-attacker at a distance.

"Marigold," I say a bit louder. I'm hoping she'll wake up so that we can get this show on the road but mostly so she can take her pig back.

How is she still asleep?

It doesn't take much for me to wake up in the middle of the night, but I'm more of a light sleeper. I've woken for a multitude of reasons: the clunk of the ice dropping in my freezer, a loud thunderstorm, or coyotes howling. Marigold doesn't have this problem; she's the complete opposite. She could sleep through anything: a truck pulling up to her car, a fist knocking, a pig squealing, and, apparently, someone calling her name.

I knock once more, even louder this time, and she mutters, "The—fishing lures—are—pigs."

Umm... Okay?

She might be having some type of work-related dream. Maybe it's a pig-related nightmare? It could be a combination of the two. It sounds... traumatizing.

Marigold continues saying more unintelligible things in a hushed voice.

I'm not sure if I should keep knocking or stand here and wait until she wakes up. I thought it wasn't good to wake someone who is sleepwalking. Does the same apply if she's sleep talking?

I'm starting to get concerned. However, after a few more knocks, I successfully wake Marigold. She stretches her arms, nearly missing the steering wheel as a pair of heart-shaped sunglasses slide down her nose. She adjusts them and turns toward me. A pink hue washes over her face, almost identical to the color of her overalls. "Sorry... Hey, Dan," she says through a yawn.

"Hey, Marigold."

"I'm sorry I fell asleep. Thanks for coming to get me. I see you've met Buttercup." She yawns again, covering her mouth with her palm.

Buttercup. So, that's the pig's name.

"Buttercup, this is Dan." Marigold gestures a hand to the pig and then motions to me. I look down at the pig. It wiggles in my arms with excitement, probably trying to inch closer to lick my face again.

No thanks, Buttercup. I shake my head. I've learned not to engage with the pig, so I keep my thoughts to myself this time.

I bob my head in greeting at the pig. Marigold laughs. She looks incredibly happy in lieu of her car breaking down. I admire her optimism. I've encountered my fair share of frustrated people while out on a tow. Marigold is a ray of sunshine, though.

"I'm glad that you two are acquainted." Her lips curve into a smile.

"Me too." What I don't mention is that Buttercup and I had a very rocky first impression; Marigold doesn't need to know that.

This is surely the longest I've ever spoken to Marigold about anything other than weather, parts, or business. Normally, we share a quick greeting in the morning as I list the parts I need for customers' vehicles. Sometimes, her nose is tipped in a notebook while she scribbles down part numbers that aren't in stock.

I like to think I'm a nice guy. Marigold is kind, at least, that's the impression I've formed from our almost-daily, brief interactions.

My musing is interrupted by a snout nudging my arm. Why am I still holding this pig? I don't know. I scratch my head, wondering how I missed the fact that she had a pet pig in the first place. "How long have you had Buttercup?"

"I just got her today. About twenty miles that way." Marigold points her finger in the direction behind us, smirking. "I can't remember the name of the road. I'm not so great with directions, but I know where I'm going... most of the time. At least this road is long enough for me to remember its name."

I nod and my lips curve into a smile.

The sun beats down on my neck and sweat pools on my forehead. I can only imagine how hot it is in her car.

"You should really get out of that car. It's too hot."

"You're right," she says, opening the door. She stands next to me, motioning for me to hand over the pig. "I'll take her off your hands."

Don't mind if you do.

Marigold takes Buttercup and leans against the side of her car. She wipes a bead of sweat from her forehead.

Dammit. I bet she doesn't have anything to drink. That should've been the first thing I thought of. I quickly grab two bottles of water from the cooler in my flatbed truck and give them to her. "There's one for the pig too," I say.

She raises an eyebrow. "Thank you. She has a name, you know."

"Right. Sorry, Buttercup." I knew that.

Marigold grins and then chugs half the bottle. She reaches into her car to grab a pocketknife from the center console. She cuts around the bottle and offers it to Buttercup. The pig eagerly pushes her snout into the water and drinks.

Marigold laughs. "She's adorable. Don't you think so?" She looks at me for a flash of agreement. Even though the sunglasses partially shade her eyes, I can tell they're willing me to agree with her.

"Yes," I agree. How could I disagree when she looks at me that way?

I shoot her a tiny grin before continuing. "I'm gonna put your car in neutral. Give me anything you want to bring with you now. I'll put them in the cab."

"Do you want to make sure you can't fix it here? I checked the oil, fluids, belts, and battery. I'm not sure what's going on. I really do feel bad for making you come all the way out here. I know you're busy," she says while handing me a paper bag and Buttercup's bed.

"I trust your judgment." It's not a lie. Marigold's extremely knowledgeable when it comes to car parts. "Don't worry about it. This is my job. It's what I'm here for."

I pack the cab full of everything she hands me, tucking the bags behind her seat and the cake between us. After she has everything she needs, I wind up the windows on her car, winch it onto the flatbed, and fasten each tire.

I get into my truck and wipe a bead of sweat from my forehead. "Sorry, there's no air conditioning. Once we get moving, it'll cool down some."

"That's alright," Marigold says as she shifts the giant cake box to her lap and sets Buttercup in between us on her bed. "I'm grateful you picked me up. How much do I owe you? I can write you a check." She opens a tiny bag, pulling out a checkbook and a pen.

"Nothing." I dismiss the thought and turn over the key to start the engine.

I pull off the shoulder and make my way into town, gripping the steering wheel and shifting as I increase speed.

I look over to her, and she shakes her head. "No way. How 'bout something for your time at least?" She clicks her pen a few times.

"Consider it part of our tradeoff. You and Harvey give me deals on parts all the time. I tow you at no charge. That was the agreement."

Harvey and I came to the agreement years ago when I first moved to town and took over the auto shop, car wash, and gas station. Fix-Its gets parts for the shop at a small discount. In return, I tow their cars and fix them at a discounted rate depending on the damage.

"Okay," she says reluctantly. "If you insist."

Buttercup oinks between us as the wind blows against her ears. I laugh out loud.

In a light voice, Marigold asks, "What's so funny?"

"Buttercup," I say as I stare out the window, watching the gravel disappear under the tires. My foot pumps the brake pedal to slow down in preparation for another curve in the road.

"I'm glad you learned her name." She laughs. "Buttercup is adorable. Probably the best thing I've ever spent money on." Marigold pats the pig's head and changes the subject. "Do you have plans tonight?"

Plans? When's the last time I had plans? I mean, Marigold's sedan and I have diagnostic plans tonight. My current obsession, a 1970 Chevy Nova, also has my mind spinning with what I'm going to start on: torching bolts out to remove the rear-end, the axle, and the rear suspension. It's more of a hobby than anything.

"No concrete plans," I say.

"Oh, good. It's my dad's sixty-fifth birthday today. We're having a little get together at Annie's. Umm, that's what the cake's for, obviously." She laughs lightly. "If you'd like to stop by, well, that'd be nice. It's up to you, of course. No pressure. I promise it'll be a small group. Nothing major. Simply cake and dinner." She taps the cake box on her lap.

"I'll try my best to stop by." Why am I saying that I will probably go? Maybe it's the look in her eyes that says she genuinely wants me to be there. It's the neighborly thing to do. I already admitted I had nothing going on. The car can wait one night. Besides, my mind needs a rest.

"You won't regret it. I promise," Marigold chimes.

When we arrive in town, the streets are bustling with chickens, tourists, and townies. The sun shines against the sidewalk, and I flip my visor down to block the bright rays from my vision. People sit on a few benches in front of the storefronts, sipping on lemonade. I know it's what they're guzzling because there is a giant sign that says "Fresh Squeezed Lemonade" mounted on a wooden stand where two kids are pouring giant pitchers of the cool drink. A few kids waiting in line lift their arms in a honking motion as I drive past slowly. I oblige by honking the horn twice. They cheer and jump with excitement. It brings a smile to my face.

I slow down as I get closer to my shop, preparing to turn when I notice a black Escalade speeding on the left side of the road, heading straight for one of the town's beloved chickens.

The scene unravels in slow-motion. My heart races. Marigold gasps. The black car screeches as the driver slams on their brakes. The vehicle weaves along the road, leaving inky skid marks in its path.

"Stop!" Marigold shouts out the window.

The chicken doesn't flinch as the driver stops a mere inch in front of it.

I've never heard Marigold raise her voice in any interaction I've had with her. She opens the door while I'm still going twenty miles an hour.

What the hell is she thinking?

I slam on the clutch and break simultaneously—my poor clutch.

Marigold shoots from her seat and sets the cake box on it. She places Buttercup in my arms and jumps from the cab, leaving me no choice but to stay here with the pig.

Marigold's long braid whips around her back as she races along the road toward the car. She picks up the white chicken and holds it tightly to her chest, whispering words that I cannot hear. She stands in the middle of the road for a moment, smoothing her palm down its feathers.

Marigold walks slowly toward the Escalade, taking her time in the middle of the road. Good thing my truck is blocking the rest of oncoming traffic, or else I wouldn't be comfortable with her being out there by herself.

There's a crowd gathering on the sidewalk, watching with bated breath. A woman in a red T-shirt holds her hand over her chest. As I squint, it becomes clear who she is: Thornwood Valley's gossip mill executive, Constance. Suddenly, the other two members of the gossip mill—Bobbie and Annie—emerge from Annie's Diner. They shield their eyes as they peer at the scene unfolding in front of us. The three of them chatter among themselves. I shake my head, knowing there will soon be an article written about what happened; Marigold will most likely be at the center of it.

My gaze flickers to Marigold as she leans an elbow into the open window of the Escalade. She clutches the chicken to her chest protectively and waves her free arm while having a conversation with the person in the car.

"You're stuck with me," I say to Buttercup. She looks at me like she wants to jump out the window and race after Marigold. "I know. I'm not her." On that note, Buttercup squeals.

The black Escalade starts my way, *slowly* this time. Marigold waves to the driver.

I move Buttercup's bed behind the passenger seat and slide the cake across to the middle. Marigold jumps back into the truck with the chicken tucked under her arm.

"What did you say?" I ask.

"I calmly told him to slow down. He's never been here before, and he had no clue that chickens roam our town. He apologized profusely, and he looked really shaken, poor guy. But he almost killed Blanche. I don't think I'd be so forgiving if that happened. Now, he knows that we are the chicken hub. And I'm sorry for making you slam on the breaks. I wanted to make sure she was okay. You didn't mind, did you?"

With the way Marigold looks at me with regret, eyes wide and head tipped, how could I say otherwise? "No, I didn't mind at all." My truck will be fine. If she doesn't stop staring at me with *that look,* I will feel so guilty for getting upset about it, though.

I set Buttercup on Marigold's lap.

A chicken and a pig are in my truck. Never in a million years would I have guessed that sentence to be true, at least not before I visited our town for the first time.

I pull the tow truck into the open bay in my shop and shut off the engine. It's mostly quiet except for a muffled clanking, probably from Mateo working on a car in the next bay.

"Thank you for picking us up." Marigold bobs her head to the pig and the chicken in her arms. The pair look curious about each other with Blanche swiveling her head and Buttercup pushing her snout in the air.

"All in a day's work." I open my door and make my way around the passenger side to open the door for Marigold.

"Thanks. I'll see you tonight, right?" she asks as I take Buttercup so she can get out of the truck.

Between all the commotion, it completely slipped my mind that I agreed to go to the diner to celebrate Harvey's birthday. There's a piglet staring at me with beady eyes—looking at me like I'm a launch pad—and as Marigold gives me that sweet look again, I'm sure no one could say no to her.

"I'll be there." I succumb.

"Good. There'll be cake, drinks, and a bunch of appetizers. It'll be fun." I can't tell if she says this as a promise or more of a reassurance to herself. "Well, I hope so..." Marigold fiddles with her necklace.

I nod and stuff my hands in my pockets. "I'll stop over at Fix-Its as soon as your car's ready."

"Take your time. I don't have anywhere to be for a while. Let me know if you need to order any parts for it."

"I will. Can I help you carry anything?"

"That would be great—"

"I can help her. I'm headed to Annie's now anyway," Char says as she emerges from the office. "Is that a piglet? What's Blanche doing here?"

Char asks many more questions as they gather Marigold's things. They walk across the road laughing as Marigold fills Char in on all the details of our morning mayhem. The pig walks alongside Marigold, and the chicken follows them. This would be unheard of in any other town but not this one. This is yet another normal day in Thornwood Valley.

Chapter 3

MARIGOLD

"I'm back!" I announce as I swing open the door to Fix-Its. The hardware store smell makes me feel instantly at home. It's a scent that's so uniquely familiar: woody, earthy, fresh, and *comforting*. My nerves settle as I take a deep breath, allowing the tension to dissipate from my shoulders.

"Mary! Is that you?" Dad shouts from behind the shelves.

"It's me!"

"What took you so long? I thought you only had a four-hour round trip. Where were you headed again? My memory isn't what it used to be." He chuckles.

"I had to go to the—"*Ahh! What is believable? Where was I?* "Paint store! I had to get some more paint and brushes, umm, the good ones!"

He's going to be suspicious. I'm blurting. I don't usually blurt things unless, of course, I'm lying or am nervous in general. I might as well have "liar" written on my forehead. At least I'm bending the truth for a good cause: his birthday. Plus, he still can't see me and my horrible acting skills from wherever he is behind the shelves.

"Oh, good. Are you still working on that wildflower piece?" he calls out.

"Yes, I am. I wasn't planning on being gone so long. My car broke down. I had to walk to find service. Then I had to wait until Dan picked me up and towed it back here."

Ugh. He didn't ask for my life story, although he knows it already. I just told him everything I did today minus my gummy worm, cake, pig, and decoration excursion.

"Well, I'll be damned. Why didn't you call, kiddo? I'm no spring chicken, but I would've closed up and got to you as fast as these two legs could carry me to my truck."

"It wasn't necessary. I knew my car wouldn't be an easy fix, so I figured a tow would be best." What he doesn't need to know is that I didn't want him to see the stuff for his birthday in my car.

"Well, okay then. Glad you made it back safe."

"Me too," I say hesitantly.

Is he on to me? It's hard to tell only from hearing his voice.

"Where are the spark plugs? Did you move 'em? They're not where they're supposed to be," Dad says while I hear him moving things around on the shelves.

It would be difficult for someone to locate anything in this place, and that's coming from me, who spends every day here.

"Aha! Got you, buggers!" he yells in triumph. "Chuck came by this morning looking for one for his mower. He'll be by later today and—" He goes speechless when he rounds the shelves and sees me standing there, holding a pig.

"Hi." I laugh.

"Hi, Mary and... who's this little piggy, kiddo?"

"Your first grandchild, Buttercup Evans," I joke.

He sniffles. "I never thought this day would come." He pets Buttercup, and she wiggles in excitement.

Is he upset?

Since I was a little girl, a part of me wished deep down he'd shed a tear in front of me—wished he'd stop pretending to be so resilient against everything for my sake. That hasn't happened. Now, suddenly, I show up with a pig, claiming it to be his grandchild as a joke, and he looks like he might cry. Will today be the day? I don't want it to be. It's his birthday: the one day a year he's supposed to be extra happy. Dang it, I feel so bad.

"I'm sorry. I didn't mean to make you upset."

"Nonsense." He chuckles. He sets the spark plug on the front desk and grabs a handkerchief from his back pocket. "I got some dust in my eye while shifting all the stuff around, looking for those spark plugs." He dabs at his nose and stuffs the handkerchief in the pocket of his T-shirt. "Why don't you set her up in the Think Den? She's probably tired from your long trip."

"On it." I laugh when I open the door to the Think Den (the office). The sign gets me every time "Important Stuff Happens in this Room." The sign was my mom's idea because my dad always said he was putting his thinking cap on when going to work on paperwork and number crunching.

I set Buttercup's bed in the corner of the Think Den. Contrary to the rest of the store, this room is tidy. The walls are painted a soft blue. At the center of the room, the desk is void of clutter. Painted on the wall behind the file cabinets in white strokes is the Fix-Its logo: a combination of tools, wrenches, and wood boards. The important documents are organized by the month and year, dating back to the grand opening. The seven-year policy of getting rid of files doesn't apply at Fix-Its. Every piece of paper is saved. This room is pretty much a time capsule.

I set Buttercup up with a bowl of water and food. Once she seems adapted to her new home, I crack the door to the Think Den so she can come in and out as she pleases.

I take my usual stool behind the register beside Dad. He pushes his reading glasses to the bridge of his nose and smiles at me. Grabbing the pen behind his ear, he shifts his attention to the stack of documents in front of him. He mumbles under his breath while surveying the papers. His hand slightly shakes as he scratches off items on his list.

The bell on the door jingles. In comes Dan. He takes long strides to the register, surveying the store, but I can tell he isn't truly looking at anything... He's thinking.

"Hey. Can I get a muffler kit for a 2010 Jeep Wrangler Sport?"

Straight and to the point, that's Dan.

I jot down the parts in a notepad as he continues to rattle them off.

"And brake pads, rotors, and calipers for a 2008 Dodge Durango." He adjusts his ballcap.

"Front, rear, or both?" I ask.

"Right and left front."

"Anything else?"

"Nope. I'll have a look at your car later and let you know if I need anything else." He smiles.

Dad speaks up, peeking over his paper mountain. "Thanks for helping out Marigold today. You're a fine young man." Dad looks down at the papers again and flips through them until he taps a line and stands. "Follow me. We have the Durango parts in stock."

The way he can know that from his notes baffles me every time.

"No problem, sir. Just doing my job." Dan grins.

My dad walks around the counter and to the fourth aisle. Dan follows him, and they disappear behind the shelves.

I grab the catalogue from the shelf underneath the counter, flipping it open to search for the part numbers. I can't help peeking at the stack of papers on the counter next to me, trying and failing to decipher Dad's notes. It's a bunch of random part numbers scribbled in no clear system.

Dad and Dan emerge from the aisle after a few minutes. Dan is now holding a mountain of parts. Since his hands are full, he nods his head toward me and pushes his back against the front door to leave. I wave and return my gaze to the catalogue.

After some time passes, I hand my dad the slip with all the part numbers. "Can you order whatever you two didn't find in stock?"

"I'll call right now." He nods and grabs the slip. He punches a number into the landline phone and starts rattling off the numbers.

"You don't have to follow me around like my shadow, kiddo. I'm only stopping for a bite to eat before going home." Dad takes long strides as I hurry to keep up.

"I thought we could have dinner for your birthday," I insist, doing my best run-walk to stay beside him. This is so typical of him to want to avoid anything to do with his birthday, but I wanted to do something special. You only turn sixty-five once, so we might as well celebrate it.

"Oh, nonsense, Mary. It's like any other day. No need to celebrate. I'm another year older and another day closer to my grave."

"Come on, Dad, you're not getting any older. Don't talk like that! You're just more retro than yesterday."

He chuckles. "That's a good way to look at it. I'm an antique, not in mint condition, and more likely a rusty, forgotten one in someone's yard."

I dismiss the idea with a wave of my hand as we continue to walk toward the diner. "I have a surprise for you." I figure I might as well give him a little warning before I open the door to Annie's. There's quite a few more people than I was anticipating.

"Surprise?" A line forms between his brows. "Oh, Mary, you know I'm too old for surprises. There isn't much that could get past me in this town."

"I'll show you. Come on." I open the door.

Everyone shouts, "Happy birthday, Harvey!"

A giant banner hangs from the ceiling tiles that reads "Happy 65th." It's one of the decorations I picked up on my trip out of town. All the shop owners and some of Dad's close friends are here. Even Dan himself showed up. I'm surprised he actually came, given that he's not normally one to go to events. Nor am I, but when I'm invited, I have a hard time saying no. It seems he has the same problem.

I'd gladly plan anything for my dad to bring a smile to his face. Without mom, someone needs to do it.

"What's going on, Mary? Is this for me?" Dad looks at me and scratches his head. "Is everyone here for me?"

"Of course they are." I smile and motion to the room. "It's your birthday. We wanted to do something special for the town's favorite tool guy." I laugh and take his hand, giving it a squeeze.

"I don't know what to say... This is... I... I never expected anything like this." He gestures his hand toward the smiling faces.

"They wanted to celebrate with you." I smile as he takes in the room, doing a spin. He scratches his head again.

People start to wish my dad a happy birthday. They clap him on the back and lead him to the table against the wall, overflowing with finger food, sweet treats, and boxes of pizza. They pitched in without a thought. I didn't have to ask. As soon as I brought the idea up to Annie to host his party here, she took the reins and spread the word.

I love it here. These people are my family. Even though I love them, I still find myself looking for a table away from everyone. I spot the perfect empty booth in the back corner. Leaning against the plush red cushion, I observe the room. Ada and Nick laugh to themselves while they fill their plates. Constance and Bobbie chat with my dad, and they keep turning their heads my way for some reason. Behind the counter, Annie is filling fountain drinks.

Dan walks toward me, hands stuffed in his jean pockets. I wave to him, and he nods in reply as he slides across from me and rests an elbow against the table's surface. I can't help but notice his grease-stained hands as he adjusts his backwards hat. His thick, dark brown hair curls around the edges of the brim. The stubble on his face is emphasized when he grins. Although it's small, I know his smile is genuine.

I may not talk to Dan much, other than business, but I know he's honest and kind. Those are his most apparent qualities. Around town, he's known as Tinker Dan because all he does is work on cars. He'll fix anything, though: engines, tools, appliances, etc. He's always tinkering with something. There's a rumor floating around town that he doesn't sleep, which is absurd, but he does spend a lot of his time working more than resting. I'm sure he doesn't get nearly enough shut-eye, but that's his business, not mine.

He places a palm against his chin, and neither of us says anything as we stare at each other. Surely, he's thinking about cars or something more interesting than having a conversation with me. It's not out of the ordinary. We don't delve into topics that aren't business related very often. I tap my fingers on the table. His eyes track my hands. We're having a silent battle of who is going to break the tension first.

I miss Buttercup. She was good at giving us something to talk about. However, I didn't want to bring her into the diner, so I left her at Fix-its. She had a chaotic day. I could tell by the way she was snoring in her bed, covered in blankets in the Think Den.

Dan continues to look at me. This is awkward. Why did I wave him over again? We're not really friends. Are we? I don't think I'd call us that. We're work partners. We talk about tools and parts or ordering tools and parts. That's the extent of our discussions.

We're very interesting people.

Dan's lips move. "Why are you sitting all alone?" His voice catches me off guard. I'm the first one to speak up most of the time.

I continue tapping my hand against the table, contemplating my answer. I might as well be honest. "Being around this many people makes me anxious. I may seem outgoing, but sometimes, no, a lot of the time, I feel... I don't know... *nervous* around this many people. I'm not sure what to do with myself. I don't know what to say." I laugh shakily.

He nods and presses his lips together.

This is awkward. He definitely thinks I'm weird.

"I didn't know." Temporarily, his gaze bores into mine. I wait because it seems as if he's mulling over something but not saying it. We seem to do a lot of silent things. "That's why I don't go to events unless I absolutely have to. I am the same way."

It's something we have in common. I try to avoid any and all town events. Nevertheless, my dad deserves this birthday party. He deserves to have his daughter here even if I'm hiding out in a booth having awkward silent conversations with Dan.

"So..." I'm curious now. "Why are you here then? What makes this one different?" I twist the end of my braid between my fingers.

He shrugs. "You asked me."

Ah, he does have the same problem as me: worrying about letting someone down, perpetually stuck in the loop of deciding whether to go to town events or not. If someone asks, I cave. If they have a bit of hope in their eyes that they really want you to be there, I'm going.

"Well, thanks. I mean for showing up and sitting here with me so I didn't have to sit with my own silence and nerves." It's nice to know I'm not the only one who feels this way. "That gives me an idea. We should start our own club or something."

"What kind of club?" He tilts his head.

"The kind that hides in the corners of events in our own bubble. We can talk, or we don't have to. There will be no one to judge us. Are you in?"

He chuckles. "That sounds great. I'm in."

"Welcome to the club." I hold my hand out to shake his. "I think we need to give each other nicknames."

His calluses brush against my palm as he shakes my hand. He releases it and taps his chin. After a few beats of silence, he says, "I think your nickname should be Goldie after Goldilocks."

"Because of my hair?"

"Yes, and because you're shy but also outgoing at the same time. Like Goldilocks, you're right in the middle."

Dan obviously has a mechanical mind. He analyzes and figures out all the parts and pieces. This man seems to have me figured out. We've talked more today than any of our previous conversations, but I guess you don't need to talk to someone very much to be able to read them. It's all in their facial expressions and the way they carry themself. With Dan, I do a lot of trying to figure him out.

"I like it." I nod in agreement. "How about I call you Danny? Honestly, you look kind of like Danny Zuko from *Grease*. So, it works. All you're missing is a leather jacket."

He's a spitting image of the greaser with his dark hair, charming smile, dark jeans, white T-shirt, and belt.

"I get that a lot actually."

"Really?"

"No." He chuckles and shakes his head. "Never have."

"Oh, well, there's a first time for everything. You're a funny guy. You had me fooled."

We smile at each other for a moment. Dan is not at all what I expected him to be like.

"Hey! Scootch over, Marigold. I'm exhausted." Daisy plops beside me, nudging my arm with her elbow. She scoots closer to me and sets a giant plate, overflowing with a little bit of every food item, onto the table. She lets out a long audible sigh. "I almost quit today. I'm sick of making pizza. Joe's being, well, Joe. I've been working there for too long. It's coming soon. I almost said it. I almost felt the *sweet* satisfaction of leaving."

I send an apologetic look Dan's way for her interruption. Daisy came out of nowhere and burst our silent bubble. Yep, that's classic Daisy. She's my best friend, and I love her to death. She gets bored, keeps arguing with Joe, and has a history of quitting jobs. It's hard to keep it all straight in my head, but I try my best.

Her last job was at The Olive Bean. She got bored of making coffee, so she started to work at The String Cheese again. She's worked there on and off for years. All the businesses seem to know how Daisy is, but they still rehire her. They don't seem to mind. They need help, and she knows what she's doing.

It still frustrates me that my dad won't hire her. I think it'd be fun to work with my best friend. It'd sure make the hours fly by.

"I'm sure it'll work out," Dan says.

Oh, poor naive Dan, you don't know Daisy well enough. My best friend will make anything work if she has to... by quitting.

"It will when I quit," Daisy retorts.

I giggle to myself. She's nothing but honest.

"How's your car doing?" Daisy plucks a hamburger from her plate and takes a giant bite. She points her free hand at the plate gesturing to Dan and I to have free rein with anything on it.

Dan and I both shake our heads in polite refusal.

"It was the ground wire," Dan says.

"You already had time to work on it?" I raise a brow.

When did he manage to do that? I was in the shop when he ordered parts. He didn't mention anything then.

"Yeah, I had a few hours to spare." He shrugs.

"Do you need me to order it? Or can you use some that we have in stock?" We have a huge selection of car parts and wire. It's just the small problem of trying to find it in the mess of the store.

"I went over while you were gone. Your dad got me some. Your car's all set." He must have run over during the hour I went to check to make sure no one needed any help setting up the decorations.

"Thanks. That was fast and unexpected." I smile and hope it shows how grateful I am.

"It was no problem," Dan says.

"So… tell me the story of how you got Buttercup. Also, how did your go-kart die?" Daisy laughs, and Dan's forehead creases.

"She calls my car a go-kart," I explain. Dan nods as the reference clicks. "But yeah, it's a long story, so be prepared."

"I'm ready, girly," Daisy says, taking a bite of her burger.

I fill them in with all the details of my hot-mess morning up until our return into town. Daisy oohs and aahs. Dan smirks. We laugh about my hawk related inner monologue and spend the rest of Dad's birthday party chatting at our little table in the corner.

People start to leave, and soon it's down to Annie, Dad, a couple business owners, and me. I squeeze Dad in a hug. "Happy birthday, Dad. I'm going to stay and help clean up. I'll see you at home."

"Okay, Mary. Thanks for today. It was great."

Chapter 4

MARIGOLD

I park my car in Dad's driveway. Buttercup follows alongside me as we take the pathway to the fire pit behind the house. The solar lights and the moon's glow illuminate the stepping stones enough for me to tell where I'm going. The darkness here is much different than in town. It's an inky black that makes it almost impossible to see my hand in front of my face.

The sounds from the fire pit fill the quiet acres surrounding my childhood home. The closer I get, the warmer the air feels against my skin. I'm surprised to see my dad still out here. It's late. It took a lot longer than I anticipated cleaning up after the party. I half expected the fire to be burned down to embers, but I didn't want to miss the warmth and solace from our Friday night tradition. It would feel weird going straight home without sitting here for a few minutes even if it were only Buttercup and me.

I sit in my chair, a wooden Adirondack, faded from years of basking in the sun. It has remained unmoved, much like everything else my dad owns. I set Buttercup on my lap, and she lies down, nuzzling her head against my overalls.

My parents' house is as much of a time capsule as Fix-Its. For a long time, I cherished the fact nothing had to change. It felt as if she wasn't gone. Lately, I've started worrying about my dad being all alone in a big house full of ghosts from a different life, though.

Dad and I sit in silence. I watch the fire as it crackles. Small bursts of sparks flit through the dark sky. My gaze wanders to the empty chair beside Dad's—Mom's chair. He rests his arm around the top of hers unconsciously. It tugs at my heartstrings and makes me wish I could go back to a time when the three of us sat here late at night, laughing, roasting marshmallows for s'mores, and telling stories about our day. Every Friday night, we'd trade ghost stories, and I'd hardly sleep. However, I'd always beg them to tell me more; I'd gladly take every bit of those restless nights. My heart aches thinking about a time when I didn't know what it felt like to miss someone so much it hurts.

"Dad?" My voice croaks from not using it for so long.

His brown eyes soften as he looks up from the fire at me. "Yeah, kiddo?"

"How was your birthday?"

"I had a good time." He smiles and runs a hand through his silver hair. "But—"

"But what?" I ask softly.

"Oh, it's nothing. I don't want to worry you."

"Please tell me."

He's quiet for a minute until he says, "Everyone keeps asking when I'm going to retire." He shrugs. "I don't know if I'm ready yet. I haven't given it much thought."

"What if you did retire? Would it be so bad?"

He laughs and then sighs. "Not you too."

"I'm sorry." I tap on the edge of the chair. "I just want what's best for you."

"I don't know." Dad scratches his head and stares into the night sky. "What would I even do with all the time?"

Suddenly, it dawns on me that maybe he shouldn't retire. The thought of him staying in his house alone all day would not be what I want for him.

"You always loved traveling. You could go somewhere," I suggest.

"You've got a point." He scrunches his eyebrows. "But who would run the store? You couldn't do it all on your own, could you?"

"I've shadowed you my entire life. I know what everything is." I just don't know *where* everything is... "I order parts every day and work well with Dan. I'd be okay. Don't you worry about me." I'm more worried about him and if this would be a good idea.

Dad listens intently and scratches his head, but I can tell he doesn't look very convinced that I could handle everything on my own.

Haven't I proved myself?

"I know that Henry comes in every morning at six-thirty to buy a container of worms. It's not some random container either. He doesn't want the red wrigglers or the mealworms. He gets the nightcrawlers and a bass jig in a different color for whichever season. Every day, he manages to snag the lure in a tree branch and ends up cutting the line. The oak tree next to the pond is covered with his jig ornaments, but he'll never admit it. He tells the same two stories." I lift my fingers as I list them off. "One: A huge fish snapped his line, therefore losing the lure. Or, two: He lost it in his truck somewhere. Then there's Constance, who shows up at two on the dot. She buys something small: a lightbulb, a screwdriver, a roll of fly tape, etc. Her goal is to make it look like she's coming into the store to shop, but Constance really only wants someone to talk to. The tourists love our selection of fishing lures and bait, while the townies love our paint supplies, hardware, and tools." I take a deep breath before continuing. "But most of all, I know Fix-Its like the back of my hand. It's not about an obligation to take over our family business. I want to run it because I love it. There's nothing else I'd rather do."

Dad smiles proudly, but it falters a fraction. "I know you do, and I couldn't be more proud of you. I just don't want to push you if you're not ready for all the responsibilities on your own yet. It's okay if you're not."

What? How can he still think I'm not ready? I've spent years figuring out the ins and outs of running the shop, put in the hours, shown up on time, and learned what each part is and what purpose they serve.

"I'm ready. I promise. I can prove it to you," I insist.

"I don't know." He runs his palms over his face.

"Please. Give me a month to prove it to you. How about a trial run?"

He taps his chin. "Okay, that could work."

"Really?" My face brightens.

"Yeah. You have one month. You'll have to hire some employees, handle ordering inventory and special-request parts, and open and close on your own. Of course, you can call if you need me. By the end of the month, we can look at the numbers and your progress. Then Fix-Its will be yours, and I'll partially retire. I'd still like to work part time though, or else I wouldn't know what to do with myself. Two or three days a week would be nice." He grins.

I smile, tipping my head. "You can work whenever you like if this month goes well, obviously. I just want you to take a break, relax, and have some fun. Let me take this month to show you that I'm capable."

The idea of him still working with me quells my worries of him being cooped up in his house alone with his thoughts.

"Fun." He chuckles and scratches his head. "I like the sound of that. It's been a while. We'll have to see how this first month goes, though."

I need it to work out. I need to prove to my dad that I'm capable. I'd really like to pave my own way in life.

Mom and Dad cultivated the store to be what it is today. Of course, Mom had the place a lot more organized than it is now. Dad was too sad to keep it the way Mom did. I didn't blame him; I was sad too.

The outside needs a fresh coat of paint. The inside is in disarray. I've wanted to work on these things for a long time, but I didn't want to step on my dad's toes. I also didn't want him to worry over Fix-Its losing Mom's touch. Plus, he has a method—one I'm not entirely sure of. He's content about knowing where everything is, but when a customer comes in, it's almost impossible to find what they're looking for without his help. I'm rooting through piles of tools here and there, fishing equipment, and car parts. It's time consuming and frustrating for a customer who has somewhere to be.

"I'm planning on reorganizing some things," I tell him, knowing he's not too keen on change in general.

To my surprise, he says, "It's yours for the month. Do as you please. You start tomorrow."

"Thanks, Dad."

He nods and stares at the sky again, tipping his head to the stars. After some time, he changes the subject. "Do you remember when we went to Ocean City?"

I smile, nodding. "I could never forget. Mom was driving me to school and then suddenly made a U-turn. She said we were going on an adventure instead. School can wait. Memories can't."

It was one of my favorite days. She was so spontaneous and would drop everything on a whim. I was wonderstruck by her way of experiencing everything life had to offer.

He chuckles softly. "She had that sparkle in her eye." Awe transforms his face as he continues. "She pushed open the door to Fix-Its, holding your hand. I thought something was wrong because you were supposed to be at school. Then your mom smiled as bright as the sun. Before a word left her lips, I knew I was in on whatever she had planned. And boy, did I enjoy every single moment of that trip. If you remember, it was a six-hour drive to the beach. The second your mom got out of the car she started setting up her canvas and paint. She never went anywhere without her supplies. She painted the view of wild horses on the beach. She stood there barefoot with paint streaks on her clothes. She was a vision."

I hold the pendant of my necklace. "I remember everything about that day and thinking I wanted to be just like her." I close my eyes and picture my mom that day. I see her blonde hair blowing in the salty air and the smile she had when turning to look at me building a sandcastle. It was a look of pure happiness.

A tear trickles down my cheek from the memory.

My eyes blink slowly open as I hear Dad's voice. "I think I might go there. Take a trip to the beach where we went. Tomorrow actually. Is that crazy?"

"No, Dad, it sounds exactly like what you need."

I smile and pat his shoulder as I pass him on my way back to my car.

"I believe in you, Mary," he calls after me.

I turn and smile. "Thanks, Dad."

I drive to my house that sits on the same property, separated by ten acres of trees and streams. I park my car and set Buttercup on the ground. She squeals in excitement as she runs beside me while we follow the cobblestone pathway to the front door. I place Buttercup's bed next to mine, and she lies down.

I find a new canvas and set it up on the back porch. I paint the moon and its reflections. The glow of the moonbeams ripple against the crick. I can't help but wonder if my mom would be proud of me—painting like her, running Fix-Its on my own, and convincing Dad to take a break for once. I think maybe she would be.

Chapter 5

DAN

I flip the comforter off and stretch my arms. My apartment is dark. I roll out of bed and flick on the light switch. Yawning, I rub my blurry eyes until my vision clears.

My morning routine is always the same: make the bed, check for missed calls, get coffee, and so on.

I set my phone on the bathroom sink and brush my teeth as I play a voicemail from my mom. Her voice is animated and bright as she says, "Hey, sweetheart. I miss you. How is my son doing?" Her tone turns somber. "You haven't called me back in a few weeks. Are you still alive? Call me back. Take a break from the auto shop for a day. Please. You're letting work overtake your life the same way your father did. I want you to be happy. Okay, love you. Talk to you soon… hopefully. Better yet, take a weekend off and come visit us. See you when I see you."

I finish brushing my teeth and brace my hands on the sink, staring at my reflection. Yep. I look as guilty as I feel inside. It's too early to make a phone call now. I need to remember to call her back later.

I click the next message that's from my brother and hit the speaker button again. "Hey, little brother. How's it going? I'm sure you're off doing important things. We're stopping by in a few weeks for the Strawberry Festival. Don't forget."

This is news to me, but I'm always glad to see Carter, Eve, and Bella.

I throw on a T-shirt and coveralls. After pulling on a pair of boots, I head down the stairs of my apartment one at a time and flick on the shop lights.

In the second bay, I line up the lift bars underneath a Honda Odyssey that I towed last night and keep the button pressed to raise it. A group of tourists got a flat tire on the way into town and drove on it for over an hour. It sure did some damage to their van. I'll have to replace the rim as well as the tire. Last night, I left a voicemail at Fix-Its to order the parts.

I glance at the clock. It reads 5:56 a.m.

Time for coffee.

The town's quiet this morning when I leave my shop. The lights flicker from the front windows of Bobbie's Freeze. They're always up early prepping for the summer rush. I pass The Chop Shop and Hoarder Emporium; both are still dark.

I get in line behind Constance at The Olive Bean. Coffee is the only reason I can be somewhat pleasant throughout the day with limited hours of sleep. The delicious smell of roasted coffee beans wafts through the small shop. Olive, the shop owner, spins behind the counter, filling an empty blender with ice, milk, coffee, and syrup.

Constance leans her elbows on the counter and lifts the glasses from her face. "Do you have any gossip for me?"

I hear her ask this same question every morning.

"Oh no! We're actually fresh out of tea, but there's still a bunch of coffee on the menu," Olive answers with mirth and a big hint of sarcasm. The corners of Olive's eyes crinkle before she turns away and starts the blender.

Perfect timing.

I'm sure she is using the loud grinding noises of the blender to drown out Constance's reply.

The second Olive silences the blender, Constance speaks up once more. "Oh, dear, that's okay. The tourists are giving me plenty to write articles about. Just last night, a bachelorette party showed up with a flat tire, and I'm writing a juicy article right now about singles—" Her voice cuts off when the bell on the door jingles. Constance turns her head, and her eyes widen when she sees me. "Oh! Dan! Good morning!"

Why does she look shocked? It's six o'clock, and I'm always second in line.

"Good morning." I nod and offer her a small smile.

Constance stares at me for a few beats then tracks her gaze behind me. "And Mason, it's nice to see you."

"Morning, Constance. Morning, Dan." Mason greets us both.

I lift a hand. "Hey, Mason."

Mason heads straight to the front of the line next to Constance. "Good morning, *Wife*. How's it going?" Mason winks at Olive.

"It's wonderful now that you're here, *Husband*." Olive is beaming ear to ear as she looks at Mason. She turns to Constance. "You were saying something about singles?"

Constance shakes her head vehemently. "I... I can't remember. I'll tell you later if I think of it."

Mason chuckles and heads toward the door leading to the kitchen.

Olive fills a cup with the blender's contents and puts a lid on it. Constance slides a bill on the counter, grabs the drink from her, and waves goodbye.

I step up to the counter as Olive pours black coffee into a to-go cup for me.

"Constance is acting strange today," Olive says, passing me my coffee.

"Seems like it," I agree, handing her the usual five dollars like I do every morning.

Olive taps her chin. "Normally she has a lot more to say. She's up to something."

"Isn't she always?" I counter.

Olive hands me my change, and I fill the tip jar with the rest. "You're right. These are typical, conspiring, gossip-mill-executive duties, and who are we to question anything that she does? We're merely pieces being played on her chess board. Now, we gotta wait for her to make a move. Look out because you're next!" She tips her head and laughs.

"I can't wait." I, for one, am not eager for Constance's match-making. I surely hope I'm not her next target. The last thing I need right now is to be in a relationship.

The door to the kitchen comes swinging open. "My wife makes the best pastries," Mason announces, pointing to the homemade toaster pastry in his hand. "Did you get one, Dan?" He takes a bite and gives a thumbs up.

"No, I didn't, but you're advertising it pretty well." I take a sip of coffee.

"Here, have one on the house." Olive holds out a bag.

"Thank you for this and the coffee," I say, accepting the brown bag.

"You got it! See you tomorrow!"

Mason calls out as I open the door. "Believe me. You'll be thanking me later. They are brown sugar cinnamon."

I chuckle, holding the door open. "I bet I will be."

The sky begins to lighten when I leave The Olive Bean. Blanche, the chicken that was almost run over yesterday, pecks the sidewalk and begins to follow me. I take a few steps and turn back. She's still there, right behind me. "I didn't save you. Marigold did," I say to the chicken.

Blanche seems to answer me with a "bawk, bawk, ba-gawk." Then she follows me as I take a few more steps.

I turn on my heel. "Please don't test me before I have coffee."

Blanche just tilts her head and lets out another "bawk, bawk."

I've officially lost it. I'm talking to a chicken. I think I need to drink my coffee faster. I take a large gulp and look around to make sure no one witnessed me losing my mind. I don't know why I'm worried. No one would bat an eye. There are annual chicken races where townies shout positive affirmations at the chickens to get them to run faster. The chickens wear Christmas outfits. There is also a Halloween chicken themed event.

I've truly found my people.

I take another gulp of coffee and let the hot liquid coat my tongue. It gives me enough sanity to head back and get some work done. I turn occasionally, but Blanche is still there following me.

"Dan!" Marigold's voice fills my ears, and I stop in place. "Wait up!" she yells, sounding winded.

I should've known wherever that chicken is, Marigold is too. I turn around and take another sip of coffee.

Marigold rushes toward me. The face-attacker, I mean Buttercup, runs beside her. Marigold braces her hands on her thighs, trying to catch her breath. When she straightens, her face flushes bright red.

She runs a hand through her wavy hair. "I only have a few minutes, but I have a proposition for you if you'd be up for an adventure."

I don't normally make time for many *adventures*, but the sparkle in her eyes intrigues me.

"Tell me more."

She rocks on her feet. "I was thinking... My dad gave me a month to prove I could run Fix-Its on my own. I have a few ideas to make the store more profitable. You know how that guy almost hit the chicken?" She pauses to wait for me to reply. I nod, and she continues. "Well, it gave me an idea. Why not make a way so that people can travel around town without driving vehicles out so much? We could reduce the traffic but still give them something to travel in."

I tap my chin, not sure where this is going and how it involves me. However, I'm in on whatever she's planning. She looks determined, hopeful even, regardless of her being nervous to ask me. "What are you thinking?"

"I saw an advertisement online for golf carts. I'd like to start with two and go from there. I could rent them out. They'd minimize traffic through town. The chickens will be easier to see from them, and they don't go as fast. I don't think the townies would warm to the idea of a traffic light or a stop sign. The carts are like a happy medium."

"It's a good idea." I voice my thoughts.

Her smile widens and falls in a few seconds. "There's just one issue. The golf carts that I found are two hours away…" She trails off and looks down at Buttercup who is currently sniffing the ground.

Ahh, that's where I come in. She needs someone to haul them for her.

I tip my coffee cup. "Let's go get them."

"Now?" Her eyes shimmer. "Are you sure? Aren't you busy? I understand if you have a lot going on. I don't want you to move your plans for this."

"We can go whenever you like."

She shifts on her feet. "Well, it is my first day running the shop on my own, but we are closed on Sundays."

"Early tomorrow works for me."

Her face brightens. "Perfect. Thank you, Dan. I'd really appreciate it."

"No problem." I start to walk in the direction of my auto shop, and she follows beside me with Buttercup. Eventually, we cross the street at Annie's Diner. "Are you hungry?" I ask.

She lifts her shoulders. "A little, I suppose."

I wedge the coffee cup between my arm and chest, opening the brown bag to find plenty more than I expected: four different kinds of toaster pastries, not just the one Mason mentioned. I wasn't expecting this much when I accepted it, or else I would've tried to pay.

I'll just leave a bigger tip next time.

"Here." I hold out the bag, offering it to her. "Take whatever you like."

"Thanks." She grabs one of the toaster pastries and takes a bite. We walk a bit more until she stops in front of Fix-Its. "This is me. See ya tomorrow."

"Tomorrow it is." I promise.

Chapter 6

MARIGOLD

I can't believe how smoothly everything is going. I convinced my dad to let me prove myself last night. This morning Dan agreed to help me with my business idea, and it'll be set into motion tomorrow.

I need to face today first. It is the first day I'm running the shop on my own. My heart races in my chest.

Hopefully, no one comes in and asks some oddball question that I wouldn't know the answer to, or else I'll have to make an excuse to use the bathroom and tap the refresh icon on my phone like my life depends on it. All the while, I'd be internally screaming, *please give me a good signal so I can search for the answer!* I really don't want to bother Dad on my first day. I need to do this on my own. I can't call him yet.

When I flip the sign to open, as I've done plenty of times over the years, it feels different. I stand and peer out the window, patiently waiting for a customer. Then I realize no one is waiting at the door.

That was anticlimactic.

I notice my reflection in the glass. My eyes widen when I see my hair. I was in a get-it-all-done mood this morning and completely forgot to braid it. I try my best to quickly finger comb my hair into a french braid, and then I begin working on Operation Improve Fix-Its.

I place my hands on my hips and stare at the shelves spanning throughout the store. I have my work cut out for me. Fishing equipment, tools, wire, car parts, light bulbs, etc., are all haphazardly stacked on every shelf. There's not one ounce of organization in the place. That was Mom's thing. She loved this place through and through. Once she got sick, she couldn't come to the store anymore and had to stay in bed. She insisted on being in her art studio, though. Being surrounded by her paintings—the walls, the stairs, every surface was her canvas—brought her happiness. The store lost her touch over the years, and Dad, well, he was too heartbroken to keep it up.

As I look at the frames on the wall, I'm reminded of a time when my grandmother was still alive and running the shop. Although I never got to meet my grandfather, a picture of him standing in front of a newly renovated home that is now Fix-Its is still in the same place on the wall. Every time I pass the picture, it never fails to make me feel as though I did know him.

I glance upward at the peeling paint on the walls above the shelves and then downward at the wood flooring full of stains and scratches that are embedded in the wood. Just thinking about it all pulls me into a warm memory.

"Little Miss. Marigold. Where's my sweet granddaughter?" Granny calls out. She sounds so far away.

I reach my arms way above my head and stand on the tips of my toes. I bite my lip and reach for the sky. Mommy always says to reach for the stars, so I wiggle my fingers in the air. The shelves are tall.

The floor squeaks as Granny steps on one of the creaky wood boards. "There you are." Granny laughs. She walks to me, stepping slowly as she braces against her cane and points to the top shelf. "Do you need something up there?"

I bounce excitedly. "Yes, please!"

"This?" She points to a box.

I shake my head no and giggle.

"This?" She taps her finger on a yellow ball. I shake my head no again.

"Oh, it has to be this then." She grabs the kitten plushie and hands it to me.

I smile and squeeze the stuffed animal to my chest.

The flashback makes tears shimmer in my eyes. This store has been in our family for three generations. The toy section was always my favorite when I was little. I cherish the memories with Granny, Mom, and Dad. Those moments were made where I'm standing. I hold them close to my heart.

I know I want almost everything about the store to stay the same. The last thing I want to do is modernize it. This place is a time capsule, and I intend to keep the charm engraved into everything: the creaking floorboard, the royal blue walls, the mixed aroma of fresh metal and wood from the lumber stacked beside the back door, the old-fashioned cash register, the first dollar made, framed on the wall next to the picture of my grandparents, and another picture with my parents holding me in front of the store. Every small item and detail holds a story that I intend to keep.

I start by tackling the first shelf. It's piled with fishing lures, ropes, gaskets and miscellaneous things. I begin sorting everything and decide to make this the fishing and tackle aisle—some of our most popular items this time of year. After all, the front shelf is the first impression people get when they enter. Maybe we can rearrange the aisles seasonally, displaying the most purchased items closer to the front. I spend the next hour organizing this shelf.

The door jingles, and I perk up at the sound. I peak over my shoulder as I hang fishing jigs on hooks.

A woman walks in. The glare of the sun follows her. Lifting her sunglasses, she smiles in my direction. She's definitely a tourist because she's wearing a T-shirt printed with "Thornwood Valley" and a picture of a rooster.

I greet her with a smile and say, "Good Morning! If you need help finding anything let me know!"

"Thanks," she replies, looking around.

As she disappears down another aisle, the door jingles again. Daisy comes in, walking with a purpose. Her eyes lock with mine, and she sighs. She rubs her palms across her flared jeans and lifts her head. "I did it again."

"Did you?" I ask, although I already know exactly what happened.

"Yep." She bobs her head, and her hair falls over her face.

"Did you and Joe have another *disagreement?*" I ponder out loud.

She shakes her head left to right. "Not this time. I got to work early, like usual. I set up the dining room. I helped wash dishes from prep. When it was time to make the dough for the pepperoni rolls, I had made up my mind. I couldn't do it anymore. I quit. Joe was fine with it. I offered to work two weeks, but he said there's no need if I didn't want to. He still has enough help and didn't mind me leaving. It ended amicably."

"You sound like you were breaking up with Joe and The String Cheese." I hang up a few more fishing lures.

"It felt a lot like one of those breakups where you say, 'It's not you. It's me.' But that's the truth. It's me. I need a fresh start. How about now? Yeah, today sounds good. I mean, I could go home and hang out with Morticia and lay in my hammock. Or take the canoe out. Or find another job." She runs her fingers through her hair.

"Hanging out with your cat all day sounds perfect, but I was thinking you could work here if you want."

"Very funny. Harvey would give a big fat *no* to that idea." She looks at the register, and her eyebrow raises. "Where is the man of the hour?"

I fill her in on last night: my trial month of sorts, Dad's trip to the beach today, and all the nitty-gritty details.

"Wow, so it's really happening? I can work here now." She pauses in disbelief and hugs me. "I can work here!" She pulls away and says, "Put me to work. What's on the agenda, boss?"

"I actually need your help with something else first. Then you can help me organize these shelves."

"Name it." She grins and plants a hand on her hip.

"Can you take Buttercup for a walk? She's zooming around the store."

She lifts her palm, and her brows draw together to form a line. "Are you kidding? You didn't have to ask. I'll gladly walk Buttercup! I'm already loving this job."

I shake my head and laugh as Daisy heads through the store, looking for Buttercup.

I continue tidying up, arranging the lures. The bait mini fridges along the wall are moved next to these shelves so everything fishing related is in one spot. Hooks are fastened on the wall, and waders and nets are hung up. Lastly, I place the fishing rods in the holder beside them, filling the wall completely.

After I'm finished, I take a seat behind the counter and flip through Dad's paperwork. It's a fifty-page list of all the inventory and the quantity of what we have in stock. He has words scribbled off and new numbers listed and crossed out.

My mind spins. He always kept track of what we sold and had in stock so that he could order what we needed. I should've learned, but I was too busy with other tasks. The way he tracked everything makes this whole do-it-myself endeavor daunting. I'd have to sort through every piece in the shop before getting an accurate count. Twirling a pen around my fingers, I continue down the list. My head muddles even more with the sheer size of it.

"Good Morning, Marigold!" Henry strolls in wearing a green fishing vest with multiple pockets. His eyes flicker with eagerness under the bill of his hat. Said bill has a fishing lure, a green pumpkin jig to be specific, lodged right in it. That's probably one of the many he has *misplaced*.

"I'm late this morning. I gotta hurry before the fish start biting. I think I'll go with the nightcrawlers today." He nods, waiting expectantly for me to grab them. Each morning he acts as if he's not sure what he's going to get.

I point to the wall behind him. "I moved them over there. I hope that's okay."

"Well, I'll be damned." He makes his way over to the mini fridge, opening the door to grab one of the containers of worms. He surveys the shelves and the wall, and his eyes glimmer. "This is great," he announces.

I can't help but smirk at the sight. I'm glad my small changes are going over well. Maybe Henry can help convince Dad of the same if he needs persuading.

He browses through the jigs and picks one. I check him out, punching the keys on the cash register. The drawer pops open, and I hand him his change.

"I like what you're doing with the place." His eyes gleam. "I'm pleasantly surprised. I didn't believe the article I read this morning. Harvey would never retire, but it looks like I was wrong. Keep up the good work. See ya tomorrow." He waves on his way out.

Henry's words of encouragement are exactly what I needed to hear this morning. I'm doing something right.

I check my phone for the article Henry was going on about. I haven't heard anything yet. He wasn't joking; there was a new one posted an hour or so ago.

Thornwood Valley Social
Big Changes at Fix-Its Hardware

Big things are happening at Fix-Its. As many of you know, the store has been a staple in our town. The building was first purchased by Granger and Lucy Rowe in 1923 to be their forever home, but they soon converted it into a hardware store. When

Granger passed, Lucy ran it for a while until she passed down Fix-Its to Iris and Harvey Evans in 2006. Now, Marigold might be the next in her family to run it.

"I heard Harvey is thinking about retiring," Beth said.

"I think she has a month-long trial," Bobbie said.

During this month, Marigold will be running the shop exclusively. Do you think she's up for the challenge? Only time will tell. I may be biased, but I think Marigold is more than capable. She's shown interest in Fix-Its for years. Plus, she learned from the best. Some fresh eyes and a younger generation might be what the store needs. There could be a lot of changes made to the town staple.

For those of you stuck in your ways, you might have a hard time adjusting to the store's sudden change in ownership. As it seems, it is happening more often in the past few years with many of our town staples.

There's a wave of changes in the air, so buckle up and get ready to embrace them. We'll keep you updated on everything as it unfolds in real time.

Constance Williams – Thornwood Valley Gossip Mill Executive

I should be relieved that Constance seems to believe in me. However, I'm not. Reading the article only intensified my nerves.

Will I live up to the reputation my grandparents and parents built?

Or will I be its ruin?

Constance is right. Only time will tell. I'd better work as hard as I can to prove myself because four weeks is hardly enough time to do so.

Chapter 7

DAN

"Hey, Mom," I say, clutching my phone to my ear with one hand.

"It's good to hear your voice. Are you doing okay? You're not working still, are you?" Her voice is shaky.

"Great and no." *Liar.*

"What are you doing right now?" she asks.

I look down at the concrete floor of my shop. "I'm making dinner right now."

If there's a world where making dinner is the same as staring at a 1970 Chevy Nova that you just took a break from restoring to call your mother, then yes, I am definitely cooking myself an extravagant meal.

"What are we having?" she jokes.

I scratch my head and try my best to not stumble on my words. "We are having—" *Damn. What am I having for dinner?* I try to conjure up what's in my fridge to my memory.

There's a container of three day old spaghetti, a stick of butter, a case of beer, and a case of soda. It's not much to work with but enough to get creative.

"Warmed up leftover spaghetti and a soda."

"I'll be right over. Save a plate for me?"

I laugh. "Unfortunately you live too far."

She sighs. "I know. Jim and I are due for a visit soon. I'm thinking we can do Christmas."

"That would be great, Mom. I can't wait."

I'll have to figure something out with Dad for another holiday. I wouldn't want to have my parents together at the same time. There'd be bickering over unresolved baggage that they've never let go of. Add in the silent way they give each other the stink-eye and plenty of eye rolls. I'd prefer to avoid that situation at all costs.

Who knows if he even plans on coming in the first place?

Watching my parents' marriage fall apart my entire childhood kind of skewed my view of relationships. Then I got married straight out of high school and divorced within a few years. That's why I swore I'd never marry again unless I knew I found the love of my life.

"Me neither." Mom's voice distracts me from my deep thoughts. "Jim will make a batch of his famous funeral potatoes. I'd like to make a honey glazed ham this year. Change things up. I'll have to call Carter and Eve. I'm sure they'd love to come. Thornwood Valley is just the most charming town at Christmas with the lights, the giant tree, the decorations, the holiday party, and the chickens. Since we did Christmas last year at your brothers' place, I'm missing your small town so much." She sighs wistfully. "I'm really looking forward to it."

My brother's voicemail from this morning comes to mind. "They're actually coming for the Strawberry Festival."

"That's right. I almost forgot. Take some pictures of Bella for me, please? I'd love to be there, but I don't think Jim or I could schedule off work this short notice. If somebody would've answered my calls a week ago..."

"About that. I'm sorry. A lot's going on. I have a bunch of business with tourists. You know how the summer season gets."

Her voice cracks. "I just... I don't want you ending up like your father. Always working. Putting work above your family. It's not healthy. You need a work life balance."

"I'm not like Dad. I love my job. It's not always this way. The summer crowds keep me extra busy. I need to take advantage of it while it's here. The rest of the year is slower, and I can take more time for myself then."

She sighs. "I know, I know. I can't help worrying about you. I love you, Dan."

"I love you too, Mom."

"Okay. As long as you're okay. Call me soon."

"I will. Bye, Mom."

"Bye."

I hang my head over my crossed arms. She worries because she wants me to be happy. I am happy. I'm not like Dad. I know I work more than I should, but I don't have a family to come home to that depends on me to be there for them. If I was in a relationship, it'd be a different story. I would want to be there to break the mold. It's not that my Dad wasn't a good parent. However he prioritized his work and devoted his life to it which in turn drove a wedge between him and my mom and put a strain on our father-son bond. In the end it was what split my parents. It was hard to watch and even harder to see them slowly put space between each other for years while still pretending that everything was okay in front of Carter and I. We knew. We just didn't say anything.

I get up from the creeper and sweep the floor, setting every tool neatly back in their place above the work bench. All this talk about ham, potatoes, and spaghetti makes my stomach rumble, and I take that as my cue to be done for the night and have some dinner.

One day later

"Mmmm. This is good. Thank you," Marigold says as she takes a sip from her cup.

I wasn't sure what her drink of choice was, so I asked Olive when I stopped in The Olive Bean for coffee. She told me Marigold doesn't really stick to the same order, normally opting for something seasonal. Within minutes, she whipped her up some kind of strawberry latte special.

"Olive said you'd like it." I turn the key, starting the engine.

"I love it," she insists, taking another drink.

"Where are we headed?" I ask Marigold, as I turn off of the town's main street.

"His house is in Maple Grove. I brought a giant map and printed out some directions too. I'm not the best navigator as we've established." She laughs, unfolding the map and squinting at it. "I'm the worst possible passenger to rely on to make it anywhere. Unfortunately, you're stuck with me."

"That's okay. I've been out that way before. I towed a few cars there. It's further out through a bunch of one lane roads. I'm confident enough to at least get us close to the area. Plus, if all else fails, I have GPS on my phone." I try to reassure her.

Marigold must believe in me because she folds up the map and leans her head against the headrest. "Good. We shouldn't get lost then."

We ride in comfortable silence for a while. The trees continue to dart by the window as the sun rises. After some time, we pass a few homes, and Marigold mutters something under her breath.

"What was that?" I ask.

"Oh, I didn't realize I said it out loud." She blushes when I quickly glance at her. "That last house we passed had a flower garden with pink marigolds. Those are my favorite flowers. The pink ones are quite rare to come across, though. Did you see them? They're beautiful."

I swallow. "Sorry, afraid not. I missed them."

"That's okay. They're just flowers."

Something tells me they aren't just flowers to her.

"I'll keep an eye out for them on the way back." I promise.

I glance at her once more. She doesn't say anything, but she smiles in reply. The next few minutes we ride in silence.

"You mind?" I gesture toward the radio.

She shakes her head. "No, go ahead."

"What station do you listen to?"

"You can put on whatever you like," she replies.

I flip the visor down, as the sun blinds my vision. "What do you normally listen to?"

"I listen to pretty much everything: pop, rock, country oldies. You name it, I probably listen to it. I guess it depends on my mood."

"I have a bunch of CDs in the glovebox if you want to pick one of those."

"Don't mind if I do." She is flipping through the discs when I look over. "Oh! I love Toby Keith and Journey." Flip. "Rascal Flatts." Flip. "Spice—" Marigold starts laughing.

"What's so funny?" I wonder out loud. *Is there anything in there that I should be embarrassed of? I think not...*

"You listen to the Spice Girls?" Her eyes glow as she meets mine.

Shit. Yep. Embarrassing.

"That's not mine." I shake my head and keep looking out the window. I fight back a smile, but I'll be damned if I admit it's mine when she's definitely judging at the moment.

I appreciate good music. Is that a crime?

"Whose CD is it?" she prods.

Don't make eye contact.

"Mateo's!" I blurt. Poor Mateo is going to be taking the blame for this one.

"Oh. Mateo has great taste. I love the Spice Girls. 'Wannabe' is my go-to road trip song. Well, that or anything by Jimmy Buffett. Like I said, it all changes based on my mood. If I need a good laugh, I listen to Ray Stevens. For a good cry, I listen to "Married Life" from the movie *Up.* Tears every time."

Dang it. I'm even more embarrassed now because I couldn't own up to the fact that all those CD's are mine. So, Mateo is looking like the one with a playlist she can relate to when it's really me. I'm the one who can relate. I'm not sure if Mateo even listens to the Spice Girls. Maybe he does too. I don't know. That wasn't really a job requirement of mine to question music taste.

I hear her pull a CD out of the sleeve and pop it into the radio. The first track is, what do you know, "Wannabe" by the Spice Girls. I do my best to keep my composure and act like I have no clue what this song is. That's blatantly not the case.

You know this song. Own up to it.

The familiar tune plays through the speakers, and Marigold sings along with the first line. She belts the lyrics and lets her hair down. It blows in a blonde mass around her head in the wind as we continue to travel along the gravel road. She looks at me with the biggest smile, singing every word from memory. I shift my gaze from the road to her occasionally. She turns her head and points at me, smiling and nodding her head along with the upbeat song.

She knows this is mine. She has to.

It's the most free I've ever seen her. It makes me want to get to know her. I want to find out what she likes, does outside of work, and what other songs she knows the lyrics by heart. I want to become more than people who only discuss business.

The song changes, and it's the perfect time for me to own up to it. "Okay, maybe it's not his. It's mine." I sigh, drumming my fingers on the steering wheel, avoiding her gaze.

She clicks her tongue. "Aha! See... I knew it." She smirks knowingly, face bright with color. "I have a feeling we're going to be the best of friends."

"Me too." I chuckle, glancing over to her. "Me too."

Chapter 8

MARIGOLD

Algae streaks the side of a dilapidated mail box marking the end of the driveway. The address is almost unreadable, but the faint outline of fifty-six peaks through the green and brown.

Dan slows the tow truck.

We're here. We just have to go up the driveway to the house.

Driveway is describing the entrance generously. It's more like a billy goat path etched on the side of a cliff.

The woods lining both sides of the road are thick and covered in bright green foliage. It's midday, but the dense forest blocks the sunlight. A few rays of sun sneak through the gaps in the leaves. Two squirrels scurry across a branch to my right where the ground slopes gradually. I turn my head and gulp as I look at the place we have to go. It's up a mountain.

My eyes find Dan's. I stare at him with silent skepticism. My lips form into a thin line as I weigh the options. *Should we park here and walk? Drive the golf carts down here to load? Or go home and call it a bust?* Any of these seem like a plausible idea. I opt to air my ideas to Dan. "Maybe we—"

Dan hits the gas and shifts the gear smoothly as he pulls up the *very* steep gravel driveway.

Never mind.

I brace the seat cushion and lean to the left so that I don't become one with the door handle.

It might be my last day on earth.

Goodbye, Buttercup. Goodbye, Fix-Its. Goodbye, Dad and Daisy. Goodbye... everything.

"Woah!" I let out a shaky gasp. "Are you sure about this?"

His reply is cool and collected. "I've been up worse." He keeps his gaze trained on the mountain and shrugs. "Don't worry."

Don't worry? I'm the worry queen!

I'll lie in bed at night restless about something I said a year ago and think to myself "Why did I say that?" I ponder it and question what I said, cringing internally.

There was this one time when I bought a shirt at Chloe's Closet, and she said, "I hope you love your new shirt." I responded, "You too!" Then I realized Chloe didn't say to have a good day, and I was embarrassed. She looked at me like I had two heads. It was awkward until she laughed it off and said, "I will." I still think about that encounter to this day every time I walk past or go into her store.

My anxiety is normally caused by something minor. However, this isn't minor. This is grand on the worry scale. It's teetering the line between *oh no* and *holy cannoli!*

Dan cuts around another sharp bend etched into the cliff. *Why am I doubting him?* He's obviously a skilled driver. My sedan would've bottomed out next to the mail box. Also, he's a professional. I mean, I'm sure he's towed plenty of cars out of not so ideal situations.

If only he'd given me some sort of warning before driving up the cliff, I could have mentally prepared. I wish that he'd said something like, "Hey, Marigold, I think I'm gonna go for it. Hang on." Or maybe, "Hold on to your hat." Although, I don't have a hat on... My ideas need some work.

Dan bites his lip and grips the steering wheel firmly. He doesn't blink as he winds around another sharp bend—one that would've ended with us tumbling down the cliff if he missed it.

I'm impressed.

That doesn't mean my hands have stopped shaking or that my clammy skin has dried. My sweat glands are currently working overtime.

The last stretch of the steep incline comes into view. I scrunch my eyes closed.

Nope. I'm not looking.

Some things are better unseen. So, I listen rather than look. My body shifts as we move. The gravel crunches. Dan hums. *That's a good sign, right?*

Google Maps did not prepare me for this driveway. It only showed the tops of the trees. That's it. Plus, when I spoke on the phone with the owner of the golf carts, he didn't say anything about the driveway. Now that I'm here, on said driveway, I'm thinking he probably should've mentioned it. It was a pretty big detail to leave out.

It's too late now. Embrace the hiccups, Marigold. Embrace the hiccups. I cling to my mom's advice and tune everything else out.

"Are you okay?" Dan's question startles me.

I lower my hands and blink rapidly. I nod slowly. "Great," I manage to say with a crooked smile.

I am out of it right now. I'm not normally like this.

"Hey." His deep voice rumbles softly. He presses his large palm over mine, calluses scraping against my clammy hand.

I look up from my lap and into his brown eyes.

"I'm sorry," he says, looking extremely guilty. "I didn't mean to scare you. That wasn't my intention. I needed to keep driving slow and steady. It's normally best when going up that steep of an incline." He looks so guilt stricken as he searches my face.

"No, it's okay, really. It was just a shock. You did great." I laugh half-heartedly and smile again. "I'm in shock, but I'm okay, really."

"You sure?" His brows knit in worry. He keeps his hand on my trembling one and rubs his thumb in soothing circles over my knuckles.

"Yes." I nod and hope that it conveys I'm all good now. I needed a moment to get my bearings. "Let's go grab these things and get out of here."

"Okay, but if you need to sit here for a while, that's okay too. I'll wait with you, or I can go get the carts and you can stay here. Whatever you prefer is fine."

It's really sweet of him to offer, but I'd rather get down this mountain sooner than later, especially before it gets dark. Who knows how long we'll be here?

I grab my clutch with the money for the golf carts, and before I have a chance to open my door, it opens for me. Dan stretches a hand toward me. I smile as he helps me. It's a high step to get in and out, so I greatly appreciate the gesture.

Wow.

I can't help myself from gaping at the most unique home I've ever seen in person. The house is made from a bunch of shipping containers. The steel is painted a warm brown, almost blending into the tree trunks. The roof is covered in plants. A large weeping cherry with drooping branches sits next to the house with bird-feeders dangling on almost every branch.

A man opens the front door. He's short, with round glasses and gray hair. He smiles as he walks up to us. There's a pep in his step, telling me that he's glad to have visitors.

He holds out a hand toward Dan. "Archie."

"Dan," he replies, short and sweet, shaking his hand in greeting.

"Hi, Archie. I'm Marigold. It's nice to meet you." I smile and shake his hand. "I was the one who talked to you on the phone."

I don't know why I said that. Obviously, it wasn't Dan. Ugh. This is going to be another moment that haunts me later.

"Ah, yes. Nice to meet you. How 'bout we take a look at the golf carts and see if you'd like to bring any home?" Archie suggests, easing my awkwardness. He walks to the garage that is separate from the house. Then he opens the door and gestures his hand inside. "Follow me."

He weaves through the garage mindlessly as Dan and I hurry to keep up. The inside is filled with boxes and tools packed into every nook and cranny. My dad would get along great with Archie. I'm sure Archie knows where everything is, just like my dad.

Archie faces us and juts out a thumb, pointing behind him. "They're behind this car. They're a little dusty, but they run. I started 'em up this morning to be sure."

I'm more worried about how we are going to get the golf carts out of the garage without moving every item in here.

Dan's eyes light up like a kid on Christmas. "A 1950s Ford Thunderbird," he mumbles to himself in awe, bending down to examine the car.

Archie looks proud as he replies, "Yes, sir. 1956 to be exact. I've had it for years. Used to take it to every car show in the area. Those days are past me now. My ol' lady likes me home. Oh, I'm sure you know." Archie gestures a hand to me, and it takes everything in me not to let out a chuckle.

"It's not what you think." Dan shakes his head. His eyes are ready to bulge from their sockets.

Thanks, Dan. Is it really that bad he thinks we're a married couple?

"I have two eyes. Anyway, if you'd want the Thunderbird too, I'd sell it for the right price." Archie stares wistfully at the red car.

"I appreciate the offer, but I have my own project right now. I don't have any more room. I'm fixing up a 1970 Chevy Nova."

"Ah, bet it's a beauty." He continues to the back of the garage.

"One day, it will be," Dan replies.

Archie pulls the fabric off the golf carts. A cloud of dust fills the air.

Did he actually start them to see if they run?

I gasp when the dust cloud clears, but I really don't mind if he started them or not. Dan can fix them. They're perfect. They're exactly what Thornwood Valley needs.

"What the—" Dan starts but doesn't finish his thought. I tilt my head at him. He jerks his chin at the carts, and I shrug. I'm not sure what he's going on about. "Is that what you were expecting?" he asks under his breath. "They're... different."

Different. *Different?* He must not see my vision because that's what someone says when they don't like something, but they're trying to be nice about it.

"Yes. They're exactly what I wanted," I say through my teeth. The carts look even better in person than on the listing.

"Where exactly does someone come across golf carts like these?" Dan doesn't seem impressed as he crosses his arms, looking to Archie for answers.

I don't know what his problem is. They're great.

"I taught a hand drafting course at Maple Grove High. This was one of the assignments. The students decorated the golf carts for the spring parade. Each student drew the front, back, sides, and top after sketching out the isometric views of their idea. Every year a new class re-decorated the carts. I've had them sitting here for years. Now that I'm retired, there's no use for em' anymore." While Archie explains further, Dan nods and listens. "The students named them as well." He points to the first. "This one is The Chicken Coop. This one is The Duck Mobile. The Robin's Nest. Then there's The Pigeon Rocket and The Hoot. As you can tell, my students followed a bird theme for my last year of teaching."

I'd take them all with me if I could fit them on his truck, but I'll have to settle on two.

Dan massages the back of his neck. He does not look convinced.

"Can my husband and I have a word, privately?" I ask Archie.

"Sure! I'll leave you to it. Holler when you need me." He winks and disappears into the depths of the garage.

"Husband?" Dan's eyebrows shoot up.

I shrug. "Figured I'd go with it since he thought we were married anyway." Dan laughs, and I continue, "Alright, now, won't you come out with it." I need to know why his expression is screaming skepticism. I trust his judgement. He's been running a successful business for years.

"Hmm, what?" He scratches the stubble on his cheek.

"What are you thinking? I want your honest opinion. I thought we were friends now."

"No, it's not that I don't like them. They're... I don't know. Interesting? I'm trying to see your vision."

That gives me an idea.

"Close your eyes." His brows knit, but he closes his eyes anyway. "Okay, imagine this. You're sitting outside your shop, lounging on a park bench, and taking in the town. The sun is shining. Chickens trot across the road. Tourists are strolling, wearing shirts with chickens on them, and sipping drinks with chicken themed cups. Out comes The Chicken Coop with a family of three, chugging along at a *slow* pace. Then you get distracted. Blanche, my favorite chicken, hops up to sit on the park bench beside you. You guys start having a conversation. She lets out a few 'bawks.' You ask how her day is going." I giggle, unable to contain my laughter any longer.

Dan peels his eyes open and scrubs a hand over his face. "You saw me yesterday, didn't you?"

"Nooo... Maybe." I look around, feigning ignorance, but my growing smile gives me away. "Okay, yeah, I did. But it was what made me think for sure you'd be on board with these carts. They're funny and perfect."

"I—"

"Hey, I'm not judging you. I say hi to the chickens every morning. Besides, I haven't finished my story. Please, close your eyes."

Dan chuckles and squeezes his eyes shut.

"Where was I? Right! The Chicken Coop golf cart fits the town theme. They're driving down the road. Then out comes a chicken. Oh, no! But they see the chicken this time because they can't go above fourteen miles an hour. I did my research. What a perfect solution to the speeding issue. Plus, a golf cart is practically silent. Also, I'm planning to propose a chicken crossing sign for each end of the main town strip. Imagine that too in your daydream. You can open your eyes now."

His eyes blink open. "I'm impressed."

"Did I convince you?" I chew on my lip and swivel my necklace. If he doesn't believe in me, will the townies even like them?

A grin tugs at his lips. "Your story telling skills are impeccable." He fixes his gaze on the closest golf cart decorated with a duck theme and nods. "I'm convinced. I see your vision. I think once the dust is off of them, they will be a hit. Bird theme and all. Which ones do you want?"

"The Chicken Coop for sure. You choose the other."

"Me?" He points to himself. "Why?"

"Because you're in this with me." I shrug. "And I value your opinion."

He studies the different carts for a few beats. "The duck is fitting and meshes with the theme you have going. There are ducks at the pond. It works."

"I like your way of thinking." I take a step closer to The Duck Mobile. The duck figurine mounted to the front like a larger version of a hood ornament is funny. The cushion is wrapped in duck fabric. It couldn't be more perfect. With a little elbow grease and cleaner, it'll look brand new.

"You're not who I thought you'd be," Dan admits.

I face him. "What does that mean?" I press my lips together, searching his face and trying to gauge whether that's a good or bad thing.

His expression doesn't give much away. "You always seemed quiet. But I misjudged you. Three days ago we barely knew each other. Hardly spoke more than a few words outside of parts. And now I'm realizing we have more in common than I expected."

"I may seem that way. Quiet. Shy. But when I get to know someone and feel comfortable around them, I open up. For some reason, you make me feel like I don't have to be anything other than myself. You are capable of embracing me. Well, if you want to."

He reaches an arm behind his head and tugs on his ball cap. "I don't ever want you to stop talking. I like hearing what you have to say."

I let his words wash over me like a hug. He probably doesn't realize how much he has touched me. I don't think *I knew* just how much, deep down, I needed it either.

When I was younger, I was made fun of for talking too much. I was always the girl who was annoying. What people don't realize is that words can hurt. It shattered my confidence at a young age, and that's why I stopped being myself unless I really felt accepted around the people I was with. Then it became my new normal or what felt like normal: keeping my thoughts to myself.

What Dan said wasn't more than two sentences, but sixteen words never felt more comforting.

Chapter 9

DAN

"Take care!" Archie yells and waves as we head down his driveway.

I lift a hand to him, and Marigold shouts, "It was nice meeting you!"

I look in my rear view mirror one last time, making sure everything looks good. Both golf carts are strapped down and secured for the long drive ahead.

It took more time moving boxes out of the way than loading. At least he had a garage door on the back of the building, or else we would've been moving stuff for the entire day. I didn't really mind because he had a bunch of antiques and hidden gems. I also didn't mind hearing the stories behind everything. It was fascinating.

At first, the carts weren't what I was expecting, but I wasn't about to say anything. This is Marigold's dream. I would've hauled whatever golf carts she wanted, especially with the way her face lit up when Archie whipped the tarp off of them.

Marigold is right, though. Thornwood Valley is known to draw tourists specifically for the chickens. The carts are quite charming and will fit right in. I have no doubt about it.

I take my time coasting along the curves and steep arches in the driveway. I didn't realize driving as I normally do in a tricky situation would be a shock to Marigold. Thinking back on it, I should've said something. I'm not used to having a passenger when I'm on the way to tow something. Fairly often, I might have someone with me on the trip back if needed. I was laser focused and confident because I've been up a million and one less-than-ideal conditions in the winter. However, Marigold isn't used to my driving. Maybe that's because we haven't spoken much before the past three days, and now I'm realizing how much I missed out on not getting to know her more.

I glance quickly at Marigold. She is tapping her fingers nervously on her lap. "Are you okay?" I ask, parking my rollback at the bottom of the driveway. I'm noticing the more time I spend with her, the more I find out about what she's really feeling but not saying.

She raises her brows. "Just glad to be off that mountain. And glad to have two golf carts. Thanks for picking them up for me." She gives me a half-smile.

I turn the way we came and shift until I reach a reasonable speed. "What's wrong?" I ask. She still doesn't seem like her usual smiling self.

"I hope it works... What if it's not a good idea? What if this whole golf cart plan fails, and I set back the business? I only have a month to prove to my dad that I can handle everything on my own. I'm not sure I can."

I catch a glimpse of Marigold's dull expression. "You won't fail," I say confidently, before focusing back on the road.

"How can you be so sure?"

I pump the brake pedal as a deer crosses the road, and I ponder her question. The answer is simple. "Because you won't give up." She's passionate about Fix-Its, that much I'm certain of. She has drive, and the whole town will back her. I'll be damned if once she announces the carts there isn't a whole line of people waiting to sign up to rent them. If no one does, I'll rent one simply to show her how much I believe in her vision. "I'm sure of it. Almost everyone around town could use them." I glance at her quickly hoping that my words are reassuring her. "They can ride to the pond. Drive to The Rhett Farm to see the goats. Or pick apples and strawberries. They'll probably just ride around for the fun of it. You have nothing to worry about."

"I... Thank you, Danny. I really don't want to let my dad down, though. Fix-Its is pretty much his everything."

I keep silent, listening to her talk as she lets me in a little bit more.

"But mostly..." Her voice is soft, barely audible. "I don't want to let my mom down."

My mood plummets with her whispered confession. I don't know what to say to prove to her that she wouldn't. I never met her mother, but I've heard a lot about her. I could tell she was a wonderful person who didn't deserve to have such a short life. No one does. However, I know, without ever meeting her myself, she'd be proud of everything her daughter is doing, no matter what.

"She'd be proud of you," I say.

"Thanks, Dan. That means a lot to me." When I look over she brushes a hand over her face. "I'm sorry. You probably don't want to listen to me talk about my problems. I'm sure you have plenty of your own things to worry about without my silly doubts and random thoughts."

"No." I shake my head. "Don't apologize. They're not silly."

Nothing about what Marigold said was silly. She lost her mom. Of course, she's worried about Fix-Its and the future. It was her mom and dad's place—a place they loved and a place Marigold loves too.

"I'm a good listener, but I'm not always great with what to say," I confess.

"You don't have to say anything," she replies. "You wanting to listen means more than you know."

We share a quiet look, and in the silence, I can almost predict the words that are unspoken. There's the heaviness that weighs on her heart from losing her mother, the pressure she feels to pave her own path, the desire to make her family proud, and how crucial this month is for her. At this moment, I vow to myself that I will help her in any way that I can. I don't know why I'm making this promise to myself. Maybe it's because I know what it's like to have a dream, or maybe it's because I feel like we understand each other.

Chapter 10

MARIGOLD

"Hi, Constance!" I greet her when she opens the door to Fix-Its.

I glance at the clock hanging on the far wall. It's two. She's very punctual.

"The place is looking sharp," Constance observes, walking leisurely around the open space with the fishing supplies.

"Thanks." I shut my laptop. "What can I help you find today?"

"Oh, nothing, dear. I just wanted to see what you gals have been up to." Constance smooths her short gray hair behind her ear. No matter the weather, her hair always seems to hold its shape: no frizz, no free flying strands, nothing but absolute perfection.

Daisy emerges from the fourth aisle and stills when she sees Constance and I talking. Constance doesn't seem to notice her as she gazes toward the wall with the waders. Daisy does a zipping motion over her lips and slowly steps out the back exit, taking care to open and close the creaking back door with as little noise as possible.

"I actually wanted to speak to you about something. I was banking on you stopping in," I say.

Constance turns and faces me, eyes gleaming. Her tone raises in pitch. "Is that so?"

I chew on the inside of my lip, working up some courage. "Would you be able to write an article for me?"

I don't like asking for favors. I like to do things on my own, but it seems the past few days have been changing my mindset. Stepping outside my comfort zone is not pleasant, but it makes a difference for the future of Fix-Its.

"I would gladly!" Constance sets her purse on the counter and pulls out a journal, taking care to unfold the leather band and securing it in place. She licks the tip of her finger and thumbs through pages of notes. Her eyes dart between them until she lands on a blank one. "Aha! What would you like the article to feature?" She sets her reading glasses on the bridge of her nose.

"I purchased two golf carts. Dan is busy servicing them now to make sure they run smoothly." I start to explain as Constance supplies a pen from her purse and clicks it on the register counter. "They'll be ready tomorrow morning. I'm gonna park them out back so that anyone can rent them."

I also fill Constance in about the incident involving the chicken almost being run over, and the reasoning behind why I got the golf carts in the first place.

"I see." She scribbles some notes on the page in cursive. "I saw the almost catastrophic collision. You are a hero, Marigold. The way you ran into the road, saving our dear Blanche. It touched me." Covering her heart, she sighs in relief. "I was already working on a piece. This will be the perfect addition." She taps her pen on the page in thought. "I like your idea of the carts. It's fresh, aptly timed, and a step in the right direction toward preventing this from happening again."

I'm relieved to hear that she's onboard.

"Don't worry about going over to Chloe's. I'm heading over there now anyway. I'll see if she can make some chicken crossing signs. I'll make sure to give you credit."

I shake my head. "Oh, no. I don't need credit." I blush. "I just want the chickens to be safe. That's all."

"Okay, perfect." She taps her chin with the pen. "I think I have enough to run with." She closes her journal and starts wrapping the leather band around it. "Expect an article within a few hours." She slides the journal into her purse and puts the pen behind her ear.

"Thank you."

"No." Constance wags a finger. "Thank you." She pats my shoulder. "I can't write articles if I don't have people like you who keep me up to speed. I'm glad you told me."

Constance leaves smiling.

Not long after, Daisy cracks the back door, poking her head in the gap. She tiptoes from the door past each aisle, peaking and darting around the shelves. When she reaches the front counter, she arches a brow. I nod at her, trying my hardest not to giggle. She tiptoes behind it and whispers, "Is the coast really clear?"

"Yes!" I giggle. "She's gone. Left a few minutes ago."

Daisy sighs and plops on the stool beside me. She leans over the counter to look out the door.

"Why were you hiding from her?" I open my notepad.

Daisy tilts her head. "I quit. She'd be all over me like butter on bread. I've already been the star of a few articles. Each one is more embarrassing than the last. She'll start asking questions about why I quit. Then I'd have to tell her it's me. I'm the problem." Daisy pokes her chest. "Then she'd prod and push until I turned red in the face. It's not worth it."

"She only means well."

Daisy scrunches her nose. "*Sometimes. She only means well sometimes.*" Waving a hand at me, she says, "You see the best in everyone. But Constance puts out articles that aren't her business. Especially when it comes to relationships and secrets. Does she really need to post an article about everything that goes on in town? I don't think so. I see straight through her game."

Maybe Daisy's right.

Constance has always been nice to me. Sure, there are a few articles I've read that seem invasive, including a few that mention me. However, that's who Constance is; it's what she loves to do. Everyone has a passion for something. Constance's passion just happens to be gossiping and story-telling.

"Do you really see through her?" I reply.

"Yes." Daisy nods. "Now, I'm taking a quick fifteen minute break. I need something. Preferably with sugar and lots of spice. I'm thinking maybe a chai latte. Want anything?" She hops from the stool.

"Sure, I'll take whatever the special of the day is. Thanks!"

"You got it!"

When Daisy leaves, I get to work organizing the next row of shelves. This one is an assortment of spark plugs, light bulbs, pliers, screw drives, etc. The items are never ending.

My phone dings with a notification for a new article.

Constance works fast.

Thornwood Valley Social
Why did the chicken cross the road?

Chickens are a hot topic this week. Let's talk a bit about Monday.

An SUV almost came in contact with one of our chickens, Blanche. This is the one and only time you will ever read that sentence. Let's be clear: there will be no more incidents. Marigold Evans is officially crowned this month's town hero after last month's hero, Dustin Rhett, saved the cat, Felix, from an awfully tall tree. On the bulletin board next to the pond, you'll find a picture of Marigold with a little bit about why she's a hero. You can read the whole story there as well. Please, if you see Marigold, offer her a thank you and a pat on the back.

In other related news, Marigold, from Fix-Its, and Dan, from Dan's Auto, are teaming up to provide a new transportation method. This is optional but highly encouraged. As of tomorrow morning, you can stop by Fix-Its to sign up to rent one of the two golf carts: The Chicken Coop and The Duck Mobile. This is a wonderful idea. Now, there's an option for tourists and townies to choose a golf cart instead of riding their vehicles through town every day. You could also walk or bring a bicycle. It's up to you. I am also working with Chloe, from Chloe's Closet, to create two chicken crossing signs for both ends of the strip of businesses. That way, tourists who aren't aware will be now. This was Marigold's idea. I'd like to commend Marigold for her great ideas and Dan and Chloe for their help. Let's not forget that we thrive with each other.

The real question is, why did the car try to cross the chicken? Food for thought.

Constance Williams – Thornwood Valley Gossip Mill Executive

I blow out an exasperated breath.

Hero. Oh gosh. I wasn't expecting that. Nor was I expecting the credit I didn't need.

I don't want to be labeled a town hero. I was just doing what anyone else would if they saw one of the chickens in danger. I don't think it deserved a billboard nomination or a story.

I ignore my thoughts. At least she wrote the article. It was a nice thing.

I head to the front desk, sit on my stool, and grab a bag of sour gummy worms from my candy stash. I pop a few into my mouth and slide my headphones on. My phone connects to the pair of headphones automatically while I hold down the power on button. I tap through Spotify until I find my concentration playlist. "Crystallize" by Lindsey Stirling plays as I open my laptop. I create a new excel sheet, titling the document: *Fix-Its Inventory*. I start by entering each line from Dad's scrawled notes the best that I can. I'm dialed in, typing away when Daisy drops off my drink. I mouth, "Thank you." She nods and heads to the back rows to continue organizing the wood shelves.

I plop another sour gummy worm into my mouth and continue typing. I create a row for each item in the store: fishing jigs, waders, paint colors, etc. I know I can trust Dad's numbers, subtracting anything we've sold in the past two days. My dad is a professional at organized chaos. Speaking of my dad, I haven't heard from him today. I scribble a note in my notepad and mutter it to myself as I write, "Call him tomorrow if he doesn't call first." Then I shift my gaze back to my laptop screen, grabbing a handful of gummy worms.

A large shadow hovers over my screen. I glance upward, searching for the source, and jump in my seat. Dan's standing there. His mouth is moving, but I don't hear a word. I do hear Lindsey Sterling bowing strings on her violin loud and clear. I click the side button on my headphones to pause the loud music.

I stare at Dan in shock. I must look ridiculous to him with a gummy worm dangling from my mouth, a pen wedged behind my ear, and a giant pair of headphones on.

Embarrassing.

How long has he been standing there?

Dan smirks, adjusting his backwards baseball cap right above his brows, hiding his dark hair. It all but confirms he definitely witnessed me shoving a handful of sour gummy worms—enough to almost choke on—into my mouth.

Was I talking to myself too?

Yes, indeed, I was... before and after I shoved candy into my mouth as if it were my last meal.

I cringe internally. *Wait a minute.* I caught him in a similar situation the other morning. He was talking to a chicken, not himself, but we're pretty much both on the same wavelength.

I take my headphones off my ears and put them around my neck.

"Hey, Goldie," Dan says. That knowing smirk is still plastered across his face.

I chew slowly, tipping my chin in reply.

We're friends now, so I shouldn't be embarrassed. However, he has the worst timing, and I'm not ready to admit I have a gummy worm addiction.

I brush some sugar dust off the counter and ask, "What can I help you with?"

"Just came to tell you that the golf carts are ready to go. Pulled them up out back." He points a thumb to the back door.

"You're a rock star."

"Call me if you have any issues tomorrow," he says.

"Will do." I drum my fingers against the counter.

Thinking about tomorrow has me nervous. Will people want to rent them, or will the investment be a big setback on our figures? I took a risk with them. I put us almost in the red for this month.

Dan's voice jolts me from my worries. "Are those sour or sweet?" He's looking at the bag of candy.

"Sour." *The best kind.*

He clears his throat. "The best kind." *Jinx. Is he reading my thoughts? I swear.*

"I got them when I went out of town. Valley Harvest doesn't have the sour ones in stock. Only the regular. These—" I tap the bag "—are soft and sour." *And delicious. And my coveted secret. I* don't usually share them with just anyone. I drive hours to secure them.

Dan squints, trying to read the bag. "I haven't had the sour ones in a long time."

I reach under the counter and grab an unopened bag. "Take some to try."

"No." Dan shakes his head. "I don't want to take yours."

"They're yours now." I hand him the bag. "Trust me. Your life will be changed. You'll never want to eat those boring ones again."

"Are you sure?"

"Yes. I have a few more bags. Don't worry about it." I have eight more bags to be exact, but he doesn't need to know that.

"Thanks," he says, swinging the bag.

I grin, knowing I'm the reason his life will be better. "You got it."

Dan walks backwards toward the door. "Call me if you need anything. No matter how small."

"I will."

He grips the door handle but stands there. It's almost as if he has something else he wants to say. I continue smiling, and his lips quirk up slightly in the corners.

I wonder what he's thinking. I can't read him.

He could be standing there thinking I'm a mad woman who talks more about gummy worms than anything else. Hmm, maybe he's thinking about the chipped paint on the wall? Oh,

I know! He's probably thinking about cars! He's got the thinking-about-a-car look. The signs are all there: lines on his forehead and eyebrows drawn together.

That has to be it!

Dan's head bobs slightly, and he scratches his five-o'clock shadow. He doesn't say anything as he turns the handle slowly and disappears from the swinging door.

I glance at the clock just as Daisy juts her head around the back aisle. "So... what's going on with you and Dan?"

"What?" I cross my arms. "Were you listening the whole time?"

"Maybe..." She winks. "Was that flirting? It was hard to see through the gaps between everything on the shelves, but I could feel the tension."

"It's strictly business." I stretch my hands behind my back and yawn.

"Mhmm." Daisy hums, picking up a pen from the cup on the counter and twirling it around her fingers. "Do business partners usually give each other their sacred candy stash?"

"I don't know." I shrug. "Dan's nice. We're friends. We bonded over them, so I gave him some to try."

"Oh. Are you replacing me?" Daisy teases.

"Never. You're my best friend, silly. There's no replacing you."

"Good. Glad we're on the same page." She tosses the pen and it lands in the cup with the others. That was impressive. "I'm heading home for the night. The wood aisle is organized and ready to go." She grabs her clutch under the counter and blows me a kiss. "See ya tomorrow, girly. Buttercup is taking a nap in the Think Den, by the way."

"Thank you! Bye!" I wave and set my headphones back on my ears. Turning up the music, I grab some more gummy worms and get back to entering the numbers into my computer.

Chapter 11

DAN

I knock on the open door of the office. "Hey, Char."

Char stops typing and looks up. "Dan, hey, what can I help you with?"

"Can you write out a bill for the Honda Civic? Oil change and a tire rotation."

She gives me a thumbs up. "I'm already on it." She types a few things and glances over.

"You're the best. Did I miss anyone coming in?"

"Chuck stopped by this morning. He needs his mower worked on. He'll be back later to drop it off. I guess it needs a new belt, has a flat tire, and won't stay running. He said he had enough trying to fix it on his own. He replaced the spark plug, but it didn't fix anything. I don't know."

"Got it. Sounds like a rough day." I chuckle. "Thanks, Char."

"No problem. Yeah, he looked pretty worked up." Char clicks her tongue. "Have you heard anything from Marigold on the carts?"

I lean against the wall and brush a hand over my face. "Nothing."

Char swivels her chair toward me and leans back. "Mateo texted. Said there was a line out the door at Fix-Its. I think the whole town wants to rent a golf cart. He went over extra early to get one for the weekend when we're both off. He got us a Saturday spot so we can ride Nova around town."

"Glad to hear it. How is Nova?"

Char's face brightens. "Great! She just started crawling. And she loves seeing the goats out at the farm. We have to make the trip at least once a week. She's sleeping pretty steady through the night now. Plus, Mateo and I have a pretty great boss that keeps us employed and both working part-time so that we get to spend as much time with our daughter as we can."

I wave a hand. "I have great employees."

Char shakes her head. "Good employees come from a good boss who cares and a great environment. You're too modest and won't accept the compliment. It's fine, but I'll keep giving them. Now, I need to get back to writing up these invoices. Don't you have a Honda to work on or something?" she teases, and spins her chair back to face the computer.

"I'll get out of your hair." I chuckle as I head back into the shop.

I love my job because it doesn't feel like one. I can always count on it. It's people that I can't. I guess not all people. It's more like a certain someone, also known as my father, who hasn't spoken a word to me since last Christmas.

I head out to the Civic and line up the lift bars, shaking the thoughts from my mind.

I don't care. If I think it enough times, maybe it will feel like the truth.

The car raises as I hold down the button on the lift. I grab a few tools from the work bench and take off the under-car engine shroud. I slide the oil drain dolly underneath the drain plug. Then I use the ratchet to remove the plug, filling the oil bin in a steady stream.

While I wait, I think about Marigold. It makes me happy to hear that she's doing well today with the golf carts. It also gives me an idea.

I shoot a text to Mateo.

Dan

Can you handle the shop tomorrow? I'm gonna head out for a tow.

A few minutes later my phone pings with a reply.

Mateo

I got it covered.

I slide the oil dolly over and remove the old oil filter when Char pokes her head out the office. "Dan, Constance is on the phone. She says it's important."

I shake my head. "Tell her I'll be there in a minute."

"Okay." Char gives me a lopsided grin.

This has to be good.

I can only begin to imagine what Constance deems is urgent news.

I wash my hands and step into Char's office. She hands me the phone. "Hello," I say, leaning against the wall.

"Dan! It's Constance! I'm sorry to be the bearer of bad news, but something's wrong with the golf cart I rented, dear. Marigold said you are servicing them, correct?"

"Yes."

"Great. I was out at the pond chatting with Henry while he was fishing. There are a few business-related topics we had to discuss that *still* aren't resolved. Anyway, I won't bore you with the details. I know you're a busy man. The Chicken Coop won't start back up. I have places to be, but I don't want to just leave it there. So, I called you to see what you can do."

"Is it cranking at all?" I ask.

"Let me have a look." The phone is silent for a few minutes. "No, dear, I don't think it is."

"Okay, I'll be right there." I guess it's best that I go and figure out the issue instead of trying to troubleshoot over the phone.

"Be sure to bring Marigold up to speed. My phone is almost dead, or else I'd do it myself. Oh! Maybe you should bring her with you since this is her golf cart business. It wouldn't hurt to have an extra pair of eyes to get the cart running."

She has a point. I wasn't planning on bothering Marigold at all, but I'm sure she'd appreciate the option to come along if she isn't too busy at Fix-Its.

"I will. Be there in about thirty minutes."

"Take your time. I have nowhere to be," Constance replies and ends the call.

I could've sworn she had *places to be*. Maybe I misheard her. Perhaps it was *no place to be*. I don't know why I'm worried about it. I, myself, have places to be.

A toddler with a lollipop larger than his head pulls on his mom's shirt and points to the pictures of the golf carts pinned to the cork board behind Marigold and Daisy at the front desk in Fix-Its. "I wanna go in the duckie. Please, Mommy."

"Let me ask the sweet lady first." His mom squeezes his hand gently.

Marigold wipes a hand over her forehead.

Oof. I think his mom just made Marigold the bad guy without realizing it. I know for sure that The Duck Mobile is rented out today and the next few days.

"We would love to rent The Duck Mobile for the day," the mother says.

Marigold offers them a sad smile. "I'm sorry. Unfortunately both carts are rented for the next eight weeks. But if you'd like to rent it for September, the fall leaves are beautiful. There's apple picking at the orchard and a giant apple-related festival in town."

Eight weeks? I can't believe they're already rented for that long. Actually, I can believe it. Marigold's idea was exactly what the town needed. Now, hopefully it proves to her that she isn't letting her parents down. She is bringing business to the store and the town. She should be extremely proud of herself.

The little boy and his mother leave with smiles on their faces, and I'm sure that means Marigold convinced them to come back in the fall.

"Hey, Goldie." I step up to the register counter.

Crimson blush paints Marigold's face. "Hey, Danny."

"How's this morning going?"

"Do you want all the details? Or the cliff-notes version?"

"Don't spare anything." Constance said she had nowhere to be... A couple more minutes wouldn't hurt.

"It's been total chaos. I had to practically hold back the mass of customers as I flipped the open sign. Most of them were familiar faces, but a few tourists trickled in. Then a few turned into too many to count. Constance was here first. She rented The Chicken Coop for today, and the line behind her let out a collective disappointed sigh. At this rate, the carts will be paid off by closing today. I can't believe it." Her smile grows. "Daisy and I had to form two separate lines. She rang out items in the store while I handled the golf cart rentals. This is the busiest we've ever been on a Tuesday. At least in my lifetime."

"That's incredible. You should be extremely proud of yourself. I know Harvey will be, without a doubt."

"I don't think my dad would believe it if I told him over the phone. If he were here, he'd be chatting with the locals and trading jokes. And he'd probably break out the photo album and tell the classic 'Fix-Its origin story' for the tourists. The one he told you on your first day in town. But right now, I'm glad he's not here even though I miss him. He's finally relaxing and soaking up some of that beach sun."

I chuckle. "I remember every detail of that story, despite my mind being elsewhere, thinking how in the world I was going to run a business in a town that I knew no one in. Your dad was the first person I met, and he made me feel welcome. And then he pointed me to Constance to introduce myself because she knew everyone." I reminisce on a time where I thought I'd never be where I am today. "Speaking of—"

Daisy's laughter fills the shop, stopping me mid-sentence. I turn my head to see Daisy scooping Buttercup up and hugging her to her chest. "Ugh. I love this job," Daisy says to herself.

"I'm glad to hear it," Marigold says through laughter. Then she turns her attention back toward me. "What were you speaking of?"

"Constance. There's something going on with The Chicken Coop. If you want to join me, I'm headed there now."

Marigold blows out a breath. "That's why you have a tool bag. Makes sense now. I'm gonna grab mine. Let's go."

Chapter 12

MARIGOLD

Today was almost too perfect. It made me wonder when the other shoe was going to drop. As soon as Dan said there was something wrong with Constance's golf cart, it made sense. Hopefully it's an easy fix because I rented it out for over eight weeks.

Oops. Another hiccup.

Sometimes, risks are worth taking in business and in life. I stepped into the golf cart rental world headfirst.

Dan pulls his tool bag over his shoulder and holds the door open for me. "Thanks." I blush and lead us across the street.

He catches up to me within seconds. His strides are long, and I find myself taking two steps to his one to keep up. He's much taller than me. I'm five feet even. If I were to guess, he's around six feet tall. He slows, probably noticing I can barely keep up.

Blanche runs toward me when we reach the sidewalk. "Sorry, Blanche. I don't have any treats on me. But, I'll bring you some mealworms later. That's a promise."

"So, you weren't lying," Dan says. "You talk to the chickens just like me."

"Yep. I don't lie." I adjust my tool bag higher on my arm.

We beeline toward the path between Bobbie's Freeze and Annie's Diner. A couple sitting on a park bench laugh at each other as their ice cream cones drip from the heat outside.

I shield my eyes from the sun as I keep walking. Right now, I'm really wishing I had grabbed my sunglasses before I left.

"Here." Dan takes his hat off and offers it to me.

"Don't you need it?"

He rakes a hand through his thick, dark brown almost black hair and shakes his head. "I'll be fine."

I don't think I've ever seen him without his hat. I'm not sure what I was expecting, but I wasn't prepared for the way it would make butterflies flutter in my stomach.

His hair is almost as dark as the night sky. If that wasn't mesmerizing enough, his mahogany gaze sparkles in the sun as he patiently holds the hat toward me.

Get it together, Marigold.

I take a moment to gather my bearings before accepting the hat from his grasp. "Thank you." I put on his hat and position the bill to shield the sun. It fits loosely around my head. I chew on my lip as I struggle to adjust the strap and buckle while holding my tool bag.

"Can I help?" Dan asks.

"Please."

Dan sets his bag on the ground and stands behind me. His hands brush my head softly as he tightens the strap. I can tell he's being careful not to snag any of my hair. It feels as though time has slowed—mostly due to the silly goosebumps prickling my arms and the butterflies swarming in my stomach.

"There you go." He hums in approval.

"Thanks." I squeak. I cover my face, trying to hide the heat I feel creeping up my cheeks.

He lifts his tool bag over his shoulder again, and we walk the rest of the way to the park to find Constance.

We reach the pond in no time. Fish jump in the air, rippling the water. The glare from the sun reflects off the water. Constance sits on a park bench beside Henry, who is casting his line into the water.

"My, don't you two look like a handy duo?" Constance observes. She raises a hand to shield her eyes from the sun and motions us over with her free hand. "Isn't that lovely, Henry?"

Henry does not look pleased with her as he says, "Lovely."

"Those two are peas in a pod. They both have tool bags and everything. They're here to save me, Henry! I'm not going to be stranded here much longer. You're probably ready for me to get out of your hair, aren't you?"

"I can see that." Henry laughs, avoiding her questions. He waves at Dan and I. "Join us. We're having a nice chat about toilet paper. Constance has a problem with the types I have in stock."

"Wha—" I stammer.

Constance purses her lips at Henry. "This isn't a *me* issue. It's a *serious* town-wide matter." She brushes lint from her shoulder and turns her attention to me. "You heard him right. Toilet paper. The two-ply is too hard on our septic system. I took a survey and at least fifty of our lovely town members agreed. I can show the results. I already spent the majority of my morning showing Mr. Stubborn the concrete proof." She holds the clipboard out to me.

I grab it and go over her survey results. Dan leans over my shoulder, shielding his eyes from the sun, and laughs softly against my ear.

I stare at the paper for a minute or so and nod my head. It's a bunch of boxes checked on a piece of paper with what kind of toilet paper people prefer. I never thought it'd be such an important topic for discussion. Constance thinks of everything.

I look up and Constance gestures for me to hand over the clipboard. I give it back, and she says, "See? We're sick of driving all the way to the next town over to get one ply. It's time he adds some more variety to the store. The same brands have graced the shelves for the past twenty or so years."

Henry casts his line. "Can't a man fish in silence?"

"Not until said man solves this toilet paper issue," Constance retorts.

Henry sighs deeply. "I like what we have. My store is simple. If it ain't broke, don't fix it. What's with you people always wanting to change things? I never once had a complaint until today."

Constance rolls her eyes. "Nothing needs fixing. Something needs to be added. You're just in denial."

"She's ruthless," Dan whispers in my ear, and I press my lips together to avoid laughing.

"People want to see some change. We're embracing change, remember?" Constance waves her arms as she talks.

"Dammit." Henry grumbles. "Fine! I'll make some calls, and we'll have one-ply toilet paper in stock as soon as the truck drops it off. Will that make you happy? Any more changes?"

"No," she replies and gets up from her spot on the bench, walking toward the golf cart.

Before I can follow her, Dans says, "Gummy worms. The sour ones." He pushes his dark hair back.

Did Dan just say what I think he did? He asked Henry to stock sour gummy worms. My heart skips in my chest. I could marry him right about now.

"What?" Henry casts his line and turns toward Dan. "You want gummy worms?" His eyebrows scrunch. "I thought we already had them."

"Not the sour ones. Can you stock those?" Dan raises a brow.

Henry scratches his head and casts his line in the water. "I don't know. Seems like too much change for one day. Don't ya think?" He mulls it over for a minute, casting his lure into the pond a few times. "Think they'll sell well?"

"I'll buy at least a few bags a week." Dan promises.

"Okay." Henry nods. "I'll try to get them in stock. That's it, though. Nothing else is changing."

"That's perfect." Dan nods. "I won't ask for another thing."

Yes! This is the best day ever!

I can't seem to wipe the goofy smile from my face.

Dan turns slowly. "So, Constance, what's—"

Yep, she's gone.

"Where did she go?" I ask. I thought she was by the golf cart...

"Walked away while we were talking." Henry points to the trail leading from the pond. "She must have somewhere better to be. She got what she wanted and left." He reels in his line. "That's Constance for ya."

Dan scratches his head. "Well, I guess we'll take a look at the golf cart."

"Have fun you two. I have a few more casts then I'm packing up and heading out," Henry says.

Dan and I go to the abandoned cart next to the park sign. Dan gets in and turns the key while pressing his foot to the petal. It makes a clicking noise but doesn't move. He gets out, and I flip the seat, pivoting it toward the front. Dan and I grab the seat together, lifting it from the latch and lowering it on the floor of the cart.

Everything looks fine to me as I lean over to check the battery. Nothing looks corroded.

Our heads are tipped over the compartment. "This is major déjà vu." I laugh. "This is my life now, checking batteries and trying to repair broken forms of transportation."

Dan chuckles. "It's contagious. Everything happens at the same time. Don't worry it's probably something simple."

Dan fiddles with some wires and after a few moments he clicks his tongue and grabs a wrench from his tool bag.

"Did you figure it out?" I ask.

"See the starter here." He points to it. I nod. "The ground wire is loose." He wiggles the loose wire. "When I tighten it, it should start. I just—" He trails off and tightens it with the wrench.

"Just what?"

Dan scratches his head. "I know I tightened it yesterday."

"I'm sure you did. I believe you. It's no big deal."

He puts the wrench in his bag, sets his tool bag in the back, and helps me lift the seat back on, pivoting it flat. He hops in and sure enough it starts.

I give him a thumbs up. "Let's go find Constance."

"Want to drive?"

"No, you can if you want." I set my tool bag in the back and trip over something on the ground. I lean down and grab the culprit, an adjustable wrench. It must have fallen from Dan's tool bag. I toss it in my bag for now and hop in the front.

I cross my legs and hold on to the handlebar as Dan drives us along the walking path. We catch up to Constance in no time as she leisurely strolls. Dan parks the cart beside her.

"Oh, my lovies! Thank you for fixing it so fast!" Constance exclaims. "Sorry for skedaddling. I have a noon lunch date with Chuck. I didn't wanna be late. I figured it'd take awhile to diagnose the problem." She fiddles with the strap of her purse.

Dan shuts the golf cart off. He swings his legs over the edge and says, "I'll sit in the back. You two can ride up front."

Constance clearly doesn't like that idea. "Nonsense. We can all fit up front. Marigold, can you scootch over? I'll squeeze in on the end."

Dan looks at me, wide-eyed. I shrug my shoulders. I don't know how in the world the three of us are going to fit on this tiny seat.

Oh, God. I'm going to become the peanut butter and jelly in the middle of the sandwich. A golf cart sandwich where I'm squashed.

I slide along the chicken-patterned seat. I inch as close as I can to Dan without getting entirely in his personal space, which is almost impossible. There's about a half-inch gap between my arm and his side.

"Just a little bit more." Constance shimmies toward me.

"Okaayyy." I draw out the word. *I don't think I can make any more room.*

I slide closer to Dan. There's about an eighth inch now. Constance sets her giant floral purse on her lap and grasps the side handle. "I'm all set."

She manages to shove me closer to Dan when she leans back. My arm brushes Dan's side, underneath where his arm stretches to hold the steering wheel. "Sorry," I mumble.

"No need to be sorry." The timbre of his deep voice cracks on *sorry*.

My arm tingles and warms where it touches Dan. It has to be attributed to the weather. It's hot outside, and we're currently jammed into this tiny seat.

"All good?" Dan asks.

"Yes." I lie through my teeth. Am I physically good? Yep, sound. Mentally good? Nope. Being this close to Dan makes my thoughts jumble.

"We're just peachy," Constance replies.

I try to avoid looking at Dan's arms, but I can't help it. I've never been this close to him to notice how strong and muscular his arms are. It's not like I ogle at him on a daily basis. On weekdays, he normally wears some type of long sleeve shirt that covers his arms. Plus, before the past four days, we barely knew each other.

Dan starts the cart and follows the path. We pass more trees and a few chickens scavenging the grass.

Constance starts talking about how well her last article did and how many likes it got on Thornwood Valley Social. I try to listen, I really do, but my thoughts are miles away.

I can't get over the feeling of being pressed up against Dan. His side is as muscular as his arms. So much is evident by the outline of his T-shirt. Goosebumps prickle my skin.

Goosebumps. It's almost ninety degrees outside, and I have goosebumps.

What is wrong with me?

"Marigold?" Constance's voice jolts me into the present and away from my very interesting thoughts. "You'll be there right?" She looks at me with a hopeful expression.

"Sure! Yeah." *What am I agreeing to?*

Dan pulls The Chicken Coop behind Fix-Its.

"Great! Thanks for the help, lovelies! I'll be seeing you both tonight then." She hops out as Dan and I slide from the seat and grab our tool bags from the back. Constance whispers in my ear. "Nice hat." She wiggles her eyebrows, winks, and waves as she climbs back into the cart and takes off toward the road.

What? I'm confused. Tonight? What is tonight?

Dan scratches his head, and I stand awkwardly, trying to piece together what just happened.

I'm the first to break the silence. "Where are we going tonight?"

Hopefully he was listening because I surely was not.

He shrugs his shoulders. "Some kind of bonfire thing. I don't know. It's by the pavilion tonight at seven. That's pretty much all I got."

"Well, guess I have plans tonight."

"That makes two of us."

"So, I'll definitely see you there?"

"Yeah," Dan says with a grin. We smile awkwardly at each other for a few beats, and he heads back toward his auto shop.

I watch him leave until I realize I'm still wearing his hat. "Wait!" I call out after him. "Your hat!"

Dan turns and scrunches his brows. I grab the brim, ready to give it back. I'm not about to steal his favorite hat. I lift it from my head and hold it out, taking a few steps toward him.

His dimpled grin makes me weak in the knees. "Keep it. It looks better on you."

My face heats with blush, and my stomach does a little flip as I place it back over my head. I'm not sure what to think, but I liked the way his voice was gravelly when he said *looks better on you*.

Chapter 13

DAN

"Dammit," I mumble under my breath as I open my dresser drawer, unfold a T-shirt, and toss it over my head.

I really got myself into a predicament. I regret agreeing to attend the bonfire party Constance is throwing. I've been dreaming all afternoon about a cold beer, pizza, and calling it a night. However, it seems life can never be so cut and dry.

I drag on a pair of jeans and slide a belt through the loops. On the way out the door I put on a pair of boots and grab a new tan hat, shoving it on my head backwards. I grin when the memory from earlier today flashes in my mind. My favorite hat has a new home, and I'm not even going to miss it.

The more time I spend with Marigold, the more I learn about her. She's funny, smart, kind, and beautiful. I can't stop making excuses to see her.

It doesn't take me long to walk to the pavilion. The setting sun has eased some of the heat from earlier in the day. The air is still warm, and the smoke from the bonfire fills my nose.

There are so many people. I'd much rather be in the comfort of my home right now.

I take a seat on a bench, leaning back, and draping my arm over the sturdy wood. I can't help it. I look for *Marigold.*

On the bench to my left there are two people I don't recognize tipping their heads in laughter. To my right, on another bench, Chloe takes a sip of her drink and leans closer to Laura, from the post office, as they talk animatedly.

Some people stand beside the bonfire beside the pavilion, holding drinks dripping with condensation. In my opinion, it's too hot to stand by a fire.

I try to conjure up what Constance was saying about tonight. There was something about a fire, dinner, drinks, and was it an activity? Oh, no. I hope not.

I had a very hard time concentrating when driving the golf cart with Marigold pressed up against me. Plus, my hat on her head was enough to make me absolutely unable to hear a word that left Constance's lips. I said *mhmm* and *uhuh* at all the right times, or so I thought.

Damn. I really did it this time. I could be at home in my bed, sleeping. That's exactly where I should be with the early morning trip I'm making out of town.

It's bad enough that I participate in the spring small business games the town committee holds every year: racing chickens, solving puzzles, treasure hunts, three-legged races where I fall on my ass, etc. I can get behind the event because it truly benefits the businesses in town.

This bonfire is unknown territory. I have no clue why I'm here or what purpose this event serves. My gaze finds Marigold walking toward the pavilion looking unsure. Now, I remember exactly why I'm here. It's so we can do this together because we both agreed to come without truly realizing the extent of tonight's festivities.

I stand by what I said earlier. My hat looks much better on Marigold. It looks infinitely better if possible. Her blonde hair falls in bouncy waves underneath it, but unlike before, she has the bill flipped to match mine. Seeing her makes all my doubts about being here fade away.

Marigold glances around as she stands just before the pavilion. She tucks her hands in the pockets of her pink overalls, turning her head to search the crowd. When she finds me, a smile tugs her lips upward, and the unsure expression she wore earlier disappears.

Marigold reaches me and takes a shaky breath. "I'm glad you're here."

I lean forward and rest my arms on my thighs. "Me too."

She takes a seat beside me. "Are you really?"

"Yes, because you're here." I massage my temple. "Otherwise? Not really. I'm wondering what the bonfire is a cover for. It's only a matter of time before Constance shows up, megaphone in hand, announcing a competition. Or maybe she will continue with more upgrades. Do you think she'll show up riding a horse?"

Marigold giggles. Her laughter is music to my ears. "I'd pay money to watch that. That's not really her style. I could, however, see her whipping in on one of the golf carts. Luckily, both of them were parked behind Fix-Its when I left. So, that is out of the question. On second thought, she wouldn't have been able to zip around going that slow anyway. Kind of defeats the purpose, don't you think? Constance needs a grand entrance, and we're not clever enough to come up with something that suits her. Guess we'll find out sooner than later."

"Did you bring your phone?"

Marigold checks her pockets. "No, I think I left it by the register."

"I didn't bring mine either. I was going to say that we could see if her article said anything."

"I'm sure it was vague. She's been unusually quiet about tonight. Yesterday she posted about the carts and the Strawberry Festival. Today she released a ten-page article on the benefits of one-ply toilet paper in septic systems. Speaking of toilet paper, thank you for asking Henry to stock sour gummy worms. Wow, those two things do not go together. Anyway, that was really... sweet." She wraps her hair around her finger.

"No problem." I knew it was something she wanted but would never ask for. What I did was not, by any means, earth-shattering. However, it made Marigold happy. It brought a smile to her face. For some reason, I can't help but want to make her smile. "On a different note, nice hat."

"Do you like it?" She smiles, tucking her hair behind her ear. "This guy I work with gave it to me out of the kindness of his heart. It was his favorite hat."

"Sounds like a decent guy."

Her cheeks fill with color. "He's not so bad." She looks around and then nudges me softly with her elbow. "So... what happened to our deal?"

"What deal?" I run my fingers over my chin.

"The hide-in-the-back-corner-of-events pact. Where we are as far away from people as we can get. We invented a club and every-thing. Even though we never named it." She raises a brow.

"Oh. This was the only available bench. I'm sorry. I can go ask the people in the back to move for us," I suggest.

Her eyes widen and dart to the tables at the far end. Marigold shakes her head.

"I'm just teasing you."

Marigold blows out a breath. "Thank God. I was worried you would actually do it."

"No, I wouldn't, not unless you really wanted me to."

"Yeah, no." She taps her fingers over her lap. "So, do you have any more guesses on what's happening?"

"I haven't got a clue."

She turns her head and studies the bonfire. "It seems quiet for a town event."

"It does—"

"Hello, lovelies!" Constance's voice booms from everywhere.

I think every single person collectively jumped out of their skin on that note. Marigold hovers a hand over her heart, and I look around, stunned.

Since when was the pavilion equipped with surround sound? I glance heavenward at the wood beams. It doesn't take me long to find the source: speakers mounted every few feet.

That seems excessive and expensive.

The speakers emit Constance's voice again. "It's time for our first ever Thornwood Valley blind date night!"

Uhh. What?

No.

This can't be happening.

What if I sneak out now before the chaos ensues? No one would notice...

I turn toward Marigold hoping she is thinking the same thing as me. There's no way I can leave without her. The flash of shock in her bright blue eyes does the speaking for her. We need to get out of here *now.*

Why did I sit us snag dab in the middle of the place?

Constance is nowhere to be found.

Plan your escape.

We could crouch-walk behind the benches unnoticed while Constance's voice projects through the speakers, distracting everyone else in attendance. No matter what, the people standing at the bonfire would see us. That's a risk I'm willing to take. I don't think they would shout, "Look! Dan and Marigold are escaping!" Would they?

Did these people know they signed up for a blind date, or was this a set-up?

Focus, Dan. Focus on the exit strategy. Don't worry about them.

"Let's sneak behind—" I start to tell Marigold. That is until a figure appears out of the corner of my eye.

Dammit.

The figure is actually Constance.

She walks slowly around the side of the bonfire, clutching a giant inflatable microphone. Her hair blows wildly around her face in a sudden burst of wind.

Is there a wind machine I'm not aware of?

The smoke rises from the fire as she moves slowly. A townie follows a few steps behind Constance, holding an electric leaf blower.

"I'll be damned," I mutter unintentionally.

Marigold's voice is shaky with laughter as she says, "This is comedy gold."

We share a quick I-can't-believe-what-I'm-seeing smile. I turn my attention back to Constance, because at this point I'm invested.

"Singles night... night... night... night," Constance says into the microphone, trying and failing to create an echo.

The crowd oohs and aahs, watching the show in front of us.

Constance reaches the—wait, is that a *podium*? Yep. It's another new thing I wasn't aware of before today.

She sets the giant microphone down and rips a piece of duct tape from the front of it, removing a miniature microphone that she clips to her dress. "Thanks for being here. We have so much fun planned for tonight." Constance waves her hand in a come here motion. Bobbie and Annie join her beside the podium, holding a poster board.

Constance hovers her arm below the first line of words on the poster board that are absolutely unreadable from this distance. "Ladies and Gentleman, as you are aware, this is a blind date singles night as described in detail in this afternoon's article, Singles Night at the Pavilion. It was pretty self explanatory." She lowers her arm to the next line of words I can't read. "Please find a seat at one of the picnic tables in front of me. Ladies, take your spot on the side with the stack of pink papers, and gentlemen, take the seat with the blue papers. There are potentially ten couples here, so it will have to be speed dating. I'm sure you'd rather not be here all night long." Her hand lowers to the next line of text on the poster board. "You will get ten minutes with each person. There's a list of questions to ask each other. You can pick and choose from it as you please. You can even ask your own *reasonable* questions. Use your time wisely because once you've had a speed date with everyone, you can choose one person to ask on a date afterwards to get to know each other further. There will be picnic baskets with a complimentary romantic dinner. You can choose to have your date here, or you can go for a walk over to the pond." She winks and says, "For a more romantic setting."

I sigh. This sounds like it's going to last awhile.

Constance drones on. "We're just here to give you a low pressure way to meet someone. Oh! Rules. That's right. The only two rules are..." She holds up one finger. "Be nice." She holds up a second finger. "And have fun. It's time to take your seats. I'll sound off the buzzer when your first speed date starts."

Marigold sighs. "Ugh. I really wish I had read the articles for today. I'm not sure that I'd be nice enough to come here for something like this. Even after telling Constance I would." She gestures around the room. "I'm stuck here now. It'd be kind of rude to leave. Might as well give it a shot." She stands and stretches her arms. "Are you coming?"

"Yeah." I wish I weren't, but it's too late now. I'm not leaving Marigold to do this on her own. I can tell she's nervous enough with me being here. Besides, we formed a club. What kind of member would I be to leave her alone?

We head to the tables, and everyone is already seated except for us. We should've rushed because now we can't be with each other for the first round of questions. I smile reassuringly at Marigold. She pats my arm and heads toward a table with a guy I don't recognize. He's probably a tourist. I sit across from Laura and stare at the paper in front of me filled with questions.

I am speed dating. My mom would be elated if she knew.

I swore to myself I was finished with relationships. After everything...

Whether I like it or not, I'm getting to know ten people. I can't shake the feeling that the only person I want to get to know is Marigold, and I don't know what to do about it. I shouldn't want to get to know anyone.

Chapter 14

MARIGOLD

I swipe my clammy hands on my overalls, and I try to shake loose the nerves bundled in my chest.

Nope. They're still there.

I'm one-hundred percent out of my comfort zone. I don't go on dates. Who am I kidding? I've never been on a date, much less stared awkwardly at a guy I don't know for this long. My mystery date has short-cropped blond hair, and his face is covered in day-old stubble. He shoots me a wide smile. I attempt a grin in reply, but my nerves are in control of my body. I'm not entirely sure I look very pleasant.

The sound of the buzzer going off makes me sick to my stomach.

"Date one starts now." Constance's voice erupts from the loud-speakers.

My *date* raises his hand to shake mine and says, "Hey, I'm Wyatt."

I'm nervous. My hands are sweating profusely. There's no way I'm going to shake this man's hand, but I don't want to be rude.

This is a dilemma.

"H-hey. Uhh I... I'm M-Marigold," I stutter. Ugh. My words are failing me.

He's still holding out his palm. I lift my hand and give his outstretched palm a knuckle sandwich.

He tips his head forward and chuckles deeply. I laugh awkwardly. I'm not sure if he's laughing with me or at me.

"I like your style." Wyatt raises his knuckles, and I give him a fist bump. "Whoosh!" he yells, pulling his hand back through the air dramatically.

He is definitely an extrovert. I haven't heard him say more than a few words, but I'm certain of it. That's not a bad thing, though. I've been spending a lot of time with Dan, and Wyatt happens to be the complete opposite.

I look at the sheet of questions in front of me.

Number one: Introduce yourself. We've done that already.

Number two: Two truths and a lie.

My nerves settle a touch. At least I have these questions, otherwise I'd have no clue what to say or ask.

Wyatt slaps the papers and says, "I don't need these. I've got plenty of questions up here." He taps his head and nods with a smug grin.

There goes my idea of scanning the questions and preparing some of my answers.

"Where do you see yourself in five years?" he asks.

I rub my hands over my lap. "Umm…" I stammer. "Here. This town. Exactly where I am now." Well, that question wasn't too hard.

He raises his brows and sets his elbows on the table. "Really? You don't think anything will be different?"

"Nope." I nod firmly.

Is there something wrong with that? I love my life here. I've never thought about leaving, especially with my dad being here. I couldn't imagine leaving him, the store, or the town behind. My heart belongs here.

"What about you?" I drum my fingers on my lap.

"I have no clue. I don't plan much of anything. My personal mantra is: live in the present, experience the in-between moments, and never worry about tomorrow. I wouldn't begin to imagine what five years from now would look like. I've never liked staying in one place. Maybe I'll travel the world. Maybe I'll be exactly where I am now if it's meant to be. I do know I'll try my best to enjoy each day. So now you pretty much know me." Wyatt stretches his hands behind his head.

"I'm sure there's plenty more to know."

"A little bit. But I'm more curious to know everything about you."

I look at my lap and pick at my nails. "I'm not very exciting." I'd rather not be the one doing all the speaking.

He lifts an eyebrow. "You don't strike me as someone who is boring."

"How are you so sure?"

"I can tell as soon as I meet a person. First impressions are very telling. And your knuckle sandwich was a curve-ball. A pleasantly surprising one."

"I'm glad to keep you on your toes." If he only knew my hands were sweltering so badly that I had to do something to divert the hand shaking, he'd be embarrassed for me.

He props an elbow on the table and rests his chin on his hand. "Tell me something interesting about yourself. Anything. The first thing that comes to mind. Don't think about it."

"I have a pet pig."

His jaw drops. "See! I knew you were interesting. I've never met someone before who had one as a pet."

Wyatt is really nice. My hands are, in fact, still clammy, but this whole experience isn't as horrible as I expected it to be.

The buzzer goes off loudly.

Constance's booming voice bursts out around the pavilion. "That's a wrap on date one. Please finish up your conversations, and gentlemen move to the next table in clockwise fashion."

"It was nice meeting you." Wyatt stands. "Hopefully, we can go on another date tonight."

"That would be nice."

I don't want to give him a concrete answer because I know I'd much rather leave after this is over.

When the buzzer goes off for the end of the ninth date, I finally feel as if I'm getting the hang of this speed date thing. My nerves settle some.

I met a bunch of people that I could see myself being friends with, but I didn't feel a deeper connection with any of them. I've wished for an 'aha' moment or a sparks-flying epiphany since I was sixteen years old. The first time I watched *The Notebook*, *A Walk to Remember*, and *Sixteen Candles* my life changed for the better. Each movie broke my heart and stitched the pieces together again, setting my expectations for what I thought every girl deserved at the bare minimum.

"Are you okay?" Dan's voice dissolves my musings. He scrunches his brows, studying me with a worry-filled expression. He braces his hands on the picnic table and steps over the wooden seat board, settling across from me. Concern still etches over his features as he drags a hand over his five-o'clock shadow.

He remembered. He knew that being around a bunch of people makes me uncomfortable. For him to *care* if I'm alright means the world to me. Dan might not always know what to say, but he *listens* to every word I say.

"Yes," I assure him.

My response seems to visibly relax the tension on his shoulders. "Good," he says. His smile is genuine as he leans an elbow on the picnic table and rests his chin on his knuckles.

"Did you find anyone you want to go out with again?" I ask.

Why am I silently hoping he didn't?

"No, did you?" He surveys my expression.

"Nope." My head tilts to the table as I trail my fingers across the smooth, wood-grain surface. "It was very awkward, and to be honest—" I flick my eyes from the table to his brown-eyed gaze "—I'm ready to leave. Not that I'm not enjoying our date. It's just... Well, this speed dating thing was not what I'd expected to be doing on a Tuesday night."

"You're speaking my language."

"Glad we're on the same page. Since we're here and all, I guess we could ask each other some of the questions, though. We're wasting our limited time." I giggle.

He rubs his hands together. "Go for it. I'm prepared."

I glide my finger down the list of questions and stop on line twenty-three. "Are you a morning person or a night owl?"

Dan taps his chin. "Hmm. I don't know. Both, if that's possible? My shop forces me to be a morning person. But if I had to pick one, I guess I'm a night owl. More often than not, I get caught up working late on projects."

"Okay, see, I can relate with that. I'm a night owl for sure, but running the hardware store is the only reason I'm up early. If we didn't open at six-thirty, I wouldn't be alive to the world until at least ten." I rest my arms on the table and lean in. "Your turn to find a question."

He lifts the sheet of paper and reads from it. "Question three: What do you do for fun?"

"That's easy. I love to paint."

He tilts his head and a slow smile reaches his eyes. "I didn't know."

"You paint too." I point out, recalling plenty of days when my dad ordered special paint for Dan. I picture the plethora of cars over the years going into his auto shop looking worse for wear but leaving beautifully restored.

"Cars and tractors. There's not an artistic bone in this body." He points to himself and sets the paper down. "What kinds of things do you paint?"

His question raises my spirits. "Landscapes mostly. Sometimes I incorporate wildlife like birds, squirrels, or deer. I'll paint anything that crosses my backyard." Dan's mouth curves into a wider grin as I talk. "Also, my favorite time to paint is when it gets so dark that I have to rely on the moon's glow to see. I can't resist grabbing a blank canvas and trying my best to do the view justice." He studies me in awe, and my face warms with blush. "Enough about me. What do you do for fun?"

His eyes gleam. "I restore cars. I'm working on a 1970 Chevy right now. But you probably already knew that. I was talking about it a little when we were at Archie's."

"I remember. I knew it would probably involve cars."

"I'm a predictable guy," he replies.

My brows draw together. That couldn't be further from the truth. "I only knew it because I work with you almost every day. I've seen how many cars go in and out of the auto shop. But nothing about you is predictable or cut and dry. You're interesting, Danny. And hard to read at times. But I like that about you. You're unlike anyone I've met."

The buzzer goes off before I can hear his response, and the pavilion turns into chaos as people move about. Through it all, Dan and I stay planted at our table. I look around, watching people grab their picnic baskets and disperse to go on dates.

Dan and I get ready to leave as the first guy I went on a blind date with walks toward me.

No. Please don't ask me on a date.

Wyatt beams, confident as ever. "Marigold." *No.* "Would you like to have a picnic dinner with me?"

Oh, no. There is hope in his eyes...

"That would be great." I force a bright smile.

"Cool! I'll grab the basket. Meet you by the bonfire?"

"Yes. Perfect."

I sag my head after he disappears toward the table filled with picnic baskets. "I didn't want to let him down," I say to Dan.

"I know." He gives me a half-smile.

"I'll see you later." Truthfully, I want to beg him to take me with him.

"Call if you need me, and I can make an excuse to get you out of there."

I smile softly. "Thank you."

Dan stands in place as I leave. I make it to the edge of the pavilion and look back at him. He's still there in the same spot. His eyes connect with mine. He smiles, but it doesn't quite reach his eyes. I can't read him. Is he upset? Is he wishing he asked me on the date? Hmmm, maybe he's unbothered and thinking about something else...

When I turn back toward the bonfire, Wyatt's there, waving me over with a giant smile. I feel like I'm stuck right in the middle. On one side is a guy I'm starting to form feelings for, and on the other, there's a guy I barely know who I'm going on a date with.

After my internal monologue wraps up, I meet Wyatt by the fire. He swings the basket ever so slightly while we walk across the street, toward the pond.

"Want to sit on a bench somewhere?" he asks.

"That sounds nice."

Make small talk. Say something.

I fiddle with my necklace. "So, what do you do for work?" I ask, keeping the same pace as him.

"I'm a mattress salesman. It's only temporary. And I also have a small photography business on the side. I'm saving up so I can travel and do it full time."

"That's impressive," I reply, honestly. "Do you enjoy it?"

"The mattress sales? Yeah, it's an honest job. I make enough to live on."

"Oh, that's great. What about photography?"

"I love it. It's almost like I get to show the world through my eyes. The best part is I get to travel to new places, notice little things I normally wouldn't, and capture memories. It's gratifying."

We have that in common. "That's similar to why I love painting. I appreciate the little things more."

"You're a painter?" He points to a park bench. "Here, good?" I nod.

"It's kind of my hobby. But, yeah."

"What do you do for work?" he asks, taking a seat and setting the picnic basket in between us.

I sit beside him, running my hands over my lap. "I run the hardware store, Fix-Its, with my Dad. Well, right now, it's just me. Running the store by myself, I mean. I have a month to prove to him I can do it on my own."

His voice softens. "Do you love it?"

My answer is simple. "Yes, I love working in a place where my family has always been. Where there's a story."

"That sounds nice." He sighs wistfully, and then we embrace the quiet for a little bit.

My thoughts begin to wander in the silence. It's weird being on a date with a man while wearing another's hat. I didn't want to blatantly turn Wyatt down. He seemed so interested in getting to know me. Maybe the thought of someone asking me out isn't a bad thing. Wyatt is nice. We're more alike than I realized, minus the traveling.

I decide to break the silence. "Where are you from? What brings you to Thornwood Valley?"

He chuckles, leaning back against the bench and stretching out his legs in front of him. "My friends and I do this thing where we pick a random spot on the map and choose to vacation there for a week once a year. My buddy threw a dart, and it landed on Thornwood Valley."

"That sounds fun. What made you come to singles night?"

"I figured why not meet some new people out of it? We're leaving tomorrow morning anyway. I had nothing planned for tonight. But it panned out because I made a friend." He turns his gaze to mine.

A Friend? I think he means me... Thank God!

Wyatt wants to travel the world. Meanwhile, I want to stay here forever. He's nice, talkative, and outgoing. *But he isn't Dan,* my subconscious whispers. With Wyatt, I don't have to try and guess what he's thinking. He just says it. With Dan, it's different; there's a mystery I want to uncover. I like that about Dan.

A part of me wishes that Dan could've been the one who I went on a first date with.

I give Wyatt a small smile. "Well, if you ever find yourself in Thornwood Valley again, stop by Fix-Its. I'd love to show you around and have my dad tell you the history of the place."

"I'd love to. There's something about this town that makes me want to come back again. It's charming here." Wyatt stares off into the distance optimistically.

"I can't argue with that." I look down at the picnic basket. "Should we dig in? The food is probably getting cold or warm. I'm not sure what they packed."

He shifts his gaze to me and drums his fingers on the basket. "Why don't you take this and go on a date with the guy you were talking to earlier?"

"What?" What is he talking about?

"You two seem... How do I put this?" He taps his chin. "It's all in the eyes."

What does that mean?

"The eyes?"

"He looks at you. You look at him. Both of your eyes say more than words do. You get what I'm putting down?"

I tip my head back, laughing. "No way."

"Way." He holds out his fist. "Now, go have dinner with him."

I fist bump him. "Are you sure? Aren't you hungry?"

He stands. "I'm sure. If I leave now, I can catch up to my friends at The String Cheese. They're having dinner there."

"Don't be late on my account. It was nice meeting you, Wyatt," I say genuinely.

"It was a pleasure, Marigold."

Chapter 15

DAN

The shop is quiet when I get back from the bonfire, and a warm orange glow filters through the glass of the garage doors. I flick on the lights and turn on the radio.

There's no going to sleep now, not with the knowledge of Marigold being on a date right now with someone else.

It stings because I should've asked her, but I didn't.

I sit beside the Chevy Nova on a roller chair, and I stretch my legs, slowly inching closer to the car. I've fallen on my ass one too many times moving fast on one of these things to mess around. I stare at the car, willing myself to begin taping off the windows to get it ready for paint when a knock sounds on the door.

"Come in," I yell, expecting it to be someone looking for a tow. I lift from my seat, peering over the car, and I'm instantly surprised.

Marigold's standing in the doorway. She takes one step in and glances around until she sees me.

"Care to have a picnic with me?" she asks, raising the basket.

Why is she here asking the question that I've been regretting not voicing for the past hour?

I round the car and brush my hands off on my jeans. "I'm confused. Didn't you have a date?"

She slowly shuts the door and takes a few steps toward me. "Kind of. But Wyatt and I are more compatible as friends. He told me to go on a date with you. He thinks we look at each other in a certain way. So, the date would be better spent with us. Plus, he's leaving tomorrow morning."

This Wyatt guy must be pretty good at reading people because he's right about the way I look at Marigold.

I never noticed her before. I didn't think about anything other than work. However, since we've spent the past four days—technically five now, counting today—truly getting to know each other, I can't get her out of my mind.

"That's too bad about him leaving." *I'm not really that upset.* "Wanna warm up whatever's in there?" I offer, pointing to the picnic basket.

"Yeah. That would be nice. I'm not imposing, am I?"

"Never." I head to the other side of the car and push the roller chair beside the work bench.

"Wow." Marigold gasps. "Is this the car you were telling me about?"

"Yep. I'm getting ready to prime it for paint."

"What color?" she asks. "Wait, no. Let me guess. Pink? Just kidding. I think it would look really nice..." She taps her chin. "A shade of blue. Actually, sky blue if it were up to me."

I tilt my head and study the car. "It would be."

I had no clue what color I was going to paint it before now, but I'm certain sky blue is the one. It's partly because she's a painter and choosing a color is second nature to her. Although, it's mostly because of the sparkle in her eyes when she suggested it.

Marigold follows me up the stairs to my apartment. I open the door for her and head to the fridge. "Beer, water, soda, or lemonade?"

"I'll have lemonade, please." She smiles and takes a seat at the kitchen table. "Your place is exactly what I pictured."

"Is that so?" I pour her lemonade and pop the top off a beer for myself. I take a seat next to her and set our drinks on the table.

"Thanks." She swirls the straw in her lemonade and takes a sip. "It's tidy like your garage. You're so organized. I love that it's all one open space. Those curtain rods are neat." Her gaze lingers on the industrial curtain rods. "The dark wooden walls are moody, kind of like your personality before you have coffee," she teases.

That comment has me beaming. She's right.

"I love the brick accent wall and antique signs. And the dark beams on the ceiling. It's all very *you*." She turns to look at me, grins wider, and takes a sip of lemonade. She glances at the picnic basket on the table. "I wonder what's in this basket." She studies it intently, pulls it toward herself, and lifts the lid. She peers into the basket and doubles over laughing.

Now I'm curious. "What is it?"

"A giant bowl of spaghetti. Two cookies. And wanna know the real kicker? No utensils! Maybe they were trying for a *Lady and the Tramp* situation. Then again, they probably used all the budget on the speakers."

"I was thinking the same thing. That's why Constance had to tape a mini microphone to the inflatable one." I chuckle. "I can warm it up, and I'll even supply some forks."

Her eyes crinkle. "Danny, that's music to my ears."

"Good. I'm glad the promise of some silverware has brightened your spirits." I smirk and grab the bowl of spaghetti, heading to the kitchen.

Opening the cabinet above the counter, I pull out a pot and dump the spaghetti into it.

"Don't you have a microwave?" she asks.

I set the container in the sink and turn on the burner. "No, I just heat everything on the stove."

"Probably better for you."

"Probably." I shrug. "I don't really have the room for one."

"Need any help?"

I turn my head, meeting her gaze. "No. Thank you, though."

I lean against the counter and shift myself to face her. She stirs her lemonade and changes the subject. "That whole singles night mixer was really interesting, don't you think?"

"I've never seen anything like that before." I grab a wooden spoon and stir the spaghetti.

"Me neither. It was quite entertaining when Constance showed up with her entourage." Marigold laughs. "And I didn't have a clue what to say on those dates. Those questions literally saved me from embarrassing myself. It's funny, thinking about it now, but I was nervous as heck."

I glance at her for a moment. "They were good questions as far as first dates go. Not really deep but enough to start a conversation."

"I wouldn't know." Marigold tips her head.

"What do you mean?" I shut off the burner and fill two bowls with spaghetti. I grab forks and set everything on the table.

She bites her lip and pushes a meatball around her plate. "I've never been on a date before today. I doubt that counted as one anyway."

"Never?"

What fools live in our town? Marigold is beautiful inside and out. She's a ray of sunshine. Who wouldn't want to go on a date with her? Absolute fools that's who—myself included.

"Well, I *was* asked out a few times in high school, but I never said yes. That was before my mom passed. Afterwards, people seemed to flock away from me. It was like they were scared to be near me, not knowing what to say or how to act. Afraid I would break. I didn't blame them. It was hard for a while. I had to be there for my dad, too. He needed me even though he never said it out loud. For a long time I was in a state of grief where I felt like my mom was still alive. I'd walk into the kitchen and wonder why she wasn't there or why I didn't smell the lavender from the diffuser she filled every morning. The house was quiet. A weird, static quiet. Then I'd remember she was gone. And it would hurt all over again."

Marigold takes a deep breath before continuing. "No one asks out the girl who's withdrawn. The girl who is sad but smiles through the pain because she knows it's what she must do. It was that way for a few years. Until I learned to live with grief and not let it overcome me. To cling to the happy memories. To smile and actually mean it."

My heart breaks for her. She lost her mom so early-on in life. It shouldn't have to be that way.

Marigold deserves everything. She deserves to be asked on a real date, not thrown into a speed dating event that she had no clue about in the first place. She deserves to let someone else take care of her for a change. She deserves it all and more.

"I—" I have no clue what to say to convey everything running through my mind, but sometimes actions speak louder than words.

"You don't have to say anything. Listening is enough, Dan."

I shake my head. This time, listening is not enough. Marigold deserves the world. "Will you go on a date with me?"

Her fork drops to her plate. "What?" She snaps her head up, and her eyes flicker. "Really?"

"Nothing would make me happier, Goldie. How about Saturday after work? I'll pick you up."

"That'd be wonderful." Her smile falters. "You're not asking because you feel bad for me, are you?"

"That couldn't be further from the truth. I don't do anything unless I'm sure of it. And to be honest with you, I wanted nothing more than to go back to that pavilion and ask you on a date."

"Oh." She bites her lip, looking down at her plate.

"So, this Saturday? Does that work for you?"

"Mhmm," she mumbles as her lips start to curl back upward. Her gaze flicks to mine, but her eyes grow somber once more.

She hasn't been this quiet for days, not since we started talking more. I wonder what she's thinking. Did I do or say something wrong?

Her voice is soft as she divulges her thoughts. "You know, I was just thinking... I was so afraid someone was going to ask me number thirty-two earlier."

"What was the question?"

"What do you think it takes to make a relationship successful? I'm sure I could've thought of a few things, but I have no life experiences to go off of. Obviously. And it's embarrassing. I'm twenty-five. I've never been in a relationship. I've never held someone's hand, well, like in a romantic way. You know what I mean. I've never kissed someone. I've never had any of those experiences." She grabs her necklace and swivels it back and forth.

"Think about it this way," I say. "You get to experience a ton of firsts. Your first date. Those speed dates don't count if you don't want them to. Your first love. Most people wish they could go back and have them again. I promise you, it's not a bad thing."

"When you put it that way, it doesn't sound as horrible as it did in my head." Her smile re-appears. "What would've been your answer?"

I take a sip of beer. "Honesty. Respect. Being present. Being friends with your partner is a good start too." I shrug. "I've only ever been in one relationship, and that turned into being married, actually. So, my answer isn't too great."

She presses her fingers to her lips. "That question was probably second date territory, right?"

"It doesn't matter. You can ask me anything."

"Same goes for you." She twirls spaghetti noodles around her fork. "Can I ask you another question?"

"Ask away." I take a small drink of my beer.

She looks hesitant as she stares at her plate. "Are you technically still married?"

I almost choke on my beer, covering my face with my hand. "No, I would've never asked you out if I were."

She raises her hands. "Just wanted to be sure. I'd be pretty angry if you were. And I don't get mad often."

"Rightfully so. I should've clarified. I've been divorced for a good six years. I got married right out of high school. We were young. We thought getting married was a great idea. Then we found out we wanted different things in life. It didn't work out."

"Oh, I'm sorry."

"It's okay. Sometimes things don't work out for a reason." Like, maybe I was meant to meet someone else even though I've been reluctant as hell to do so for six years.

"If you don't mind me asking one more question, how old are you?"

"Twenty-nine."

She grins, bobbing her head. "That explains it."

I lean back in my chair, tracing my fingers over the condensation on the outside of my beer. "Explains what?"

"Why you're so much wiser. You've got four years on me."

"Now, you're being ridiculous. You created a successful business idea a couple days ago. You're much smarter than you give yourself credit for. And I probably spent those four years trying to figure out what I was going to do with my life."

She quirks a brow. "Now, who's the one not giving themself credit?"

"Touché."

"Maybe we should eat before our food is freezing," she suggests, shoving the forkful of spaghetti into her mouth.

"Good plan." I laugh, spearing a meatball.

After we finished dinner, Marigold insisted on doing the dishes, although I tried to convince her otherwise. It was a failed attempt. So, that's how we ended up at the sink, washing them together.

Marigold hands me a soapy bowl. I rinse it and place it on the drying rack.

"How's the hardware store coming? Was it a good day?" I ask.

"Yes." Her voice is light. "I paid off the carts in one day, Danny. *One day*. My dad will be speechless."

I look up from the sink. "That's incredible, really. You should be extremely proud of what you accomplished so far."

She hands me a cup covered in bubbles. "Thanks. Let's hope my dad thinks that too."

"You haven't told him?"

"Not yet. He's been at the beach all week. And he's hard to get a hold of. He hates the phone I got for him. He doesn't like newer technology in general, which you probably know."

"Yeah. It's obvious by the way his face turns red when he's on a computer."

"Yep. I have to walk him through how to do things, but most of the time, he lets me handle anything computer related. It's for the best.

"Anyway, he wanted to go somewhere my mom loved. She took us on a trip to Assateague Island when I was younger. We were reminiscing about it, and that's where he decided to go. He was only supposed to stay a day, but he's still there. He called once he got there and yesterday too. I haven't heard that much excitement in his voice since before we lost my mom. His happiness is all I could ask for.

"I just hope he meets someone. I don't want him to be alone forever. We tried the whole dating app thing, but that didn't work out because there is no one to match with in town. Plus, he wasn't so thrilled about the idea of meeting someone online."

I set a cup on the drying rack. "I'm glad he's enjoying himself. I think he will meet someone if it's meant to be. Maybe give him time. You are helping him now even though he isn't sure he needs it. It's good for him. Ever since I moved here and worked with him, he's never taken a day off."

"You don't either." Marigold smirks while scrubbing another dish in the sink.

"Nor do you," I counter.

"Okay, fair point. But I go home at night. You live where your business is. Does it feel like you never leave work?"

"No." I shake my head. "I love it. It doesn't feel like a job. Every day is a new adventure. Literally. I never know what car is going to come in the door with a new issue I haven't encountered before."

"Did you always know you wanted to be a mechanic?" Marigold asks.

"No, I went to college undecided." She hands me that dish, and I rinse it under the running water. "I took a lot of classes, but I couldn't find a knack for anything. I dropped out to go to trade school and started with the automotive program. Right away, I knew I found my calling. Then I got a job at a shop, moved out, and leased my own apartment. I lived there for a few years, close to my parents, who were getting divorced at the time. And not long after I was in the same situation. So, I took a trip to Thornwood Valley after seeing an ad for the auto shop. I took a risk. The rest is history."

"I'm glad you found your way here." Marigold holds out a soapy pot.

I lean toward her, and our shoulders brush. "Me too. It was the best decision I ever made."

Chapter 16

MARIGOLD

I brace my hands on the counter and yawn. The shop is mostly dark, except for the glow from a small lamp on the corner of the front desk. I'm not ready to wake myself fully by turning on all the lights yet.

I jump at the sound of the phone ringing. I pick up, still yawning. "Hello."

"Good morning, Mary," my dad says.

"Hey, Dad." I yawn again.

"Tired?"

"A little. It's still early."

"I can't help getting up at five. Been doing so for decades. Old habits never die. I just called to check in. It feels like I've been gone for a lifetime."

"You doing okay?" I can't help but worry about him.

"Never been better!" I can tell by his warm tone that he's being honest. That quells some of my worries.

"Good. Are you having fun? Staying out of trouble?" I joke.

His voice raises in pitch. "You'll be pleased to hear I'm going out on the town tonight."

"Like going out? Or *going* out?" I needed clarification. If he's *going* out—like, on a date—I'll be so happy.

"We'll see. Just two friends taking a stroll on the boardwalk grabbing some food." His tone sounds almost hopeful.

We'll see was all I needed to hear to give me hope.

"I'm so happy. You don't even know. I have a lot of questions. How did you meet? What's her name?"

"Don't you have to open soon? It would take too long, but her name is Eleanor." He pauses. "Everything going okay with the shop?"

Although I'm bummed that he changed the subject, I want to tell him how well Fix-Its is doing with the golf carts and the small changes that people are embracing.

"Well, her name is lovely. And yes, I have a bunch of updates for you."

"Save it for the end of the month. We'll go over the numbers then. I may stay a few more weeks. I'm having a wonderful time here. I almost forgot to tell you. I could've sworn I saw your mother on the beach yesterday. A woman was looking out at the waves. She had this long flowy dress similar to the one your mother never left the house without. Her hair was long and blonde. For a few moments, I believed it was her. When she turned, it was someone else, but it was a sign that I'm where I'm supposed to be."

"Dad, that warms my heart. You sure you're okay?"

"Kiddo, you've been taking care of me, *worrying* over me for too many years. Don't worry about your ol' man anymore. I'm happy. This trip is exactly what I needed."

Tears cloud my eyes. "I'm glad to hear it, Dad. I miss you."

"I miss you too. Have a good day. I'm glad I caught you before you opened."

"Me too. Have fun at the boardwalk." Anticipation fills my voice.

"I will. Talk to you soon." His words come out cheerful.

"Bye." I swipe a happy tear as I set the phone on the receiver. I sniffle and try to get myself together. Everything in my life is changing. Most of it is for the better.

Buttercup comes rushing toward me; I pick her up and hug her to my chest.

I gather my thoughts, set Buttercup down, and delve into my opening routine. Wipe the counter. Check each shelf. Stock the worm fridge with this morning's shipment. Re-stock shelves with things that sold out. Update inventory numbers on my laptop.

By the time I finish getting ready, Daisy walks in the back door. "Good Morning," she says as she sets her clutch underneath the counter. "Where's Buttercup?"

I lift my chin. "Exploring the aisles."

"Oh, she's too funny." Daisy takes a sip of her coffee. "So, we're tackling the mower abyss today?"

"Yeah, if that works for you."

"You're the boss. Whatever you say goes."

"That's not how this works. We're best friends first. If you'd rather start somewhere else, you can tell me."

"Nope. I'm ready for everything mower related." She sets her drink down and heads toward the third aisle. I follow her and we begin organizing mower belts.

I break the silence after a few minutes. "I'm going on a date."

Daisy hangs up a belt and turns toward me. Her eyes glow. "No way! Your first date ever! When? Where? Who with?" She shoots her hands in the air. "Wait. I know who. It's with Dan, right?" I nod in confirmation. "Good. Ah! Your first date! What are you going to wear? Do you need help picking something out?"

"I was going to wear one of my dresses. When I asked, Dan said to dress comfortably. He told me it will be dinner, but he didn't say where."

I swivel my necklace feeling a pit of nerves in my stomach.

"I'm so excited for you!" Daisy grins. Her excitement settles my worries a little and I smile.

"Do you want to come over on Friday to help me choose a dress?"

Her face lights up even more. "One thousand percent yes! I'm in."

"Awesome. I gotta go make some phone calls. I'll be back in a little bit."

Daisy shoos me away with a hand and lifts another mower belt. "Good. You better get to work. You're distracting me!"

I head to the front desk grinning.

I make a few phone calls and then help Mateo when he comes in to order some parts for Dan's Auto. I feel kind of bummed that it wasn't Dan who stopped by. Our conversations last night brought us closer, and now I can't stop thinking about him.

The rest of the day goes by relatively fast. I help Daisy sort the mower parts for a while until I get another phone call. One call turns into two, and then it's almost time to close. I begin putting away items beside the register when the front door jingles. Violet, the town's florist, comes in carrying a giant bouquet of flowers.

"These are for you," Violet says with a bright smile. She blows the bangs from her eyes and sets the vase next to the register. "Sorry, I have a hard time seeing through these bangs. I need to get a haircut."

"You're good. These are stunning. Who are they from?"

She leans in close to me and whispers, "A florist never tells." She heads for the door and calls over her shoulder, "See you later!"

"Thank you!" I yell after her.

I look at the bouquet and smile.

The flowers are Marigolds. *Pink Marigolds.* I gasp at the significance. I mentioned how I loved them a few days ago to Dan in passing. He remembered. They must be from him. Tears threaten to fall as I shakily pluck the note from the vase.

Marigold,

I saw these and thought of you. A dozen Marigolds for one Marigold. Isn't that fitting? I hope these make your day just a little bit pinker. And you were right. They are beautiful. So are you.

Dan

Daisy pops out from the mower aisle. "Who are those from?"

"Dan," I say, unable to look away from the flowers.

"You have hearts in your eyes," she observes.

"I know," I whisper as I glance at the note once more. Happiness courses through me. I feel weightless, reading his words again.

Chapter 17

DAN

"Do you have a minute? There's something I want to show you with the golf carts." I jerk a thumb to the back entrance in Fix-Its.

"I don't know. I'm very busy right now." Marigold folds up a bag of gummy worms and fastens the bag shut with a binder clip. She brushes sugar dust from her hands and smirks at me.

I grin. "I can see that."

A little grunt distracts me from our conversation. "Hey, you." I crouch down and pat Buttercup's head. She squeals and takes off. She must still hold a grudge against me after our first meeting.

Marigold shuts her laptop and stands. "Is something wrong with the golf carts?"

"No, nothing's wrong." I try my best to fight a smile because I know it'll give me away. I spent the entirety of today keeping this from everyone, and I'm not about to blow it in a matter of seconds. "It's something minor I fixed and wanted to show you." That sounds believable enough, I think.

"Okay. Lead the way."

I open the door for her. Once we're outside, I nod my chin to the two golf carts.

Marigold gasps, covering her mouth. "What? Dan... you didn't!" Her wavy blonde hair flows around the hat she's wearing. It's not just any hat; she's wearing mine again.

My head was fuzzy the moment I walked into Fix-Its and saw her with it on. I can't think straight when she looks so beautiful.

"Did you seriously pick these up for me?" Her voice trails off.

"Yeah." I lift my shoulder in a half shrug. Marigold smooths her hand over the side of the golf cart decorated as an owl. "What are you doing?"

She shakes her head. "Making sure they're real. This isn't a dream, right?"

I'd hoped she'd be happy about the golf carts, but I worried this could be overstepping. Seeing her smile now is everything I could've wished for.

I can tell how much Fix-Its means to her. This month is not only about proving to her dad she's capable; it's about proving it to *herself*. It's also about her mom's legacy. This is Marigold's dream, and I would do anything to help her see it through. I know what it's like to have a dream and wonder if it will ever be attainable.

"It's not a dream," I assure Marigold.

It's hard for me to read her. She almost looks like she's in shock.

My heart sinks when it dawns on me... She's not used to people doing things like this for her. That's a shame. I want to be the person that shows her she doesn't have to do everything on her own.

"Is this why you were gone all day?" Her eyes glimmer.

"You noticed?"

"Of course I noticed. Mateo ordered parts instead of you or Char. He never does that." She takes a few steps in my direction. "And the flowers..." Her cheeks pinken. "What were those for?"

"Thought you would appreciate them."

"They're beautiful, Danny. Thank you." She rocks on her feet.

"I'm glad you like them, Goldie." I take a few steps toward her.

Her mouth curves into a smile. "I absolutely do. You don't know how much they mean to me." The tremble in her lower lip and the glossy shimmer that appears in her eyes suggests there's more behind those words than I could begin to understand.

She hugs herself and sighs softly. "Before I forget, let me grab a check." She points to the golf carts.

"There's no need."

Marigold tilts her head. "Huh? I will be paying you for these."

"I can't take anything for them," I insist. "They're a gift."

"No, they're not, Dan." She shakes her head. "They're too much. I can't accept them."

"They're a business investment." I want to help her any way that I can, and this is also true. I see how well they did already. They are an investment in this town and in the chickens' safety. That's good enough for me.

"How's that gonna work?" Her nose scrunches.

"When they need to be serviced, I'll fix them."

She looks unsure. "And you'll let me pay you?"

"Yes, when I work on them. Archie practically gave them away for nothing. He just wanted them out of his hair. You don't owe me a thing."

"Okay..." Marigold says, not looking convinced.

"I promise you."

"Good," she replies softly. "As long as you keep it. We're in a club, remember? Club members aren't allowed to break promises. And if they do, there are extreme consequences."

"Is that so?" A smile stretches my lips. "What are the consequences?"

She gives me a lopsided grin. "You get kicked out of the club."

"Well then..." I swallow. "I won't break my promise."

Her lips purse, and her eyes sparkle. "Perfect."

I'm glad that her smile is back. I hope that whatever was troubling her is distant from her mind.

We stand like this, staring into each other's eyes, for a lingering amount of time. I don't know when exactly the shift between us started, but I do know there's this feeling in my bones that something more is going on between us. It's something tangible that I want to grasp onto and never let go of.

I could stand here, rooted to this spot forever, and watch as the most beautiful woman I've ever laid eyes on smiles at me. I have to leave eventually. There's work to catch up on after being gone all day, but for a few more moments, I ignore everything else. A thought crosses my mind: *I'm not like my dad.* Thank God. That feels like growth for me. I know when work can wait; this is one of those times.

Chapter 18

MARIGOLD

"Strapless, spaghetti straps, or short sleeves?" Daisy's voice is muffled as she browses through clothes in my closet.

"Umm. I'm not sure." I stand behind her, looking into the depths of my closet.

"Really narrowing it down, aren't you?" she teases, pushing a few dresses aside. "This is going to take a while. You might wanna sit down. Get comfy."

If she insists.

If it were anyone else, I'd feel guilty for watching them choose my outfit while I do nothing, but Daisy loves this sort of thing. I never understood why she didn't go to school for cosmetology or apply for a job at Chloe's Closet. Then again, she always insisted she loved it so much that she didn't want to turn her hobby into a career.

Daisy's good at styling anything. The outfit she's wearing is a testament to having such talents. Her light brown hair is straight and smooth with the slightest curl at the ends. Those bell bottom jeans have little embroidered flowers on the pockets. To top it off, the wedges pair perfectly with that white lace cropped tank top.

I wrap a pale pink comforter over my arms and sit on the edge of my bed. Buttercup rushes up the pet stairs and nuzzles beside me.

Daisy turns, holding a stack of dresses. "Are you cold right now?"

"A little," I admit, wrapping the blanket tighter around myself.

"There's something wrong with you. It's gotta be eighty degrees in here."

"The air is set to seventy-two." I point to the window unit. "It also doesn't help that I'm wearing a sports bra and compression shorts."

"True." Daisy continues to choose dresses. She sets another few on the rocking chair for me to try on.

"I'm kinda nervous," I say after a few minutes.

"That's normal." Daisy sets another dress on the chair and sits next to Buttercup and I. "You are going to have a great time."

Am I? What if I get nervous and freeze?

"Maybe I should prepare. Should I make flashcards? On the speed dates, I had the questions as a crutch. This time I won't have anything..."

"Woah. Okay, Paris. You might as well call me Rory. You will absolutely *not* be taking note cards on your date." She shakes her head.

I sink back on the bed and stare at the ceiling. "I don't know. Maybe I should cancel. Dan probably feels bad for me after I told him that I've never been on a date."

"Nope. Not happening. Dan sent your favorite flowers. He also spent an entire day driving to surprise you with the golf carts. He is definitely interested in you. Be yourself. He likes you. The rest of the cards will fall into place. It doesn't hurt to try. To go. It doesn't mean you have to marry the guy. It's just a date."

I sigh softly. She's right. No one has ever done anything like that for me before.

I'm starting to really like Dan and I think that makes me more nervous. I don't want to ruin it so soon. Still, if I never give him a chance, there'll be nothing to worry about at all. Maybe that would be even worse, though. I'd never know if there were sparks between us, just like the romance movies I grew up adoring.

I scan my eyes over the stucco ceiling while my thoughts run rampant, wondering where Dan will take me. He said dinner, so I'm expecting Annie's Diner or The String Cheese. I wonder if he'll—

Daisy jolts me from my daydream. "Stop that."

I sit up slowly and stare at her with a small smile.

She can see right through me. Her arms are crossed, and she has a look that says I-mean-business.

"What?" My mouth twists.

"I can see you overthinking. You want to be prepared. Let's prepare."

Oh no. She's got that look in her eyes.

"Pretend I'm Dan for a minute." Daisy's serious expression doesn't falter.

I cringe at that. "What? No."

"Come on. I'm serious," she insists.

"Okay..."

Daisy, or better yet, *Dan*, gives me a once over. "Hey, Marigold, you look nice."

I didn't know her fake man voice could drop that low. I fall backwards on the bed, clutching my stomach with laughter. "I can't."

"You can. Come on," Daisy insists.

I sit up and she starts over again. "Hi, Marigold."

"Hi—Dais—Dan—umm," I answer, scratching the back of my neck. "This isn't working." I burst out laughing. "You—look—nothing like—him. And—sound nothing—like him."

"Give me a minute. We can fix that." She hops from my bed and goes into my closet. She grabs a baseball cap, twirls her hair into a bun, and puts the hat on backwards. "Better?" She tries her best to imitate a deep voice while I shake with laughter again.

She giggles but waves her arms. "Let's try again. Be serious, Marigold. I'm going to help you practice." She sits on the edge of my bed and grabs my hand, getting into character.

"You look beautiful tonight." She tries a deep voice again, that's not so convincing, but I play along, trying my hardest not to laugh.

"Thank you." My voice cracks.

"You got it." She clears her throat. "And your eyes, they're stunning. Light blue orbs like the ocean in the morning. Deep and captivating and rare and unique. Ohh, like a waterfall flowing into never-ending blue water. Just like my love for you. Endless."

I try to imagine Dan saying these things, but he would never say that.

She continues. "And you are just the most wonderful person. In here." She pats her chest right over her heart. "Oh, Marigold, will you go on another date with me?" Daisy laughs. She quits doing the deep voice impersonation. "You're right. This isn't working."

We fall into fits of laughter.

Although Daisy's impression of Dan was not even close, the silly exchange was enough to boost my spirits. I think I'm ready to go on a date with him. Don't get me wrong. I'm petrified, but I'm also kind of excited.

We laugh for a few more beats until we can't breathe. Then Daisy gets up, grabs a dress from the top of the pile, and insists I try it on right away.

I unwrap the blanket from my arms and pull the short-sleeved yellow dress over my head. I turn and ask, "How's this one?"

"It's beautiful. It could possibly be the one," Daisy says. "But I need you to try on the rest anyway. Something else might be the one too.

I peel off the yellow dress and put on a white one with pink flowers. "What about this one?" I shrug.

She taps her chin. "Hmm. What if you get barbeque and end up wearing it?"

My eyes bulge. I didn't even think about that. What if I end up wearing food on my first *real* date... Should I pack a spare dress just in case?

"Stop it. I see you spiraling. Forget I said anything. It'll be smooth sailing. No condiments will end up on your dress." Daisy looks serious.

For my sake, I hope she's right.

I try on multiple dresses until we land on the final one: a light blue spaghetti strap with a form fitting bodice. The end of the dress falls a touch below my knees. This time, when I look in the full-length mirror, my breath shudders.

This was my mom's dress. I look like her.

I stare at my reflection. Is the woman I see in the mirror really me? She looks confident, independent, and self-assured. I feel as though I'm staring at a new version of myself.

Although I'm still working on the confident and self-assured part each day, running Fix-Its on my own is paving my way to finding myself. I'm closer to finding where I belong. Confidence will follow with time. I'm sure of it.

The dress is beautiful. The neckline sits perfectly. Groups of ruffles cascade over the silhouette, flowing as each section fades into the next.

I'm glad I kept this dress, plus all of Mom's other dresses. They may only be material things, but the memories are woven into every fiber of fabric.

I really do look like her. The dress grasps onto a different life. It holds a piece of her I never want to let go of. No matter how much I change, I know she'll always be in my heart. Her spirit will live on through me.

Tears threaten to fall.

"Was that your mom's dress?" Daisy asks.

I nod silently, fighting the pools welling in the corners of my eyes. I'm not strong enough to hide the growing urge to cry, but I don't need to, not with Daisy. My lip trembles. The tears fall. Daisy pulls me into a hug, squeezing my shoulders.

I wipe my cheeks and sniffle. "When I looked at myself in the mirror... for a tiny moment, I swore I saw her looking back at me. It felt real. Like she was here."

"You did, Marigold. You did. You are a splitting image of your mom. And I know she's looking down at you right now, telling you how much she loves you and how proud she is of you."

My heart warms with Daisy's words.

"This is the dress." I smile through tears, sure of my decision.

"I know," Daisy agrees. "It's the one. Really this time. You were meant to wear her dress. I think it was a sign from your mom that everything will go well and not to be nervous. You'll be just fine." She squeezes my arms reassuringly. "Dan won't know what to say when he sees you wearing this dress." She winks. I laugh, wiping at the remnants of tears. "It's time to pair this dress with some jewelry and shoes." Her eyes gleam.

I sit on the edge of the bed, holding the key pendant of my necklace over my chin and moving it across the gold chain.

Daisy goes through my shoes, pulling a pair of white converse from the closet. "These are so you. I think they'll go well with the dress. And that way you don't have to be uncomfortable. You can be true to yourself," she says.

"I love that idea."

Chapter 19

DAN

Marigold's house is pink. That doesn't surprise me because almost everything she owns is in a different shade of the color.

An effortless smile graces my face every time I see something pink now because it reminds me of her; Mateo even commented on my grinning a total of three times yesterday.

She has completely enamored my thoughts in a matter of days.

I grab the flowers from the passenger seat and leave my car. Instead of grass, the entire landscaping surrounding her home is made up of flowers. It's extraordinary. I follow the stone path to her porch and knock on the front door.

Her home is welcoming. There's a wicker bench with plush floral cushions facing the walkway, and flowerpots on either side of the door. Bird feeders and windchimes dangle from hooks above the railing, wrapping around the entirety of the porch.

My observation is halted as the door cracks open. Buttercup comes rushing from the gap, catapulting herself at me.

"Missed me?" I ask as I scoop up the tiny pig in one arm. She squirms, pushing her snout close to my face. "We've been over this. Not my face."

She wags her tail and squeals. She looks devious. I already know she's plotting how she can climb higher in my arms and attack my face. She's also kind of adorable, though.

"You two look like you're getting along well." Marigold's voice distracts my inner monologue.

"She's growing on me," I reply.

My breath hitches when I catch a glimpse of Marigold in the doorway. Her blonde hair flows in loose waves around her face. Plus, the dress she's wearing hugs her as if it were made with her in mind.

She's always beautiful but there's something about the glow in her eyes, the blush painting her face, and the warmness in her expression that makes me temporarily forget words.

I hold out the bouquet of flowers, her favorite ones. It's not because I want to make this go any faster. My goal is simply for her to smile; she does exactly that.

My gift is small in comparison to the flowers flowing from her front garden and the surrounding fields, but she doesn't seem to notice. Marigold's face lights more as her cheeks flush a deep crimson. She tries to hide that gorgeous smile, covering her face with her palm. I don't miss the slight trembling in her hand. I want to give assurance that she has nothing to be nervous about, so I say, "Goldie, you are beautiful."

"Thank you." She tucks a section of hair behind her ear. "Am I too dressed up?"

"No." I swallow. "You are perfect."

Marigold blushes. "You look nice yourself." She takes the flowers from me and holds them close to her chest. "Water. I'm going to put these in some water. Do you wanna come in?"

"Sure." I set Buttercup down and follow Marigold into her house. I stop in my tracks, taking a moment to soak it all in. Crisp white walls are covered in paintings—canvases of wildflowers, streams, moonlit paths, and beaches. The walls themselves are decorated with painted flowers, trailing over every open surface. Coffee cans filled with paint brushes are on end tables beside a floral couch.

Marigold was humble when she said she only paints on the side. She's extremely talented. She has a gift.

I lean down to untie my boot laces as Buttercup circles me.

"You don't have to take your shoes off," Marigold says.

I lift my head. "Are you sure?"

"I'm sure. It's a mess in here right now anyway." She opens a cabinet, pulls out a crystal vase, and starts clipping the stem of the flowers. "Who am I kidding? It's always like this. I hope you don't mind."

"It's not a mess. I'm completely mesmerized." I fix my shoelaces and meet her in the kitchen.

Her house isn't crowded or messy. It has character. Everything has a place. In a way, her house resembles a museum. It's captivating. I want to know the story behind each painting on the walls.

"Really? You're just being polite." She clips another flower.

I shake my head. "Really." *Doesn't she see how talented she is?* "Did you paint all of these?"

"Some of them." Marigold points to the living room. "The moon, stream, and wildflower ones are mine. But the charcoal and watercolors are my mom's. The beach paintings and the ones with people in them are hers too. This was her art studio before I moved in. She'd paint in here every morning before going to Fix-Its with my dad."

I knew her mom was an artist. Some of her paintings hang in Fix-Its as well as Annie's Diner. I never realized how truly gifted she was until today.

"Thank you for the flowers by the way. They're beautiful." She changes the subject.

"You're welcome." *They're not as beautiful as you.*

She puts the flowers on the windowsill above her kitchen sink. Then she washes her hands and pats them dry on a towel. "Where are we headed?" she asks so nonchalantly that I almost tell her instinctively. Nevertheless, I want our date to be spontaneous since it's technically her first one.

I smirk. "You'll find out soon enough. Nice try."

"You almost told me, didn't you?" Her lips curl into a playful smirk.

"Almost," I admit as I head to her front door.

"Be good, Buttercup. Daisy will be over in a little bit to pick you up. You're having a sleepover," Marigold calls out as she closes the door.

When we reach the car, I open the passenger side for her. She wears a smile as she steps in, and I close her door softly.

After I start my car I ask, "Ready?"

"Ready." She smooths her dress over her lap.

As I reverse the car down her driveway, my mind wanders.

I spent the past few days planning how tonight would go. I wanted her first date to be special. Now that I know Marigold better, I know that she doesn't feel comfortable around a lot of people. I didn't want to take her to Annie's Diner or The String Cheese. They'd be too crowded. I ended up opting for something better. Hopefully, she'll love it.

I pay attention to the road for a little while until I turn my head quickly to catch a glimpse of her. Marigold is tapping her fingers on her lap apprehensively.

I try my best to think of something to settle her nerves and make her laugh. "Did you know pigs can fly?"

"What?" Her voice is warm with the question.

I hold back a smile. "Yep. It's proven."

"Is it really?" She giggles. "Sounds impossible to me."

I keep my voice serious. "Nothing's impossible, Goldie. I've seen it with my own two eyes."

"Have you?" she asks with mirth.

"Yep. Buttercup took flight when I came to tow your car. Right off your lap at my face."

"What? Oh no. I feel so bad. I'm sorry."

"Don't be. It was funny. It was a sight to behold. A man was almost killed by a piglet on the fourth of July."

Her laughter is music to my ears. "Oh my gosh. That could've been a perfect article name. But it's kinda hard to believe a little piglet could take down a grown man."

"There's a first for everything."

"That's true. But hardly believable, Danny."

I wind my hands around the steering wheel, following a curve in the road. "I guess you'll never know. You were asleep."

"Darn it. I can't believe I missed seeing a pig fly. Next time I'll have to stay awake."

"Next time." I promise her. I'm sure there will be plenty more times Buttercup will attack me. I look forward to it if it means that I get to see Marigold smile.

After another few minutes, I shift my gaze from the windshield to Marigold. I can tell she's visibly relaxed, and I'm glad.

I park in the lot between Cat's & Novels and The Valley Harvest. I open the door for her, and take her hand. We walk behind the shops instead of on the main street, avoiding any run-ins with townies. The small town gossip can wait for one night.

Chapter 20

MARIGOLD

Dan and I walk slowly, following the path behind the shops in town. The sky is a fascinating blend of colors: persimmon, apricot, aquamarine, and indigo. Wispy clouds and the setting sun have me almost wanting to stop and paint the view. Although, Dan's hand in mine reminds me that I want to be in the moment with him.

All my doubts floated away the second he started talking about flying pigs on the ride here. I know he was doing it because he thought I was nervous. I definitely was, but now, I'm just excited and happy to be with him.

My heart skips a beat when we walk to the edge of the park. A wooden bench between two maple trees is covered in a tablecloth. The table is set for two. At the center there is a bouquet of flowers, two sets of plates, and a picnic basket. Soft music plays while twinkling lights dangle between branches of both trees. As Dan and I get closer, I notice what is hidden behind the picnic basket... It's the key to my heart: a giant glass container filled with gummy worms.

He is literally fulfilling all of my dreams.

We sit across from each other. Dan opens the flap on the wicker picnic basket and pulls out a variety of containers. He fills our large plates with pepperoni rolls and sauce. Then he places jelly filled croissants on the smaller plates. He twists the lid off the sparkling cider, and sends me the most dashing smile. His dimples make my heart do this weird fluttering thing. To top it off, his dark, shaggy hair that he usually keeps underneath his hat is on full display.

I don't normally paint people, only landscapes, but if I were to paint him, I'd match the wisps of his short, wavy locks. I'd use a round brush to perfect the strokes of his slight, bristly mustache and beard. I—

"Are you okay?" Dan's voice pulls me from my daydreaming.

"Yeah. Sorry." *I definitely wasn't just ogling you in my mind.* "Everything is wonderful, Dan," I say, trying not to let my voice crack as I motion my hand to our surroundings.

He smirks while pouring our drinks and says, "It was no trouble, I had a little help."

I grasp the glass from him, grazing the tips of my fingers slightly against his. I take a small sip of the bubbly liquid and set it on the table, trailing my finger over the condensation forming on the glass. "You did?"

"Constance actually."

"That was really nice of her."

"Yeah, she made sure the park was clear. She has plenty of con-nections." He flexes his fingers in an air quoting motion.

A laugh bubbles from my chest. "She does."

"Yeah. Well, this town's pretty great too," Dan says.

"It is." I pluck a slice of pepperoni roll from my plate, dunk it into sauce, and take a bite.

I've lived here my entire life, and this is all I've known. However, Dan hasn't. It makes me wonder where else he's lived. My curiosity gets the better of me, so I ask, "Where did you grow up?"

"Maryland, actually. Pretty close to the PA border. My mom still lives there with my step-dad, Jim, in my childhood home." He takes a sip of his drink.

"Was it a small town like ours?"

"It was more of a suburb since the houses were pretty close. But there was a park behind our house that my brother and I would walk to every day. We'd spin each other around on a mer-ry-go-round until we were sick." He chuckles, reminiscing. "My brother, Carter, would lay on the grass, staring at the sky for a good hour before we went home."

I laugh, covering my mouth. "That reminds me of when my parents took me to the beach and we would ride the roller coasters.

Dad would get sick every time, but I'd jump up and down and beg to go one more time. One day, I convinced him to go on a rollercoaster five times in a row. He was green in the face by the last round. But, Mom and I could've gone a few more times."

"I can't imagine Harvey on a rollercoaster."

"Picture it. Actually, I might have a photo album somewhere. I can show you if you'd like."

"I'd love to see it," Dan says, smiling. Then his face falls. "I wish my dad was like that when I was younger."

"I'm sorry."

"You have nothing to be sorry for."

"If you don't mind me asking, what was he like?"

"He was... well... it's hard to really put a word on it. He was never there." Dan grimaces.

I reach out and rest my hand in his. "I know you don't want me to apologize. But I'm sorry that he wasn't there for you."

He traces his thumb over my knuckles. "It's okay. My parents fought so much when he was home that it was better if he wasn't there. He lives in Delaware now. They needed to live in different states. One wasn't big enough for both of them. They divorced right after I left to move here, but their marriage was broken for a long time before that."

The hurt etched in his features makes my heart sink. Maybe I shouldn't have asked. I don't want to dredge up bad memories and make him upset. Daisy might've been wrong. I think I need those flashcards on the appropriate date questions right about now.

"That sounds... horrible. I didn't mean to bring it up." My parents were always so close. I can't begin to imagine what he went through. I wish I could hug younger Dan.

"I don't mind talking about it with you. I could talk about anything with you."

"Me too." He makes me feel as though I could tell him all my thoughts.

We finish dinner and move onto lighter topics: our favorite colors, food, and what we're working on inside and outside of work.

I pick out a few gummy worms and hook my feet around the chair legs. "So, have I converted you to these now?"

"I can't stop buying them," he admits. "I bought out Henry's stock for tonight."

"What? This is news to me! Henry already has them in Valley Harvest?" I'm baffled. How did I not find out about this development? Hmm... it's probably because my fridge is bare, and I need to go grocery shopping as soon as possible.

"Yep." He grabs one from the container. "The rest of these are for you to take home."

"Really?" My eyes widen.

"All yours. You can go crazy."

"I like you, Danny," I say before I have a chance to think.

He replies instantly, "I like you too, Goldie."

The sky starts to fade a deep orange and purple. The strands of lights continue to twinkle, and not long after, Dan walks me to his car, holding the door open for me. We exchange small talk on the drive back to my house.

I keep thinking about how well tonight went. I honestly thought that I'd never go on a date in my life. I had come to terms with it, but Dan opened my eyes to a whole new world. I'm starting to really fall for him. While that comes with hope, excitement, and wonderful feelings, it also scares me a little bit because this is all new and unknown. Yes, I've liked people before. I've never liked someone so much that the thought of losing them would scare me, though. With *like* comes *love*. I couldn't bear the thought of losing another person I love. Now, I'm spiraling. *Stop it, Marigold.*

Dan walks me to my front door, holding the giant container of gummy worms.

We stand in the dim light of my porch. He towers over me as I lean toward him. "Can I show you something?" I ask, not wanting the night to be over or to be alone with my thoughts just yet.

"Yeah." His voice is deep.

I grab the container from his arms and set it in the house. I take his hand and lead him to the edge of the wildflower field behind my house. I bend down and begin untying the laces on my shoes.

"What are you doing?" he asks.

I take my socks off and shove them into my converse. "Taking my shoes off, silly. It makes the experience more fun. You can take yours off too. If you want."

"I'm up for anything." He takes his boots off and stands in the grass in his socks.

Dan has made today spectacular, and I want to show him my favorite place in the world. It's the place I go to think and to escape. I want to show him this piece of me.

I place my hands on my hips. "Run with me if you want." I pose the challenge. "I'm sure you couldn't keep up." I wink and run barefoot through the flower fields on the grassy path I've taken many times before. The wildflowers are a blur in my vision, never quite seeming to begin or end. Dan follows me through the flowers, running alongside me for a while. Our laughter is like music. I turn my gaze to him, not worried about tripping because I know the path like the back of my hand. His eyes crinkle as he reaches his arms out to feel the wind, and right now, I'm sure he's feeling as free and alive as I do.

I run as fast as I can, picking up speed, following the trail of the solar lights, but Dan's quicker. He catches me, lifting me off my feet with one arm. The other wraps around my legs. I giggle into his chest, breathing deeply and short winded from running so fast. I pull back my head and stare at him in awe as he continues to run. The flowers flit by my peripheral.

We're at my favorite place, but I can't focus on anything other than him. Dan is absolutely mesmerizing. His dimples appear as he laughs, and his deep brown gaze softens when he looks at me.

He slows to a walk and lays me down in the middle of the field. Wildflowers surround us: black-eyed Susans, Queen Anne's lace, and butterfly milkweed. The moon hovers as the sky fades to a deep black. We lie facing each other. Although I can barely see him anymore, I can make out the hard features of his jaw and the smile painted across his face. The grass tickles my bare feet. Crickets sing while lightning bugs dot the sky everywhere as if it were just for us.

Dan whispers, "You're gorgeous." I bite my lip. His eyes track the movement. He practically devours my lips with his gaze. When his eyes lock with mine, they glow in the moonlight. He mutters, "So stunning." His lips hover over my forehead, and he kisses me there. I blush. His lips hover over my ear. "You're easily the most interesting, captivating, and beautiful woman in the world." Those twelve words send goosebumps over my entire body. His fingers dance on my arm. "I'm a fool, Goldie."

"Why?"

"Because I never noticed what was right in front of me. You."

"Me neither, Danny. Me neither." I bite my lip again, wondering what it would feel like to be kissed by him.

Chapter 21

DAN

I scrub a hand over my face, staring at my car. I can't focus.

Last night is still fresh in my mind. Marigold let me see a part of her that I doubt she shows many people. When she ran through the flower fields and her dress blew in the wind, her beauty made my breath catch. I wanted to spend the rest of my life there with her, running with her, carrying her in my arms, watching her hair flow, and listening to her laugh.

I opened up to her too. It felt freeing to tell her a little bit about my parents. I don't normally do that. I find myself wanting to tell her everything because I think she'd get it. She'd listen. That strained part of my past is just that—the past. I don't always say what I'm thinking, but with Marigold it's different. For the first time in a long time, I want to see where this thing goes.

Focus. I remind myself of my current project. The shop's closed on Sundays, but that doesn't mean I don't have work to do.

I spend the day priming the Chevy Nova and tidying up. Once I'm thoroughly exhausted, I step outside for some fresh air. It's dry and hot, but not unbearable since the sun has almost disappeared.

The street lights flicker on as the sky darkens. I take a seat on the bench beside my shop, stretching my legs in front of me. There's a bench in front of every storefront. This one is in honor of Marigold's grandparents. The one in front of Fix-Its is engraved to her mom. There's also one in front of Rooster's Bar, but that one is in tribute to the town's late, beloved rooster.

It's unusually quiet. The town bustle normally slows on Sunday but never comes to a complete stop. It probably has something to do with the fact that Constance's daughter, Chelsea, got married today. They're probably all at the reception.

I stretch my arms in front of me, taking a long, deep breath as I lean my back against the bench fully. I'm physically and mentally exhausted. I'm ready to hop into bed and become one with the mattress.

In the back of my mind, I think about my mom and what she said. Maybe she's right; maybe I'm starting to become my dad. Have I been making my job my focus and letting other things fall to the wayside? Maybe I need to take a couple days of vacation. I should visit my family more often. I haven't taken a day off in years. When my brother and his family visited last year, I worked every day and only spent the evenings with them. It's time to start changing my routine and fit in a few days for resting. I should make time for people I care about.

I grab my cellphone from my pocket and dial Mom's number. It rings three times before she picks up.

"Hello?" she answers.

"Hey, Mom. How are you?"

"Dan, sweetheart, this is a nice surprise. Jim and I were just talking about you."

"Were you really?" I ask. "Maybe that's why my nose was itchy."

She laughs jovially. "Yes! That's how it works. We were looking through old pictures and found one of you at prom. You looked so dapper and grown up."

"Oh, yeah?" That was a picture I hoped would stay hidden.

"I haven't seen you wear a suit since prom. No, wait, I almost forgot. You wore one when you got married to Kate." Her voice trails off. "Sorry."

"I save my good suit for special occasions. And you don't have to be sorry for bringing it up. I was married. It's a part of my life. We can talk about it."

"I know, but I remember how hurt you were. You've been doing well for yourself. We don't need to talk about the past." Her voice becomes animated as she changes the subject. "So your suit. Any special occasions in mind?"

"Uhh, not really. But I'm seeing someone," I tell her.

Technically, I'm not sure what Marigold and I are. We only went on one date. It was the best date of my entire life, but I'm not going to rush anything.

She gasps audibly. "Wow! What wonderful news! Jim! Jim! Hey, Honey! Dan's seeing someone!" She steps away from the phone, and everything between Jim and her is hard to hear.

"Jim says he's happy for you." Her voice is breathless when she returns to the phone. "What's her name? What's she like?"

"Marigold." I find myself smiling when I say her name.

"That's a beautiful name. I bet she's as stunning as her name is."

"She is. She's nice. She's funny. I really like her," I say.

Thinking about Marigold lifts my mood. I can't stop making excuses to stop over at Fix-Its just to see her for a few minutes.

"Christmas can't come soon enough. I can't wait to meet her. Send me a picture of you two."

I don't have any pictures of her yet because I've been more focused on enjoying every moment we've had together.

"I'll send you one later. I promise." *Hopefully, I won't forget.*

"I'll hold you to it." She sighs. "This is great news, Dan. I'm elated for you. Jim and I both are."

I take my hat off, and run my fingers through my hair, massaging my scalp, and yawn.

"I hear you yawning." She yawns. "It's contagious. Call me again. It was nice to hear from you. Love you, Dan."

"Love you too, Mom."

I am still smiling after I end the call. It was nice talking on the phone with her. I need to call her more often. I also make a promise to myself to take a few days off when my brother and his family get here. It's time to take a break and be with the ones I love. Even if I need to close the shop for a few days, there's nothing that needs to be worked on right away. If there's a towing emergency, the calls will get directed to my cellphone. So, I have no excuses.

A few clanks erupt from my left. I turn my head, looking for the source of the sound. No one's on the sidewalk or benches. The chickens are most likely perched in their coop for the night.

A yellow glow emits from the front of Fix-Its. I didn't think Marigold was in tonight. I figured she'd be at the wedding. I put my hat back on and head over to Fix-Its.

Through the glass of the front window, I see Marigold on an A-frame ladder, reaching toward the wall with a paint roller. She bites her lip in concentration as she moves the roller up and down. I wait until she steps down the ladder and sets the paint tray on the floor before I knock on the door. She tips her head up from her crouched position and grins when she sees me.

The door was already propped open, so I push it the rest of the way, stepping inside. The paint fumes hit me right away. Soft music bubbles from the radio. Marigold hums as she wipes a brush around the rim of a paint can. Blue paint splotches decorate her overalls, face, and braided hair, but I don't think she's ever been more breathtaking.

"Hey, Goldie." I smirk, unable to hide my amusement.

She smiles through a yawn, looking as exhausted as I feel. "Hi, Danny."

"It looks really nice." I take in the fresh paint on the walls above the shelves. "Want some help or are you finished?"

"Thanks, but I'm almost done here. Just have to clean up the drop cloths and wash these brushes." She raises the brush, sets it in a paint pail, picks up a hammer, and taps the lid to close the can.

"Can I drive you home?" I offer.

"No need," she says. "I'm sure you're exhausted too. Go home. Get some rest. I'm headed out in a few minutes anyway." She wipes her hand against her forehead.

"I know, but I'd much rather make sure you get home safe." If I drive her, I'll know she made it home okay. I won't stay up worrying.

Marigold relents. "Okay, thanks." She yawns again then covers her face with her palm, in turn dabbing a small blotch of paint on her lips. I chuckle.

Her eyebrows draw together. "What?"

"There's more paint on you than the walls," I reply, failing to hold back a grin.

"That's impossible," Marigold protests. "Logically..." She taps her chin in thought. "I'd be practically swimming in paint if there were more on me than the walls. I used two and a half gallons.

These are high ceilings, and you are not taking that into account." The corner of her lips quirk up as she leans against the front wall.

I take a few steps closer to her. I'm close enough to feel her hot breath against me. She looks into my eyes, and I brush my thumb over her forehead, swiping over wet paint.

She quirks a brow. "What are you doing?"

I show her my thumb. "Showing you the paint you smeared on your face. The paint I *am* taking into account."

"Oh." She clicks her tongue. "Cold, hard proof. You're pretty sly, Danny. I'll give it to you." A soft laugh escapes her lips.

Electricity courses through my veins. Her laughter is mesmerizing. Being this close to her is making it difficult for me to concentrate on forming words.

Say something...

I poke her nose. "There's some more over here."

Her lashes flutter. "Is that all?" she teases.

I rest an arm on the wall and lean toward her. I find myself searching her face, wondering if she feels as pulled to me as I am to her. The sparkle in her eyes is almost like confirmation that she might.

I made a promise to myself that I'd get to know Marigold as much as I could. Do it right. Take it slow. I was clear headed then. Now, my head is foggy.

I don't know if I can do this anymore. I don't know if I can keep myself from kissing her.

This is agony.

What she doesn't know is that it's taking every fiber in my body not to close the gap between us. I inch closer and place a kiss on her forehead.

She gasps softly, and it damn near crumbles the resolve I have left.

When I pull back, her cheeks are her favorite color, and her eyes sparkle that bright sky blue that I adore so much. She reaches upward and smears her fingers over my lips. I smirk as she pulls them back and shows me the paint.

Now, we're both wearing paint, and I'm reeling because I'm already falling for the woman in front of me.

I step backward after some time to get some space from her, not that I want to. I have to before I throw every plan of taking things slow out the door and pull her against me for a kiss.

I massage the back of my neck and bring up something else to derail my thoughts. "I didn't realize you were over here today. I thought you'd be at the wedding."

She bends down and picks up a drop cloth. "I thought about going, but I really wanted to get this painted. I need to have every-thing finished before the end of the month. And I'm not gonna lie, I'd rather skip it than socialize. What's your excuse?" she teases as she starts folding the drop cloth.

"Nearly the same reasons." I shrug my shoulders. "Working on my car." I pick up a drop cloth and fold it, setting it on the stack.

She places another folded cloth on a chair and glances at me. "I always dreamt of getting married one day and having a wedding, even though I avoid going to them. But, now, it's sad thinking about it. My mom was supposed to be there."

"Hey." I take a few steps in her direction, and my voice softens. "Your mom will be there. She may be gone, but she's always with you. She's in your heart. She's in your memory. She's always there."

"You're right. Thank you." Her eyes turn glossy. She's silent for a few beats and tilts her head as she fiddles with her necklace. A laugh bursts from her lips. "All this talk of weddings reminds me of when I was little. I'd wear this flowy white dress. I'd pretend I was getting ready for my wedding. I think this goes without me saying, but don't tell anyone this. It's embarrassing. Promise me?"

I shake my head. "I would never. I promise." I'd never tell a soul something she trusted to tell me.

Her nose crinkles, and she gives me a small smile. "Okay, you seem trustworthy." Her eyes dart to her hands as she picks at the corner of her thumb. "I'd dress my teddy bear in a suit." She bites her lip. "I'd run into the flower fields, and my mom would help me make a flower crown to wear. We'd have a fake ceremony and everything."

"Did your bear have a name?"

She laughs. "Mr. Fluffy."

"So you're already married to Mr. Fluffy?"

She smirks and looks to the ceiling, shaking her head. "It wouldn't hold up in a court of law." She covers her face, trying to hide the blush creeping up her cheeks.

"You don't have to hide yourself from me. I think it's sweet."

She uncovers her face. "Really?"

"Yeah." I nod, reaching out and brushing a lock of hair that had fallen loose from her braid around her ear. *She's so beautiful.*

She grabs her necklace and swivels it. "I still dream of wearing a pretty dress, surrounded by the people I care about. To say vows. The heart-wrenching ones that you don't prepare for. When you stand there looking into the eyes of the person who makes you whole. And the words just tumble from your lips." She sighs. "That's exactly what I want. Maybe it's me dreaming. Wishing for too much."

I want the exact same things as her. I want to be so in love that everything feels undoubtedly right. When Kate and I got married in the courthouse, we were only eighteen. It felt rushed. We were high school sweethearts who thought it was us against the world. Then she moved for college, and I wanted to stay at the only place I knew as home while still finding myself. We thought everything would work out no matter what, and a few years were but nothing in the long run. Turns out the long distance was too hard, and we grew apart.

The thought of being with someone now that I'm settled and comfortable in my life doesn't scare me as much as it used to. To me

Marigold's dream is not too much to ask for. It's what she deserves and will have one day. *Maybe I will too.*

"It's not too much. Don't ever think your dreams are too big. It's exactly what you deserve and more, Marigold."

She smiles wide. "That's nice of you."

"I'm being honest." *She deserves everything.*

"Well, I appreciate it." She smooths her hand over the top of the drop cloth. "What about you?"

I almost say *it's complicated* out of habit. I don't share much about myself with anyone. Marigold's not just anyone, though. I want to tell her. "After my parents... Their divorce... My divorce... I'd sworn off marriage. As I've gotten older, I realized that maybe I would want to get married again one day. But only for love. True love. For someone I couldn't imagine waking up without being next to them every day for the rest of my life."

"I'm sorry you had to go through that." Marigold shoots me a somber expression. "I don't blame you for having reservations about getting married again. I would too. It's hard to see the good in something that you've mostly seen the bad parts of. And it proves how strong you are to realize it and overcome it."

"Thanks." I step back and pick up the last drop cloth to fold. "My mom's happy now. I think my dad's doing well. That's all I could've ever wished for. I turned out all right, I guess. So did my brother."

"You turned out more than alright, Dan." She puts out her hand and lifts a finger. "You're amazing." She lifts another. "You're genuine." A third finger shoots up. "Smart." A fourth is added. "Kind." A thumb is thrown in. "Funny." She raises her other hand and lifts that thumb too. "And handsome."

"Thank you." My voice chokes.

We're silent for a few minutes as I hand her the drop cloth and follow her around the front counter. We put away all the supplies, and I look at the picture behind the counter of her family in front of the shop. It reminds me of something that I promised Mom.

"By the way, I need to take a picture of us together if it's alright with you?" I ask as she grabs her keys and turns out the lights. "We don't have to take one tonight. It's late, and I know you're tired."

"Of course. We can tonight. It'll only take a second."

"I talked to my mom earlier, and she asked for one," I explain as I head into The Think Den and pick up Buttercup from her bed.

"You told your mother about me?" she asks when I walk from the office, holding Buttercup. Marigold blushes, covering her face as we head out the front shop door. "Good things, I hope."

"There's only ever good things to say about you," I say.

"So what did you tell her?" she prods as she searches through the keys, looking for the right one.

"That there's this girl. This girl I really like. And she's pretty and smart and funny and has an obsession with gummy worms and the color pink."

She finds the key and locks the door. Then she turns to me, eyes aghast. "You didn't." She pokes my arm playfully.

"I did. Well, everything except for the gummy worms and pink part."

She sighs in relief. "Good."

"Everything I said was true. I really like you, Marigold."

She smiles, tipping her head downward with that blue paint-speckled hair on full display. "I really *really* like you too, Dan."

Chapter 22

MARIGOLD

"**W**ere you asking to rent a golf cart for a week?" I lift my head from my notebook.

Mason, the owner of Rooster's Bar, adjusts his glasses as he flips through a wood working magazine. "Yes, please, if that's doable."

"The next four weeks are fully booked. Can I pencil you in for sometime in late August? We just got two more golf carts, so the list moved up." It's all thanks to Dan. My heart pitter-patters thinking about how sweet the gesture was.

I can't believe I already booked four carts that far out. I had no clue my golf cart idea would create this kind of reaction.

"That works for me. There's no rush. And I'd like to get this." He places the magazine on the counter. "I'm making two rocking chairs, and this has a few different plans in it for them. I'm gonna surprise Olive, so keep this between us." He makes a zipping motion over his lips.

"That's so sweet. Your secret is safe with me. I'll pencil you in and ring you up for that." I drum my pen on the counter.

After Mason leaves, promising to be back to pick out some hard woods to make the chair, I open my laptop.

A few days ago Constance updated the town's website. I know… yes, a website. Our town is really embracing change this summer. Constance and her gossip mill have been working on it for a while. The website features a town event calendar and a place for people to learn about the town. There's a dedicated tab on the chickens, of course, and also a special tab for the golf cart rentals. They can look through pictures of each one to choose their favorite or learn a little about the bird associated with the cart. There's a section for contacting Fix-Its to rent one. The tab has a special calendar with the available renting dates. Ever since Constance made the website live this morning, Daisy and I have been fielding calls left and right.

I update the booking calendar on my laptop with the week rental for Mason. Then I continue flipping through different programs—updating the inventory numbers, sorting through parts I need to order in, and checking my email for any golf cart inquiries.

Daisy's voice pulls me from the computer. "Another cart rental?"

"Yeah." I drum my fingers over the keyboard. "The Chicken Coop is rented for another week. Can you believe that?"

"Holy moly." Her eyes glow with excitement. "Your dad is going to lose it when he comes back. You've already exceeded the past two months of profit. I'm sitting next to the new CEO of Fix-Its."

"CEO might be far-fetched." I lean against the counter. "I know I'm starting to prove myself, though. I'm doing this thing. My dad is going to be blown away when he gets back. I mean, in a good way! At least, I hope so."

She rounds the counter and sits beside me. "He will be. You've already gone above and beyond. It's looking great. The paint. The shelves. The organization. The golf carts. I'm proud of you, girly."

"Thanks. I couldn't have done it without you."

"You could have. But, it was more fun together," she points out.

"Exactly."

Daisy scratches her head. "So... give me the four-one-one on your date. You gave me the cliff notes version when you picked up Buttercup Sunday morning. But I see it went really well." She raises her eyebrows suggestively and grins at another bouquet of flowers that Dan had sent to the store, sitting next to the register. "Buttercup," Daisy calls. "Cover your ears, little one."

"She doesn't need to cover her ears." I roll my eyes. "It went—" How do I put the most amazing first *real* date into words? Dan went way beyond any expectations I had. I really wasn't expecting it to be life altering. It's easy to talk to him, to tell him things I haven't told anyone else, and to be myself around him.

I glance at the flowers. He doesn't need to keep getting me flowers. I can't deny they're the sweetest thing, though. They're on the counter in front of me. They're on my windowsill at home. Everywhere I turn, I'm reminded of him: the words he shares that cover me in goosebumps, those dimples that appear when he smirks, and the look he gives that's only reserved for me. Well, at least I like to imagine it is.

"Marigold," Daisy says.

Oh, crap, that's right, I was supposed to be saying these things to her.

"Your Dad is on the phone. He's asking for you." She holds the phone out toward me.

I completely missed hearing it ring.

"Thanks," I whisper to Daisy as she puts her thumb up and heads into the Think Den with Buttercup on her heels.

I laugh and talk into the phone. "Hi, Dad."

"Hey, Mary. I'm glad to see you've got yourself some help."

"Yeah, it's Daisy. I know what you said, but she's actually pretty great—"

He interrupts me. "No need to explain yourself. I trust you. Whatever you think's best. Anyway, I was teasing you about that. Daisy is a great worker. I've seen her fling pizzas around and tackle a line out the door without breaking a sweat."

I spin a pen on the counter. "She's pretty great."

"You sound happy," Dad observes.

"You do too. And that makes me happy."

"I am." He's quiet for a moment, and I can hear the lapping of waves and birds chirping. "I needed this trip. It's medicine for my soul. It's incredibly refreshing. I ate some soft serve, fed the seagulls, and now I'm going to soak in some sun. Maybe I'll take a nap on the beach. I have no concrete plans, and that in itself is true peace."

"You're making me jealous. That sounds perfect."

He chuckles. "Well, I need to return to reality soon, or else I'll get used to this and never leave."

Although I want him to be happy, a part of me doesn't want him to stay there because I'd worry about him... I'd miss him. Then there's the logical voice in my head saying that this is a good thing. He is happy. If his happiness is at the beach, maybe he should make it his home. He's got enough saved up to make it happen.

"When are you coming home?" I ask.

"The plan is next Friday," he says, making it sound more like a question. "You'll still have a week on your own with Fix-Its. I won't step on your toes. I'll just hang out at home and stroll around town. Are you all good there? If you need me, I'll come home right now."

"No, Dad. I'm great. Everything is running smoothly. I have Daisy's help. And Dan's been helping with things that I've been working on too."

"Dan's a great guy."

"I know. And uhh... that's what I've been meaning to tell you. He took me on a date." I smile, tapping my fingers on the counter.

"That's great news," he says. "Uh-oh, my phone is making an annoying dinging noise. What does that mean?"

I laugh. Dad still doesn't know how to use the cellphone I insisted he carry with him. He never had one and refused the idea. I got him one anyway, and I'm glad of it now. He's obviously figured it out enough to call me.

"I think it means it's dying. You better charge it. Did you bring the charger?"

"Yeah." He grunts in frustration. "Stop beeping. Dang technology. You kiddos are all high-tech. I'll plug it in so I can call you in a few days."

I try really hard not to laugh, but it's pointless. "Good. You better because I'll worry if I don't hear from you."

"Don't worry. I'll get it charged. Bye, Mary. Talk to you soon. This thing won't stop pinging in my ear."

"Bye, Dad. Love you," I manage to say, laughing.

"Love you too."

After I end the call, I get back to figuring out this month's expenditures. I type away until a blue spec of paint on my nails ends up distracting me.

Last night flashes in my head. I spent two hours in the shower scrubbing myself with a loofah like my life depended on it. I was ready to grab sandpaper. That's how desperate I was, but I thought better of it. Trying to peel the blue flakes out of my hair took the most time. Dan was right; I almost had more paint on me than the walls. I was letting go and having fun. Singing along to the music playing, I didn't even notice when I flung paint all over myself. I definitely regretted that decision yesterday and this morning as I plucked stray pieces of blue from my head.

At the same time, the paint reminds me of last night's conversation with Dan. I can't believe he almost kissed me. I wish he had. I was ready to kiss him. I wanted him to break through the space between us and kiss me, but he did not. Now, my mind can't escape the thought of him pressing his lips to mine.

"So—" Daisy taps on the counter, fizzling my daydream of Dan. "Are you going to fill me in yet?"

"Oh, yes. Starting with the picnic we had in the park."

"Yes! I need to sit down for this. Tell me everything. Don't leave any of the juicy details out." She rushes to the seat beside me and props her head in her hands.

This is going to take a while. I smile as I recount everything about Saturday and last night.

Chapter 23

MARIGOLD

I tap my fingers on the desk in the Think Den. The bell on the front door jingles, announcing a customer. I hop from my chair and leave the office to help whoever just came in. Buttercup rushes from her spot in her bed underneath the desk and follows me.

"There's my two favorite girls," Dan says from his spot in front of the register.

Buttercup races to him. He picks her up and pets her head. A smile warms my face as I watch the two.

"Buttercup loves you," I say.

"I'm beginning to love her back." He pats her head and looks up at me. "She's not trying to lick my face anymore. We're making progress."

"I can see that." I smirk at the sight. "Char already ordered the parts for today," I say, not sure if that's why he's here.

"I know." He nods, setting down Buttercup. She squeals happily as she zig-zags through Dan's legs and mine. Dan chuckles, watching her take off to The Think Den. He turns to me, face beaming with mirth and says, "I came to see you and to ask you something."

My stomach does a flip when he adjusts his backwards hat with his free hand.

"Oh." I lift my chin.

"My brother's visiting tomorrow with his family. We're gonna go to the Strawberry Festival. Since we're pretty much smack-dab in the middle of it, I thought maybe you'd wanna tag along with us. It could be... I don't know... kind of like another date. Well, you'd be my date."

Dan actually seems nervous to ask me. It's really sweet that he wants me to tag along with him and his family. My heart swells at the idea of officially meeting them and even more so that he *wants* to introduce me to them. It speaks volumes.

Even though I'm nervous, I'm also excited. "I would love to. What time?"

He scrubs a hand over his face. "How does six sound?"

"Perfect." I rock on my feet. "Are you sure your family won't mind me being there? I know they haven't seen you in awhile, and they probably want to spend time catching up with you. I'll be fine here."

He takes my hand. "They won't mind. They will love you. You have nothing to worry about."

"Okay, I'll be there then." I smile, stepping closer to him.

"I see you're wearing my hat today." He winks, sending a rush of butterflies in my stomach.

"I was hoping you'd notice." I smirk, tipping the bill forward.

He sticks his thumbs in his pockets. "Oh, I noticed. It was the second thing I spotted when you walked from your office."

"What was the first thing?"

"Your smile."

I giggle and blush a thousand shades of deep crimson. This man knows exactly what to say to make me swoon—consider me swooning.

"What are your plans after you close?" Dan asks.

I shrug. "Nothing earth shattering. Go home. Paint. Hang out with Buttercup."

"I'm headed to Valley Harvest. I need to grab some things to stock my fridge for when they come tomorrow. You're welcome to join me if you want," he offers.

"Actually, yeah. I need to grab a few things."

I check the clock on the wall. I'll close things now, leave Buttercup here, and pick her up before I head home.

Once I lock up, Dan and I walk to the grocery store. He reaches for my hand, looking unsure, but then a soft smile paints his face.

I take his hand, feeling butterflies in my stomach as my fingers interlock with his.

For a moment, I can't help but wonder what we are. Are we just two people who go on dates and hold hands? Would I be considered his girlfriend?

None of that matters because I'm happy with whatever *this* is.

As we walk, my mind wanders to this town. This is all I've ever known. I'd like to think Dan fell in love with Thornwood Valley when he first visited here. Who wouldn't? The summer sun makes the windows of the shops sparkle. The houses converted into stores are charming. Stunning flower arrangements overflow from pots in every nook and cranny. Chickens roam the sidewalk. No one's in a hurry, and townies aren't afraid to stop to talk for hours.

Dan and I pass Paula's medical practice as people filter in and out the wide open front door. Next is Cat's & Novels, where an adorable orange tabby cat sleeps on a cat tree behind the glass window. Daisy's Aunt Ada, who's one of the owners, waves from the door when we pass, beaming a warm smile. Then as we walk past the parking lot, a few more chickens strut by.

Dan holds the door open for me at the Valley Harvest and a rush of cool air greets us.

"Thank you," I say as I pass the checkout section. Dan grabs a buggy, and we head to the local produce table first.

"Will this fit everything you need?" he asks, surveying the bell peppers.

"Yes, I'm only grabbing a few things."

He chooses a green one and grabs a paper bag from the shelf to put it in. "Get whatever you want. It's on me."

"No, I couldn't let you." I shake my head. He already got me plenty of flowers, plus the golf carts, and our date the other night.

He puts a few more peppers in the brown bag and glances down at me. "Please?" He looks adamant.

"Okay, but next time, I'll cover yours?"

He pauses, bracing his arms on the buggy. "We have a deal. But I'm only getting a few things then."

"Touché." My shoulders shake with my laughter.

Dan chuckles as he grabs a large Vidalia onion and a head of lettuce.

"What are you making?" I pick out a zucchini, putting it in the buggy.

He surveys the vegetables. "Steak and Italian hoagies. A giant salad. And then my famous pancakes for breakfast."

"That sounds delicious." My eyes track the blueberries, and I grab a container. "So how famous are we talking... on a scale of frozen pancakes to Annie's Diner?"

"My pancakes surpass the scale." The corners of his lips tilt into a full-fledged smile, dimples and all.

"Well, I'm sure your family loves staying at your place if the pancakes are that good."

He picks out a cucumber and chuckles. "They probably wouldn't come if it weren't for the pancakes."

"Yeah, right." I lift an eyebrow. "I think they mostly want to see you." I nudge his arm playfully. "The pancakes are just a perk that comes along with the trip."

He sets a tomato and a purple cabbage into another bag then shifts his gaze to me. "Cooking something while they stay has pretty much become a tradition." He scratches his chin. "Every time they've visited, I worked through the day and only spent the small moments I have off with them. This time, I'm gonna take a few days off from work, though."

"That's a good thing. I think that would make them happy."

I can clearly see how much Dan's family means to him by the effort he is making. Plus, I know they will appreciate more time with him. Life can be unpredictable. I learned that from losing my mom. Therefore, time should be cherished.

"Me too. And it will be good for me. Taking a break." He sets another paper bag full of produce into the cart.

"I can't disagree with that."

He pushes the cart and nods to the aisles of dry goods. "Come on. I want to show you something I think you'll like."

I follow after him.

"We're making a quick detour."

"Okay." I laugh, following him down the breakfast aisle.

Dan taps his chin and crosses his arms as he flicks his gaze over an array of boxes on the shelf. When I catch up to him, I realize what he's looking for.

He grabs a box of *Bisquick* and holds it proudly. "See, I told you they were famous pancakes. World famous." He drops the box into the cart.

"You'll have to make me some then."

"I will." He promises. "Okay, now let me show you the reason I wanted you to come with me."

We walk to the next aisle. Dan leads the way, stopping the cart halfway.

"Take a look at this." He stands nonchalantly in front of bags of candy and points to his left.

"No way!" I cover my mouth, realizing I just shouted in the store. It's too exciting. Not one, not two, but three rows of my favorite gummy worms are on the shelf!

"Henry said he stocked so many since they sold out right away. And now, they'll be permanently stocked every week."

"Brace yourself." I warn Dan as I envelop him into a hug.

Dan chuckles, and I laugh into his chest. I squeeze my arms around him tighter, and he rests his chin on my head. I don't want to let go. Dan makes me incredibly happy. He doesn't cease to amaze me with his kindness.

Gummy worms might simply be candy to anyone else, but they're more to me. They embody the effort Dan goes to. He spoke up for me when I wouldn't. He thought about me. He listens. To me, this is a *grand gesture.*

I feel myself falling for him more every day.

Chapter 24

DAN

"Uncle Dan!" my niece, Bella, sing-songs.

I tuck this month's invoices away into the desk drawer, making a point to put away any and all work for the next few days.

Out of sight, out of mind.

I make my way to the office doorway and lean against the door frame. I watch Bella survey the garage with anticipation until her dark brown eyes lock on me. Her entire expression brightens, and I smile at the sight.

Found you, I'm sure she's thinking as her feet pitter-patter across the concrete floor. Her happy-go-lucky laughter echoes off the brick walls as she beelines to me with her arms outstretched for a hug.

I step just outside the door and crouch to my knees. I open my arms, and she squeezes her little arms around my frame. She pulls back to look at me and giggles. She mutters, "Hi." Then her eyes sparkle as she asks, "Can we go get some ice cream?"

I laugh lightly, shaking my head. The kid knows her priorities.

"Later. Pinky promise?"

"Pinky promise," she repeats. She raises her arms and then locks her pinky with mine, sealing the promise.

"We're going to have lunch first. Then we can go to the park and feed the ducks by the pond. After that, you can have as much ice cream as you want."

My brother, Carter, joins us by my office and gives me a look that says, *Bella can't have as much ice cream as she wants.* So, I say, "You can have as much ice cream as your parents let you have."

Carter gives me a thumbs up.

Bella wiggles her eyebrows. "Strawberry ice cream?"

"Yes," I reply, laughing.

She pumps her arms, probably remembering last year and hoping for the same thing. They spent hours eating ice cream, sweets, and strawberry themed foods, trying a little of everything at the festival while I was working... I shake the thought from my mind.

This year will be different.

Anyway, they all went to bed in a food coma, or so I thought. I peeled my eyes open in the middle of the night when I heard a strange sound coming from the kitchen. The freezer light was emanating in my studio apartment. I flipped the covers off me and tiptoed across the floor to shut the freezer. Instead of an abandoned freezer door, there was little Bella, hidden by the counter. Her arms were stretching to reach the leftover ice cream in the freezer. I scooped us both a bowl while Carter and his wife were dead asleep on the pull-out couch.

Bella had me laughing, trying not to be too loud, but Carter's snoring was a telltale sign we wouldn't be caught. It was our secret.

Bella stands in front of me, one hand propped on a hip. She looks taller and more grown than when I saw her last year. "Look at you. All grown up."

She giggles. "I'm four now."

"I know. I can't believe it." I shake my head in disbelief.

Where does the time go?

This is exactly why I want to spend as much time with family as I can; I'd miss out on these moments if I were working during the few days I get to see them a year.

"Can I put my backpack in your house?" Bella asks.

I look to Carter to see if he's cool with it. I see him nod. "Go on ahead," I tell her.

She smiles and rushes to the stairs leading to my apartment.

I stand, stretching my legs from being crouched over for so long.

"Hey, little brother." Carter pats my back, embracing me in a hug.

"Hey, man. I'm not so little anymore." I chuckle, releasing him.

"You'll always be little to me."

"That's sweet," I mutter.

"Oh, come on. Just because you had a growth spurt in the tenth grade means nothing. You may be taller than me, but you'll always be a little kid to me. In here." He pats his chest over his heart.

"That's fair." I grin. "Hi, Eve." I greet Carter's wife as she walks in.

"Hi, Dan! Sorry it took me so long. I saw the lemonade stand in front of The String Cheese. Strawberry lemonade looked really good, so I got everyone one." She laughs, balancing a tray filled with cups and her own cup in her other hand.

"Here. Let me help you," Carter offers, before I have a chance to. He settles the tray on his arm.

"Thanks, honey." Eve smiles at her husband. "That was a long drive. But it's so nice to be on a vacation. This is obviously our favorite stop because we get to see you."

"She's right," Carter agrees. "We're going to stay for three days this time. If that's alright with you? Then head to Mom and Jim's. Try Dad's if he's home. And finish the week off at the beach on the way home."

"Perfect. I'm taking the next three days off work, so I'm up for anything." I shift on my feet.

"You are?" Eve gasps.

Carter splays his fingers over his heart. "Is there a full moon or something?"

"I don't know, why?" I ask.

"You never take a day off." Eve takes a sip of her lemonade.

Carter nods. "Never."

I shrug. "I'm trying something different."

"Good for you, Dan." Eve smiles at her lemonade. I'm guessing she's thoroughly enjoying it. She shifts her gaze, beaming at me. "It'll be good to have some plain old fun and get some rest. I'm sure it'll do you good." She smiles at Carter, and they share some kind of nodding look that I don't quite understand. "I should see what Bella's up to. Is she upstairs?"

"Yeah, she went up a few minutes ago," I say.

"She's probably looking for ice cream in your freezer." Eve winks, taking the tray of drinks.

Damn. The cat is out of the bag.

Eve doesn't give me a chance to pretend I have no clue what she's talking about. Instead, she points a finger at the tray of drinks and says, "You both need to have one before the ice melts. They are delicious. I drank half of mine while waiting for the rest of them to be freshly squeezed."

"Thanks," I say, taking a cup.

Eve gives one last I-know-about-your-late-night-icecream smirk and heads up the stairs.

Carter and I are quiet for a moment, well, more like busy slurping on the strawberry lemonade that is addicting. Half of mine is gone before Carter speaks. "You look different. There's something about you."

"I'm the same person you've known for your entire life," I reply nonchalantly while taking another gulp of the drink.

"No." Carter brushes a hand over his chin. "You're smiling more. You took time off. You seem more laid back... I don't know, man."

"I smile. I'm a happy guy." I shrug my shoulders.

"I never said you don't or weren't." Carter rolls his eyes. "But you're smiling nonstop. For whatever reason. I'm happy you're happy."

I have no clue what to say to that. "Well, I'm happy you're happy too." It's the truth; he looks happy as ever.

Is the smiling thing that obvious? I run my fingers over my lips to see if they are indeed curved upward into a smile. What the hell? They are. First Mateo, now my brother has noticed. I am truly happy, and it probably has something to do with Marigold. Dammit, it has everything to do with her. Thinking about her makes me smile. It's not a bad thing nor is it something I should try to hide. I lower my hand. I'm done hiding. I need to embrace it.

Just when I decide to tell Carter about Marigold, he changes the subject. "Is this your new project?" Carter prods, running a hand through his short clipped hair and pointing to the Nova I primed.

"Yeah." I nod. "Been working on it for a while here and there."

Carter clicks his tongue. "This looks immaculate. It'll look great once you paint it." He walks over to the car, sipping on lemonade. He side steps around the car, looking at the quarter panels and fenders. "I don't think I'll ever get over how impressive you are, man. You really found your calling. The patience and talent this takes is incredible. Are you gonna keep this one? Or is it for a customer? Do you already have a buyer? If not, I'd be interested."

I think, I almost say but stop myself. "I'm going to keep this one." I shove my hands into my pockets, rocking on the balls of my feet.

"Wow, you have changed, brother. You never keep them for yourself. I'm damn proud of you. It's good to keep something you worked hard on for yourself once in a while. You deserve it."

"Can I have a mini cheese pizza?" Bella bites her lip while looking up at her mother.

Eve surveys the menu. "Yes. What do you want to drink?"

Bella tilts her head. "Chocolate milk?"

Eve relays the question to Joe, or Pizza Joe, as everyone in town refers to him. He smiles as he jots down their order on a guest check. I place my order as well, and we head to a table outside, shaded by an umbrella. Bella sets our table number in front of her and sits next to me. She begins coloring a placemat Joe handed her.

"How's business been?" I direct the question to Carter and Eve.

"Booming as ever." Eve supplies the answer, smiling. "There's never a shortage of four-legged clients."

Carter nods in agreement. "Oh, and don't forget birds!" He grins and wraps his arm around the back of Eve's chair.

"Ever think of opening a veterinary practice in PA?" I joke.

"Texas has my heart."Eve sighs wistfully. "Although, it'd be wonderful if we were closer to you."

"I was just kidding with you." I reassure her.

"Ever think of opening an auto shop in Texas?" Carter raises his brows.

"I love it here too much."

"I can see why. There's something about the chickens roaming town that really feels homey. Plus, the pizza here is almost worth staying for." Eve smirks.

"You could say that." Both are small reasons why I love it here. The biggest reason is the people in town. I've come to see them as family. *Or maybe it's more specifically one person. The girl one shop over. The one that has captivated my every waking thought.*

"Here's your pizza." Our waitress, Jamie, hands out plates from a large serving tray, steaming with warm food. "Can I get you anything else?"

I shake my head no, and I look at Carter, who gives a thumbs up.

"We're perfect here. Thank you, darling," Eve replies to Jamie for the table.

"Holler if you need me." Jaime tucks the tray at her side and heads back inside.

The four of us waste no time as we dig into our food. Bella abandons her crayons in favor of the kid-sized pizza she gets all to herself. She grins, doing a dance in her chair as she lifts a slice and takes a giant bite.

"Is it good?" I ask her as she goes in for another bite.

"Mmm." Her little eyes light up.

I laugh and take another bite of my pepperoni roll.

"Can I still feed the ducks?" Bella asks after some time.

"Only if Dan has time," Eve replies.

"Of course. That was the plan. We can head to the park after this and from there to the festival once it starts," I say.

"Great." Carter smiles.

"Yay!" Bella cheers. She takes a gulp of chocolate milk and slides the placemat in front of her, coloring between the lines once more.

I dip my pepperoni roll in sauce. "We just have to stop at Fix-Its before the festival. I hope you don't mind if Marigold tags along?" I take a bite and watch for their reactions. Eve and Carter lift their heads in tandem. I definitely have their undivided attention now. Their pizza is all but forgotten.

Carter leans back and wraps an arm over Eve's chair.

Eve leans into the table and says, "We don't mind one bit!"

Carter looks at her and smiles. Then turns to me, wearing a smirk. "Nope." He shakes his head. "The more the merrier. Is she the one that was at the front desk over there when we got Bella's fishing gear?"

"Yes, her." I nod, remembering how I spent that Sunday evening with them at the pond last year.

Bella pokes me on the arm. "Fishing? Can we go fishing too?" she asks excitedly.

"How does tomorrow morning sound?" I ask everyone.

Carter and Eve nod.

Bella's eyes dance. "Yay! Tomorrow!"

I can't believe I spent years missing out on them by not taking off work, which I've desperately needed to do. Time with family is irreplaceable. Seeing the excited look on Bella's face right now is enough to prove that to me.

Chapter 25

MARIGOLD

*J*ust a little bit more.

I bite my lip in concentration, staring at my reflection in the tiny bathroom mirror. I jump and pull my high-waisted jean shorts upward with determination. They're stiff, and I always end up doing the hop-tug-dance to wear them, but they're so cute and definitely worth it. I've got it down to a science now, with about four repetitions of this method being the sweet spot. The denim is embroidered with tiny strawberries, pairing perfectly with my red T-shirt.

I take a deep breath in and out, counting backwards from three. *Three... two... one*. I jump and tug again, successfully latching the button. I don't breathe until I zip up the shorts. I sigh in relief once I get it and tuck in my red top. I put on a strawberry headband

and pull a few strands of hair on both sides loose. I run my fingers through my loose waves, trying my best to untangle any knots.

After my outfit is set for the evening, I hang out with Buttercup, catching up on some paperwork as I wait for Dan and his family. I tap a pen unconsciously on the side of my desk while flipping through a stack of invoices from this month. I try my best to concentrate, but I find myself losing my train of thought.

Will Dan's family like me? Will I say something that I'll regret later? Most likely. Will I be imposing on their time together? I'm not sure. There's one thing I am sure of: I'm making myself anxious wondering these things.

I leave the office and wait by the front desk. I look out the front window, holding Buttercup in my arms. A few townies walk by occasionally. The muted sound of "Strawberry Wine" by Deana Carter plays outside. I hum along, petting Buttercup.

A few minutes later, Dan walks into Fix-Its, holding the hand of his little niece. My heart melts instantly. In such a short amount of time, I can already tell this is a side of Dan that I haven't seen much of. He already seems calmer and brighter with his family. I know he spent the whole day with them.

Dan grins, and the dimples carving his cheeks are prominent. He's so handsome. His presence in the room is captivating. I smile back and twirl a strand of my hair, getting lost in his brown eyes.

I almost miss Dan's brother and sister-in-law, following behind him. I stand up quickly and set down Buttercup. She rushes to greet Dan.

"There's my favorite pig," Dan says, bending down to scoop her up into his arms. He holds her out to his niece.

His niece's eyes light. "She has a pig?" she asks in excitement.

"Yes." Dan lets out a deep chuckle. "Here, you can pet her." He cradles Buttercup in his arms, and his niece reaches out her hand to pet Buttercup's head in soft pats.

After Dan sets Buttercup down, she runs off, zooming around the shop in excitement. Everyone laughs.

"Bella. This is Marigold." Dan introduces me to his little niece.

"Hi, Bella!" I exclaim. She pulls me into a hug, and it's the sweetest thing ever.

"Hi," she says and pulls backward. She turns to Dan. "Uncle Dan, is this your girlfriend?"

Dan doesn't miss a beat as he replies, "Yes, she is."

I am?

I blush. Did he just call me his girlfriend?

"She's pretty," Bella says.

"She's very pretty." Dan smirks at me, and I'm sure at this point my face is deep red.

Dan said I'm his girlfriend. Me? My heart won't stop its persistent fluttering.

"I'm Eve." Dan's sister in law introduces herself to me. I go to shake her hand, but she laughs, avoiding my hand and hugging me instead. "We are huggers in this family." Eve smiles when she pulls away.

"I'm Carter. Nice to meet you, Marigold." Dan's brother gives me a quick one armed hug as he holds Buttercup in the other. I didn't notice him pick her up. She sure has made rounds to everyone.

"It's nice to meet you all. Dan has told me so much about you guys already," I say.

"Don't listen to a word he said... unless he said some good things. In that case, I guess you can believe those words." Carter pats Buttercup's head.

Dan laughs, shaking his head. "I don't ever say anything bad."

"Like we're gonna believe you." Eve teases.

"I swear, it was only good things." I reassure them for Dan's benefit. "He told me about your practice. About Bella. Only positive, glowing things."

"I guess we oughta thank Dan then." Carter laughs. "For leaving out all our negative attributes."

"Marigold, it's a lovely shop you've got here," Eve says, surveying the shelves.

"Thank you." I smile, not wanting to get into the details of how it's actually my dad's place, was my parents' place together, and before that, belonged to my grandparents. The generations of Fix-Its is a long story. Today is about strawberries, having fun, spending the evening with Dan and his family, and more strawberries.

"We'll be by tomorrow morning to get some worms. Dan's taking us all on a fishing trip," Eve says as she looks around more.

"Are you gonna come with us?" Bella asks with a hope filled gaze.

"I wish. I have to work tomorrow. You'll see me when you come here actually. But I bet you'll have so much fun. I can try to come next time." I do my best to keep my tone excited, not to let her down.

"Yay!" Bella cheers.

"Ready to go get some strawberries?" Dan asks everyone, and we all agree.

I lock the door behind us, leaving Buttercup at the shop while I'm gone.

Bella, Carter, and Eve wander ahead of Dan and I. They cross the street, passing booths set up in the road that is closed for the festival. Bella clings onto her parents hands as they swing her in the air. She giggles and says, "Again."

I feel Dan grasp my hand, and I look up at him. "You look beautiful, *girlfriend*." With a playful smile, he raises his eyebrow.

There's that word again. *Girlfriend.* Am I really his girlfriend? We've never spoken about it. Maybe he's just teasing me. Then again, maybe he's serious.

I wouldn't mind being his girlfriend. I really like him. I like our quiet moments spent together. Now that I'm thinking about calling Dan my boyfriend, I'm quite liking the idea of us. Hearing the word *girlfriend* coming from his lips is nice.

"Thank you," I say while fiddling with my necklace.

He waves to Dustin and Violet who are set up with a goat cheese and flower booth.

Ask it, my subconscious whispers. *Just ask him.*

I take in a deep breath, willing all the confidence I can muster. His grip on my hand is steady as we walk down the sidewalk, passing more booths. "Am I really your girlfriend?" I ask it so quickly that I almost wonder if I said it or not. I avoid his gaze nonetheless, twirling the pendant of my necklace.

He squeezes my hand reassuringly, and I tilt my chin, looking at him. He grins, answering with a deep timber in his voice. "I'd like that. That is... if you want to be my girlfriend?"

Umm. Yes! Now who's asking silly questions?

"I'd love to be. That is... if you want to be my boyfriend?" I bite my lip through a smile, already knowing the answer, but wanting to hear the word regardless.

"I'd love the title. So you ready to get some strawberry ice cream with me, *girlfriend?*"

"I've been dreaming about it, *boyfriend.*" I wink.

Dan and I hold hands as we follow his family into Bobbie's Freeze. Dan and I both order chocolate soft serve in strawberry-dipped cones. Bella gets a cup of strawberry ice cream topped with fresh strawberries and pretzels. Eve opts for a strawberry cheesecake ice cream cone, and Carter picks a cup of vanilla soft serve.

"You don't like strawberries anymore?" Dan asks, raising a brow at his brother as we all take a seat at one of the booths by the window.

Carter gives Dan a dirty look that almost makes me burst into laughter. "Love 'em. Just trying to cleanse my palette before I devour every strawberry related pastry I can get my hands on."

"You're going to make yourself sick," Eve says. I'm uncertain if she's serious, but then she smirks. "And I'll be there right with you."

They start chatting back and forth about everything they're planning to try.

Dan leans into me, whispering, "They do this every year. As soon as they get back to my place for the night, they pass out from a strawberry related coma. It's the Stone family tradition."

"Sounds like the perfect tradition to uphold."

"This is so good!" Bella's voice shifts Dan's and my conversation to her, filling the ice cream shop with laughter.

Chapter 26

MARIGOLD

I can't get over how amazing today is. The sun shines over us, the booths dot the street, and people walk past chitter-chattering. When I'm with Dan, I don't get as nervous as I normally would. He makes me feel at ease.

"Carter and I are gonna grab something. You okay here with Eve?" Dan asks, voice low enough that only I can hear.

It's sweet, him making sure I'm okay alone with his family while he's gone. Dan gets me. I think he's the first person that truly sees me.

"Of course," I say.

Dan kisses my cheek and takes large strides toward Carter. Bella jumps up and down, tagging along.

I sit on a park bench—my favorite bench in the whole town, Mom's bench.

"Is this seat taken?" Eve asks, gesturing to the empty spot beside me.

My lips curl into a smile. "It's all yours."

"It seems they've abandoned us." Eve laughs.

I hum in agreement. "They did."

"I can't complain. Sitting down for a moment is just what I needed."

"Me too." I'm exhausted from the long day of working and walking around town for the past few hours.

"I love coming here." Eve sighs, pulling her sunglasses off her eyes and placing them on her head. She gestures around her. "To this town to do the Strawberry Festival. And to visit Dan. You know, this is the happiest I've ever seen him." She pauses briefly, looking out at the booths. "I was hoping to catch you alone because I wanted to thank you. I'm sure it has something to do with you."

"Oh, no. Nothing to do with me. Dan always seems happy."

"That's true. Dan is a happy guy. But not like this. This is unusual. He never takes multiple days off to spend with us. And he has never mentioned having a girlfriend after he got divorced. Until you." Eve smiles. "I see the way he looks at you. Whatever you're doing, just keep on doing it. This is good for him. He needs to slow down a little bit. He needs a bit of joy in his life. And I'm almost positive *you* are a big part of that joy."

My face blushes. "I will." I promise Eve. I honestly have no clue what I'm doing, but I'll try. If it's spending every day with Dan, I can do that. He makes me happy too. I'm finding that I want to be with him all the time.

"There they are." Eve points between a group of townies and a table covered with crocheted strawberry plushies, quilts, and doilies. Bella skips between Carter and Dan. A pretty red daisy is nestled behind her ear.

Dan smirks when he sees me. He tugs on his backwards hat and winks. His charming smile makes my stomach fill with butterflies. "This is for you." He holds out a pink marigold. I go to take it from him, but he says, "Here let me." He brushes some hair behind my ear and tucks the flower there. Goosebumps coat my arms. The flower smells wonderful, and when he steps back, there's still a hint of floral notes and Dan's lingering woodsy cologne.

I am swooning.

"Are you gals ready for the tractor ride to pick some strawberries?" Carter asks.

Eve stands. "I am."

The five of us walk to the edge of town and wait at the end of the shops by Dan's car wash.

George, Dustin's grandfather from The Rhett Family Farm, pulls his big green tractor around, backing the wagon just before the line of waiting people. Everyone steps up to get on the uncovered wagon. Dan gets on and then helps me up. I sit on the hay bale at the edge, since we're the last two to get on.

Dan stands. "Switch me," he says. "I'll take the end."

"Okay, sure." I take his place next to Bella.

"Sorry. If anyone were to fall off this thing, I'd rather it be me," Dan says, settling himself on the end.

"It's me and you brother," Carter chimes in, clutching his stomach through laughter or maybe he had one too many strawberry desserts and isn't feeling too good. "We're going down together."

"I don't remember George going that fast last year." Eve scrunches her face.

Dan chuckles. "Dustin got him a new tractor. Trust me. It's better that we're at the end. We can jump off if we have to."

I don't know if that's a good thing or not. They can be the first to jump off, but they might be the first to fall off.

George revs up his tractor even more, heading toward the farm and fields of strawberry plants. The sound of laughter and giggling erupts from people sitting beside us.

Dan was right. The ride turns from smooth to bumpy in a matter of seconds. George chugs away as I grip the hay bale underneath me. Dan's strong arm wraps around me, pulling me to his side.

"You okay?" Dan asks softly into my ear.

I bob my head. "Yes." I'm even better now, nestled under his arm. I like being close to Dan. I like that he's always noticing me and checking on me.

Through every curve, hill, and bump, Dan holds onto me.

George doesn't look back once the entire time. Maybe that's a good thing, though; at his speed, focusing on the road in front of him might be best for the sake of everyone on this wagon. George slows the tractor to a stop in front of the rows of strawberries.

Dan helps me off the wagon and then ends up helping everyone else too.

Bella runs toward the far right row with Eve and Carter in tow. They follow the group of people carrying baskets and picking strawberries.

I grab two baskets from the wooden stand and hand one to Dan.

Dan and I veer to the left away from the group, walking alongside the strawberries. The rows are narrow between the plants, so Dan follows closely behind me.

A slight breeze blows my hair backwards and the scent of the flower behind my ear fills my nose. I walk for a while, breathing in the fresh air, taking in the stunning view surrounding me. It's so breathtaking that I almost want to paint the view, but a painting couldn't capture every last ounce of beauty before me.

My thoughts wander to my mom and how she used to adore going berry picking. Every year we'd go to the festivals in town. We'd take the tractor ride over to the farm, much like today, and pick four baskets of berries to make a plethora of homemade pies. I was never any good at cooking, but she did pass down to me her secret touch of baking pies. Dad would always appear when the scent of the pie started to waft through the house. The three of us would grab a slice and sit by the campfire. I still bake a pie every year and share it with Dad. He says the scent evokes wonderful memories, and he doesn't ever want to lose them. I agree. The smell, the taste, and the process of baking the pie fills my heart with warmth and a deep connection to my mom.

After some time, I stop moving, realizing I'm at the end of the strawberry patch. Letting the reverie slip my mind, I catch sight of Dan following at a steady pace behind me. There's no one else in sight but us. His eyes meet mine, and I can tell he's deep in thought.

I tilt my head to the left, raising an arm to shield my eyes from the low-hanging sun. "What are you thinking about?"

He smirks in a way that almost suggests I should know the answer to my own question. "You don't know?"

"No." I shake my head. He could be thinking about anything. There are so many possibilities... I couldn't begin to put my finger on one.

"About you."

Oh.

"Wha—why?"

"Because you're amazing, Marigold, and I can't stop thinking about you," he says. "Not even for a few minutes."

Dan looks at my lips, and heat fills my cheeks. I'm certain my face is blushing a deep red matching the strawberries beside us. I bite my lip, hoping he will finally kiss me already. There have been at least a few moments that I wanted him to kiss me: in the wildflower field, the time he had his arm draped over my head and my back pressed against the wall when I was painting, and while he showed me the gummy worms in stock at Valley Harvest. I almost said it then. If he doesn't kiss me this time, I might have to kiss him myself.

Dan's empty basket is discarded by his feet in a matter of seconds. He takes large and steady strides toward me. I part my lips, and he brushes his calloused finger on the base of my chin, tilting my head upward to look at me.

Is this finally happening? Is he throwing caution to the wind?

"I want to kiss you, Marigold," he says with a gravelly tone.

"Please, do. Kiss me, Danny." I barely manage to get the words out.

He leans down, lips hovering over mine for a few beats. My eyes flutter closed. The stall in time feels like hours. When his lips finally brush against mine, fireworks erupt in my stomach. He kisses me softly. He kisses me tenderly. He kisses me as if nothing else in the world exists but us. I melt against him.

I've never kissed someone before, but with Dan, it feels like I know how. I drop my basket, letting it fall wherever it decides to land.

His stubble brushes against my face in a delicious way. His hand threads through my hair. His lips are perfectly soft.

I wrap my arms around his strong frame, wanting him to be even closer than he already is. The kiss deepens, goosebumps form on my arms, and my heart throbs fast in my chest. A hint of the sweet strawberries fills my nose, but I'd have to say this kiss is even sweeter.

I bunch my fingers in the back of his shirt. His other hand wraps around my waist. Dan's lips continue to brush mine.

At some point I pull away, breathless, having lost track of time. Dan's grin is contagious, and I smile so big it almost hurts. I miss him being close to me already.

"Should we maybe pick some strawberries?" He lifts his shoulders.

I giggle. "That might be a good idea." I smooth my hair down.

Dan hands me my basket, and I can't help laughing, thinking about how I just threw it.

I touch my lips, feeling the ghost of that kiss. It was the best first kiss I could have ever dreamt of.

Chapter 27

DAN

"Good morning, *Goldie*," I say to Marigold as she opens her front door.

Marigold yawns and blinks at me for a few moments. "Good morning, *Danny*." She opens the door fully. "Thanks for picking me up. You know you didn't have to drive me home last night. You're supposed to be with your family right now, mister." She nudges my arm playfully.

"They won't even know I'm gone. They're still in a strawberry coma. The three of them passed out as soon as we got home, and they were still snoring when I left."

"Ah." Marigold giggles softly. "I know the feeling." She scrunches her nose. "I think I need a couple days without any strawberries. I went a bit overboard. I was planning on making a strawberry pie, but that might have to wait. Maybe I'll make it and freeze it instead. I need to use all the strawberries we picked before they go bad."

"I don't want to look at another strawberry for at least a week."

"Same here."

I'm glad Bella didn't wake up in the middle of the night last night for ice cream. I couldn't handle one more bite of anything.

Marigold rests her shoulder against the door frame. "Do you want a coffee or tea for the road? I've been on a tea kick the past few days. Irish Breakfast with some milk and honey."

"Will I be putting you out if I ask for coffee?"

"Absolutely not." She laughs, covering her face. She motions for me to come in. "That's right. You're moody before coffee." She turns, winks, and continues to the kitchen.

It's true. I am. "And proud of it," I say, following her. I take a seat at the bar stool along the kitchen island.

"You have your coffee, and I have my gummy worms," Marigold says. She opens a cabinet, pulling out a box of tea bags, a bag of coffee grounds, and coffee filters. Marigold clicks her tongue. "I almost forgot that you're on vacation. Shouldn't you be sleeping in? You should've let me drive last night."

"I wanted to see you," I admit.

Marigold turns around and smiles at me. "I can't deny it's nice seeing you too."

Buttercup nuzzles against my leg, distracting me from responding.

"Good morning," I say to Buttercup. She snorts and then runs off. She must not be a morning pig. I can't blame her.

I rest my elbows on the island. "Do you need any help?"

"Nope," Marigold insists, filling a kettle and the coffee maker with water from the sink.

I lean back on the stool and watch her spin around the kitchen. The flower I put behind her ear yesterday sits in a vase of water on her windowsill. It's a reminder of the strawberry fields and our kiss. Yesterday was nothing short of incredible. I've never felt anything close to what I feel when I'm with her. I want to spend as much time as possible getting to know everything she loves because I find myself falling for her even more every day.

My phone vibrates in my pocket. I see it's just a spam email but then notice I also missed a text from my mom yesterday.

Mom

Can you send me a picture of you two?

I send the picture of us the night Marigold was painting Fix-its. A few minutes later my phone vibrates. She must be up for work.

Mom

You two look lovely. I'm happy for you.

I hope we get to meet her soon.

Dan

Thanks. Soon.

That last text to her is a promise. I'd really like them to meet one day.

The tea kettle whistles, and I put my phone away. Marigold shuts it off, pours a thermos of tea, and fills another with black coffee. Then Marigold, Buttercup, and I get into my car, heading to town.

After I get back from dropping Marigold off in front of Fix-Its, I take the stairs up to my apartment quietly. I creak open the door slowly, peeking inside to make sure I don't wake anyone. The three of them are still asleep. So, I slide off my shoes and lie in bed.

I stare at the ceiling for an hour, unable to fall back asleep. I can't lie that it's weird not doing anything so late in the morning. It may only be six, but I'm used to getting up for work. It's also a breath of fresh air to clear my mind and focus on being with my family.

Bella wakes up first. Then Carter and Eve follow suit. The three take turns with the bathroom as I get up and start making pancake batter.

"Can I help?" Bella asks.

"Of course! You know I can't do all this by myself." I slide a chair from my kitchen table and lift Bella to stand on it in front of the mixing bowl. I add the ingredients while she stirs the batter with a wooden spoon that looks giant in her little hands.

"Can I crack the egg?" Her eyes widen as she peers up at me.

"Yes, you can." I place a turquoise egg in her hand.

She raises it and says, "A green egg. Wow."

I chuckle. "The Ameraucana chickens lay those blue-green ones."

"Is the egg green inside like *Dr. Seuss*?" She tilts her head. The curiosity in her eyes makes me wish I could be the cool uncle and tell her it is green inside. However, they're not.

"The outside is blue-green, but the inside is like a normal egg."

"It's pretty." She grins.

"Just like you," I tell her.

She giggles. "You're pretty too. And your girlfriend is very pretty."

"Thanks, kid." I smile. She's right. Marigold is pretty.

I place a towering plate of pancakes in front of Marigold and Daisy at the front counter inside Fix-Its. "Thought maybe you two would want some of my famous pancakes. Bella even helped make them this time."

Marigold's eyes light up. "Thank you! I've been dying to try them."

"Are you kidding? Yes!" Daisy answers. She turns to Marigold and says, "Wow. When are you going to marry him?" Marigold's eyes widen, but she stays quiet. "That was rhetorical," Daisy clarifies.

Marigold fiddles with the end of her braid. "I know. But technically we are married in Archie's eyes."

"I'm missing something. Who is Archie?" Daisy asks while filling a paper plate with a few pancakes.

"The guy we got the golf carts from. He thought we were married." Marigold bites her lip and fills a plate with pancakes and syrup.

It's strange. Daisy was just joking. I'm not ready to get married again, but being with Marigold has shown me what it's truly like to be with someone who makes it worth wanting once more.

I shake the thought away. It's too deep to be contemplating today. I need to focus on buying some worms.

Bella walks up to the counter and reaches to set the container of worms next to the pancakes.

Daisy grabs the stack of pancakes with her free hand, slides them under the counter, and takes a bite of the ones on her plate. She gives me a thumbs up.

I pick Bella up, giving her a boost.

"These are delicious, you two," Marigold says after she finishes chewing. "The best pancakes I've ever had. But I was wondering if maybe you could share your recipe with me?"

"It's a secret." Bella covers her lips with her finger.

Marigold sighs. "Aww, man. I guess you'll have to stay and keep making them for me."

I shoot Marigold a smile because I know she knows my secret recipe is actually *Bisquick*.

Bella giggles.

"Bella, do you want to come with me?" Marigold asks. "I have something for you."

Bella nods her head excitedly. I lower her to the ground, and she takes Marigold's hand.

Marigold turns the corner, and I follow them. "Pick any toy you want," Marigold says. "You know, when I was little, I always loved the cat plushies. They were my favorite. They used to be way on the top of the shelves, and I could never reach them. But now, I moved them to the bottom shelves, so you can pick one out."

"I want a cat too," Bella says.

Marigold smiles broadly, covering her heart with a palm.

Bella adores her, and it only makes me like Marigold even more.

We head to the front counter, check out the worms and a few fishing items, and wave goodbye to Marigold. Eve heads toward Chloe's Closet to look around as Carter, Bella, and I take the path to the pond.

When we get to the pond, I help Bella set up her fishing rod and cast it into the water. She dangles her feet from her tiny folding chair and watches the bobber intently. It's almost comical how she won't look away from it even for a second. She shushes us the entire time if we talk louder than a whisper.

I cast my rod and reel it in as Carter unfolds his chair next to mine. "I like Marigold," he says.

"Me too." I nod, taking a sip of lemonade that we picked up on the way here.

"Do you love her?" Carter's question makes me choke on my drink.

"Subtle question—brother." I choke some more while Bella shushes us with a finger over her lips, giving me a no-nonsense look. I keep choking. "I'm good. Thanks—for—asking." I sputter between coughs.

It went down the wrong pipe, and not one person here cares.

Bella squints her eyes at me. *I'm dying over here,* and she's worried about me scaring the fish. Honestly, I'd be laughing right now if I weren't choking. I taught her well: no loud noises while fishing, so we don't scare the fish. However, there are exceptions to that rule, like when someone is choking, dying, or if it's an *emergency*.

Carter slaps me on the back a few times, and my coughing subsides.

"You good, brother?" Carter asks.

I give him a thumbs up in reply.

"You didn't answer my question," he prods, tapping on the arm of his folding chair.

I roll my eyes at him. "I'm getting there. Let me get some air."

Carter holds up his hands. "Sorry."

I take another sip of lemonade to soothe my throat. His question caught me off guard. It was the last thing I thought he'd ask.

"I don't know," I say after I relax, leaning back against my chair.

Carter's gaze doesn't veer from his bobber. "You don't know?"

"We haven't been dating very long. I don't know yet. But, yeah, I could see myself falling in love with her. She's great. I've only ever been in love once, as you know, but I can't really remember what it was like. It's been a while."

"You'll know when it's love," he assures me. "Don't mess this up." He gives me a shit-eating grin.

"Thanks for your confidence in me," I say in a sarcastic tone.

"I'm just trying to rile you up. I know you won't."

I laugh. "Sure you are." I'd like to hope I wouldn't mess things up between us.

Bella shushes us, making me laugh harder. Her bobber shoots under the water and she yells, "Fish on! Help!"

I shoot from my chair and help Bella reel in a small-mouth bass. She lets it back in the water and grins.

"Best day ever," Bella says.

It warms my heart, seeing her happy. Today has been pretty great.

Chapter 28

MARIGOLD

This must be the worst section in the store. Maybe that's why Daisy and I have been avoiding it. It's like the kitchen junk drawer full of everything that doesn't have a place, except it's an aisle full of hundreds of tiny parts, pieces, and knick-knacks.

I start at the end of the aisle, sorting similar things into bins. My head spins trying to figure out what goes where to form any semblance of organization in the chaos. It's much harder doing this all on my own. I take Daisy's help for granted.

A set of pliers, wood glue, and a door knob are the next items I grab from a low shelf and put into a bin. It's remarkable that my dad kept inventory straight and found anything someone needed.

I wonder how he's doing. I try my hardest not to worry, but he hasn't said a word since Monday. If he doesn't call by tomorrow, I will be calling him, whether he likes it or not.

After a few hours of working on the disaster aisle and helping customers, the bell on the door chimes.

"I brought lunch." Dan's voice is music to my ears. "Where are you?" he calls out.

"Here," I say as I step out to greet him. Buttercup beats me to it, rushing toward Dan as fast as she can.

"Hey there, little Buttercup. I missed you too." He scratches her head and lifts her into his arms. "There are both my girls." He smirks as he sees me and sets Buttercup down.

"Hey." I shift on my feet, grinning.

He shoves his hands in his pockets. "Hi."

I don't think it would be us if we weren't still a little awkward.

I take a step closer to him, and he says, "Come here, Goldie. I want to properly say hello to my girlfriend."

"Oh, really? And how do you plan to do that, Danny?" I take another step in his direction.

"How about I show you?"

"I'm up for that." I stop in front of him. He tilts my chin and leans down to kiss me. I feel light and dizzy when our lips meet. Same as the last time, butterflies swarm in my stomach and a smile transforms my face.

"Lunch." He kisses me softly again. "We should eat." He kisses me again.

"I'm not hungry." I giggle and kiss him back.

He brushes my hair behind my ear. "Did you have breakfast?"

I trace my fingers down his arm. "I had tea."

"That doesn't count. Let's have lunch."

"Okay." I pout. I like this too much. I like being close to him, listening to the rhythm of his heart as I rest my head on his chest and feeling his arms wrap around me. I may never move, but my stomach rumbles, giving me away. I mumble against his chest. "Just give me a second to flip the sign."

My feet stay planted as he says, "It's already been a second."

I let go and wave my arm at him as I head to the door to flip the welcome sign. "There. It only took me like ten seconds. Let's eat outside. I could use some fresh air."

A relaxed smile crosses his face. "Your wish is my command."

He grabs his lunch box from the front counter while I call Buttercup over and put on her harness. Dan takes my hand, and we head to the pavilion. Tourists and townies mill about, waving as they pass us on our walk. A few people stop to chat about the article that was apparently written on our new relationship. I pay no mind to it. Constance means well, and I like her, but I'd rather not read what was written about us. I know what is building between Dan and I is great. Anything the article has to say isn't going to change a thing.

Once we get to the pavilion, Dan sets up our table with the lunch he brought. Then he hooks up Buttercup's retractable leash so that she can still run around. Plus, he pulls out a bowl of water for Buttercup.

He thinks of everything.

"I could get used to this." I sigh in content.

"Good. You should."

I look around at the pavilion. "You picked a bench at the far-end corner this time."

"Yeah. Making up for the last time, I suppose. Our club depends on it." He takes a sip of water.

"Taking notes, I see," I say with mirth, and take a few bites of my sandwich.

His dimples make my stomach flutter. "I'm observant when it comes to you. What can I say?"

I spin the key pendant on my necklace between my fingers. "Are you now? What things do you notice?"

"A lot of things." He scratches his chin, searching my face. "You love pink and would do anything for gummy worms." He pulls a bag out of the lunch box, sliding it across the table.

True. "Very observant."

"And you twirl that necklace of yours when you're nervous or thinking. You bite your lip when you want me to kiss you." I cover my face with my palm because I didn't know I did that. "You cover your face when you're trying to hide that beautiful smile." His words encourage me to uncover my face, and my smile widens. He's right again. "I also know pink marigolds mean more to you than you let on. There's a story there."

"You get me." I look down at my sub. *Dan gets me.* "There is a story. It's a long one, though."

"I have time. But you don't have to tell me if you don't want to."

"No, I want to." I take another bite of my sandwich and finish chewing. "My dad told me this story after my mom passed." Dan reaches out and places his hand on mine. "When my mom was pregnant with me, she started the garden surrounding the studio. She wanted a sea of pink calendulas. My dad left to pick them up for her at The Not So Secret Garden (NSSG), but they didn't have any. He went to the next town over. He found flowers that he thought were the ones she asked for. When he came home hours later, my mom pretended they were calendulas even though she knew they were marigolds. She knew he'd leave to get the right flowers and be gone the rest of the day. And for years she never told him. She must've forgotten. One day, they were drinking tea on the front porch, looking out at all of the flowers. She finally told him, and they had a good laugh over it. It's actually how she came up with my name. It was an ode to the flowers, I guess. After he found out, he'd bring home pink marigolds all the time because he loved the story behind them. He still brings them to her grave every Friday before our weekly bonfire." Dan smooths his thumb over my fingers. "The NSSG has carried the flowers just for my dad. You getting them for me and noticing how much I love them... that's everything and more to me."

Dan's smile is genuine. "That's a beautiful story. And I will never stop getting them for you."

His words touch my heart. They truly do.

I head toward dad's place, even though I know he's not home. I feel compelled to stop there. It's Friday. I miss our weekly tradition. So, Buttercup and I will have to uphold it. The lights inside the house are all off when I park my car in the driveway. The porch light is still on, but it always is. I take the path, carrying Buttercup. I stop in my tracks. The fire is lit. I take a few steps toward the fire pit.

Did Dan come out here?

No. It's my dad.

I rush to the fire and stop beside him. He's sitting in his chair like usual, staring at the dancing flames.

"What are you doing here?" I ask him.

He turns his head. "Nice way to say I miss you, kiddo."

"Well—I did miss you." I breathe heavily, catching my breath. I pat his shoulder and slouch in my Adirondack chair, setting Buttercup on my lap. "Is everything okay? Should I be worried?"

"No, I'm great." He smiles, but it doesn't reach his eyes. That reaction in itself tells me I should be worried.

He's quiet for a while as he studies the sky. "I couldn't miss another Friday. It felt wrong." His voice is somber.

Oh.

"I get it. I really do. It's my way of being close to Mom too. Not being here last Friday didn't sit well with me after years of us never missing one. Being here feels like we're keeping her memory alive."

"We are. And she will always be a part of our hearts. Our souls," he says almost as if he's reminding himself of this.

My throat tightens. "I know. I don't know about you, but it doesn't feel like it ever gets any easier."

"Because it doesn't. We simply learn to live with it and think of the good moments."

He's right. I cling to the happy memories, and they are what remind me to be grateful for every one I had.

We're both silent for a few minutes until I ask, "When did you get back?" However, I'm actually wondering how long he's been here alone.

"This morning."

"Why didn't you stop by Fix-Its?" Buttercup shifts on my lap.

"I didn't want to break my word. I said you'd have a month."

I shake my head. He did not have to stay away. "Dad, you should've come by. How 'bout tomorrow?"

"Yeah. That'd be nice," he says, sounding troubled.

There's something wrong. I just know it. I don't want to push him, but I'm worried.

"We can go over the numbers tomorrow of what I have so far. And you can see my progress. I think you'll be happy." *I hope so.*

"I like the sound of that," he agrees.

I try my best to lift his spirits. "Me too. It'll be fun."

It seems to work. He chuckles, but then that same worry-filled look falls over his face.

"I—never mind. I don't think it's the right time to talk about it."

I chew on the inside of my lip. "You can tell me anything."

He looks at the fire. "Do you recall when I called and told you about going to the boardwalk with my friend, Eleanor."

"Yeah." I wonder if that is the reason for his somber mood.

"I—she—"

"It was a date." I finish for him, knowing that's what he's hinting at.

His eyes meet mine, and the guilt eating at him hurts my soul. "I suppose. I don't know if this is the place to talk about this sort of thing."

"Why not? Mom wanted you to fall in love again... She made you promise, remember?"

"I know, kiddo."

"And she's always with us. She'll hear you everywhere."

He chuckles. "You're right." He scratches his head and wipes a palm over his face. "That's another reason I came home early.

Eleanor is great. That's why I left without a word like a nincompoop. It felt real. I haven't felt anything like it since your mom."

"You're not a nincompoop, Dad. You were scared. What Mom and you had was special. I don't blame you in the slightest. It's going to take time."

Dad opening up to me like this is unheard of. It's nice having him voice things with me.

He looks at the watch on his wrist and massages the back of his neck. "Speaking of time, I better hit the hay now since I have an early morning."

"Okay." I get out of my seat, setting Buttercup down, and we head for the path. "Goodnight, Dad."

"Night, Mary," he calls out. He still sounds off. Like something else is bothering him, and I can't put my finger on it.

Chapter 29

MARIGOLD

"Your tea," Daisy says, handing me a to-go cup. "It's a chai latte. Careful, it's still hot."

"You're a lifesaver." I take off the lid, blowing on the drink to cool it down. "My dad's back, and he's coming in to see what we've done. I woke up at the crack of dawn to finish the junk-drawer aisle."

"You should've called." Daisy takes a seat beside me, sipping on her iced coffee. "I would've come in early."

"I know you would've, but I didn't want to wake you."

"Girl, you can wake me anytime you need something." She gathers her hair and puts it in a ponytail.

"I will next time." I won't, not unless I'm desperate. *I hate bothering people if I can help it.*

Daisy swirls her drink and tilts her head. "You won't. But thanks for pretending. It was nice for a moment."

I laugh, at least she knows me well enough to infer that. The back door creaks open, and I dart my gaze to it.

"Good morning, kiddos," Dad says as he opens the back door to Fix-Its.

"Hey, Dad." I yawn and take a sip of my hot tea.

Daisy waves from the stool next to mine. "There's our famous tool guy!"

"Daisy, good to see you." He walks in our direction.

She leans her elbows on the counter. "I'm still here. I'm trying something different. We'll see how long it lasts."

"I'm glad to see Marigold had your help with—" He gasps, shifting his gaze around the store.

Oh no. He hates it.

The silence is loud.

"You kiddos really are something," he says.

Does he mean a good or bad *something*? It's hard to tell.

"Doesn't the place look crisp?" Daisy asks. At least she can be the one to bring it up.

My dad clears his throat. "It hasn't looked this way in a long, long time—I—I need to have a seat. I'm gonna head to the Think Den for a minute. You kiddos hang out here."

My heart sinks. *He's disappointed in me.*

Daisy and I share a concerned look as he shuts the door to the office. Then my mind begins to spiral until I ignore the thoughts and his request, heading straight toward the office. I knock, but don't wait for an answer. I open the door to find him sitting behind the desk holding Buttercup in his arms.

"Are you okay?" I open the door fully and shut it behind me. "If you don't like what I've done, I'm sorry. I never meant to change anything. I just wanted to organize the tools and freshen up the paint. Like it used to be."

"Have a seat." He points to the chair across from his desk.

I sit down and drag my necklace over my chin, swiveling it back and forth.

He sighs. "I am proud of you, Mary. Incredibly proud." He shakes his head and pets Buttercup. "This place is extraordinary."

All my doubts fizzle into thin air... *He's proud of me.*

"You are?"

"What you've done here. It's incredible. I—it looks as good as the day I first stepped foot into the store. I don't need to see any numbers to know you're more than capable."

I arch a brow. "But—"

"No buts. I never doubted you for a second."

I scratch my head. I'm pretty sure he said otherwise... I've been worried about being capable for weeks. "But you said—"

"I know what I said. It was a lie. Everything was."

A lie? What is he talking about? I didn't even get to show him the golf carts.

His expression turns somber, marring his face the same way it did last night when I knew there was something else bothering him. "I knew you could handle Fix-Its on your own. You're smart. You're capable. I taught you everything I know."

"But why did you say otherwise?" My brows draw together. "I'm lost."

"There's something I've been meaning to tell you for a while."

I stay silent. I can't for the life of me think of any reason as to why he would have to lie or hold something back from me.

"Promise me you will listen to it all before you leave."

"Leave? I'm not going anywhere."

His expression hardens. "Promise me."

"I promise..." I trail off.

He rubs his arm. "And you truly want to run this place? You love it?"

Even though I'm confused, I smile thinking about how much I love it here. "Yes, Fix-Its means everything to me, Dad. I spent my whole life here. This is our family's legacy... Grandpa and Granny. Mom and you. I couldn't imagine myself anywhere else."

He nods. "I need to come out with it now. This can't wait any longer. After your mother passed, her attorney contacted me to discuss her trust. I didn't know she had one. But, once she was diagnosed, it seems she took matters into her own hands while

I was busy being in denial. The cancer took her from us so fast, Mary." The pain in his voice is evident as a few tears run down my cheeks. "She set up a living trust. Fix-Its was in her name, as it was her parents'. She made me the successor trustee, and she left you as the beneficiary on some conditions." He sets Buttercup down and leans back in his chair.

I have a feeling the conditions aren't simple because he's giving me a look full of trepidation.

"If you're not married by your twenty-sixth birthday, you won't inherit Fix-Its." His voice is shaky. "Your birthday is almost here. I didn't know what to do, Mary. I knew I had to tell you. I waited as long as I could, but I didn't want to push you to get married. And then the time flew by. You were twenty-five faster than I could blink. When you suggested running Fix-Its on your own this month, I went along with it. It was the best thing. I needed to be sure Fix-Its legacy was something *you* wanted. I knew you'd get married just so I could keep this place. But I didn't want that. This isn't about me. I want you to want it for you and only you."

I have no words to reply with.

Me... Married? I have to be married to keep Fix-Its... My birthday is in two weeks.

My mouth goes dry, and the room spins. *Marriage.* I shake my head. Why? Why would she make that a condition? I don't understand.

"I know you're probably wondering why," he answers me, as if reading my thoughts. "I'm not sure. But she was my other half. I've thought long and hard about the reasoning. Why would she make it a condition? I don't know for sure, but I can guess. I think she did it out of love. She wanted to ensure your future since she wasn't going to be there. She wanted you to be happy. I know that. I guess she thought that marriage was the key to your happiness. It was a different time when we were younger. Maybe that was partially my fault. What we had was special. A once in a lifetime love." He pulls an envelope from his pocket. "She left you this to open on your wedding day. I haven't read it."

"Thanks." I take the envelope from him.

"If you need some time off, I understand. Why not take the rest of the day? We're closed tomorrow anyway. Think about this before you make a decision. You can try to combat it in court. If you do go that route, I'll be by your side through it."

I wipe the tears from my face and try to compose myself. "I—okay. Umm—I'll see you on Monday, Dad—thanks?" I stand, heading for the door.

"Hey, Mary, please don't be upset with me. I was only trying to protect you." His eyes are filled with worry.

"I know, Dad. I'm not upset with you." I shake my head. "I just need some time to process. To figure this all out."

I stumble out of the office, feeling confused. I'm uneasy on my feet because my brain is swirling with questions. I will most likely never get the answers, unless they're in this letter weighing down my hand. Buttercup follows me, and I shut the door to the office.

When Daisy looks up from the computer, her face fills with concern. She closes the laptop. "What's wrong?"

I want to tell her, but I can't find the words. "It's a long story." I walk around the counter. With trembling hands, I get Buttercup ready to go, putting on her harness and leash.

"Do you want to talk about it?" Daisy's voice is soft beside me.

I let out a breath. "Not yet. I need some time to think." I stand and brush my legs off. "Are you okay here? I'm gonna take the day off."

"I'm all good. Please, call me if you want to talk or not talk. I'm always here for you, Marigoldie."

"Thanks, Daisy Dollup," I say, trying my best to hide the tears that are threatening to fall again.

Chapter 30

DAN

Nothing is better than an early morning coffee and some fresh air.

The sky is still dim as I step out the back door of my shop. The rooster's crow rings out in the distance. I sip on my coffee and walk toward the golf carts to give them all a quick once over.

I crouch down to examine the tires on The Duck Mobile when I hear what sounds like a door opening and shutting. I stand and squint, looking for the source of the sound.

Does Mateo need something?

It's actually Marigold. She heads to the back door of my shop with Buttercup, raises her hand to knock but then lowers it. She stands there for a moment and then heads for a park bench and lowers her head in her hands.

Something's wrong.

I set my coffee down and meet her at the bench as fast as my legs will carry me.

"Marigold," I say softly. "Hey." I kneel in front of her, taking Buttercup's leash from her hand.

She lifts her head. It damn near rips my heart to shreds when I see the tears falling from her eyes.

"I—" Her lip trembles as her tears continue to drop.

"Shh. It's okay." I wipe her tears away with my thumb. "Do you want to come to my place for a while?"

She nods her head up and down. That's all the answer I need. I pick up Buttercup and take the envelope from Marigold's shaky hand, putting it under my arm. My hand grazes her lower back as I guide her to the back door. I shield her with my body the best I can just in case Mateo's here. I know he wouldn't say a word, but I think she would appreciate not having to face anyone right now.

He's not there, so I follow her up the stairs and into my apartment. Buttercup squeals when I set her on the floor, and I place the envelope on my kitchen table. I turn to look at Marigold on my couch.

I've never seen her upset like this. I want to give her space, but it's killing me not helping her in some way. She looks broken... defeated... worry-stricken.

"Do you want me here? I can give you some space if not. You're welcome as long as you like."

"You have to work." Her voice is but a whisper.

"No, I can stay. Only if you want me to."

She pats the cushion beside her. "Stay, please."

I kick off my boots and hang up my hat. I sit beside her and pull her into my arms, letting her cry. She wraps her arms around me, crying into my chest. I smooth my hand down her hair, and I hold her. There's not much I can do if I don't know what's troubling her. However, this is something I can do—be here for her. She cries for some time until her sobs subside, and she falls asleep against my chest.

After an hour, I lower her against the couch slowly. I gently lift her head, slide a pillow underneath, and cover her with a blanket.

Buttercup follows me around my apartment. Eventually, I take her outside to use the bathroom. Then I have a quick conversation with Mateo and head to grab Marigold lunch.

When I open my apartment door, Marigold's awake, sitting on my couch with her legs pulled to her chest. She wraps the blanket tighter around herself and smiles at me with puffy eyes. I hope she wasn't crying while I was gone. Also, I hope she didn't think that I left her for work. That is the last thing I would do.

I shut the door and take Buttercup's leash off. She hops onto the couch. Marigold smiles and hugs her.

I bring Marigold a to-go container with lunch. "I picked you up a club sandwich and fries."

"How did you know that's my favorite?"

"Daisy was there ordering lunch. She said I would get even more brownie points if I got that for you."

"Daisy sure is something." She grins, picking at her fries. "Did she say anything else?"

"Just asked about you. If you were okay. Asked me to be good to you. And that's it."

"I'm sure you're wondering about what happened." She holds her necklace. "My dad told me some things this morning that are hard to believe. It really shocked me. I felt lost. And the first person I thought of was you. I needed you."

"Why didn't you knock or come in? The only reason I saw you was because I was already outside checking the golf carts."

She chews on her lip. "Because I was worried it might be too much, too soon for me to come crying to you about my problems. And I figured you were working. I didn't want to bother you."

I shake my head. If she only knew, she's all I think about. "You, Goldie, are never a bother. Not to me. Work can wait. Nothing's more important than making sure you're okay. My dad always worked like I told you. He was never there. I want to break the mold. I want to be there for you whenever you need me. No matter what time. What day. What I'm doing. I want to be your safe place. I want to be someone you can always rely on. And the first one you think of when something's wrong." *Because I'm falling for you hard and fast.*

"That means a lot to me." She grabs a fry and chews. "I think you already are."

Marigold explains everything over lunch. Her dad coming home, his reasoning for holding this truth from her for so long, the trust, and the letter sitting on my table.

I'm beside myself. She is stuck in an almost impossible situation. It seems like there's only three options. Option one: She could get married. Option two: She could contest the trust, but that comes with lawyer and court fees. Option three: She could ultimately not get married, let Fix-Its go, and buy it on the market. All of the options are near impossible if she wants to come out the other side debt-free. There's only one that seems the least time consuming, and it's the one I can help with: *marriage.*

I saw my dad never be there for my mom, brother, and I. Then my own marriage failed. Well, those things make this decision harder. The scars on my heart after Kate left cut me as deep as the ones when my dad left. He didn't exactly leave. He just wasn't present. The last six years of my life have been spent swearing off the thought of marriage, but within the past couple of months, I've been toying with the idea of it. I was young. I made mistakes. This is a completely different circumstance. The stakes are higher. I'm rushing into it again, but this time I'm mature. I'm clear headed and comfortable with every aspect of my life.

Would I actually marry Marigold? I would. I would marry her. There's no other way. For her happiness and her family's legacy, I'd do probably anything to help her keep both.

"So, your birthday is in two weeks..." I trail off.

"Yeah." She fiddles with the end of her braid.

My decision is clear. I'm going to help her save Fix-Its. "Since you don't have much time, well, I'm just going to come right out and ask. Will you marry me, Marigold Evans?"

My sentence stuns her into silence. She whispers, "You couldn't, Dan. Not after everything you've been through. It'd be wrong of me to ask that of you. I wasn't planning on asking."

"I know you weren't. But I'm asking. You have to save Fix-Its. You love it." *And maybe I'm starting to love you.*

"Are you sure?" She holds my hands as a tear trails down her face.

I wipe her tear away with my thumb. "I'm positive. Let's get married." I've never been more sure of anything in my life. If it were me in her position, I would do anything to save it.

"So, will you marry me?" I ask once more.

"Yes." Her answer is soft.

I wrap her in my arms and kiss her forehead. "Everything's going to be okay," I whisper. "I'm here." She rests her head against my chest, and I know it to be the truth because I will do everything I can to make sure it will be.

Chapter 31

MARIGOLD

"Goodbye, PA. Hello, Maryland," Dan says as we cross the state border.

I drum my fingers on my lap while watching houses flash by the window. "How much further?"

Dan flips the sun visor and squints at the road. "Not much. We're almost there."

"And they're really not expecting us?" I'm sure Dan can hear the apprehension in my voice.

"Nope. They don't know we're coming. But they'll be home. Sunday is game day," he says with a calm and collected demeanor.

"Football?"

"No, more like a crossword from the Sunday paper, a 3,000 piece puzzle, and a Ping-Pong tournament."

"That sounds like fun." They sound like fun people. I always loved playing Ping-Pong, so I'm at least eager for a good game of that.

"It is. But they can be pretty competitive. And loud about it. Just warning you now." He massages the back of his neck and shoots me a quick half-smile.

I smirk. "Thank you for the warning. I can play a mean game of Ping-Pong, though. So, don't worry about me."

Dan twists his hands around the steering wheel, following a curve in the road. "They'll love you then."

I trace my fingers over the window frame. *Will they?* They won't when they find out I'm marrying their son because I'm trying to save a business. I plan on telling his parents the truth. It's only right. They're probably going to think I'm using Dan which is the furthest thing from the truth. I really like Dan. It could almost be love, if only we had more time together. Everything was going so well.

The last thing I wanted to do was ask him to marry me. He offered out of the kindness of his heart, and I accepted because I was desperate to keep Fix-Its. Now, I'm wondering if it was too easy of a solution.

Dan's voice pulls me from my thoughts. "What are you thinking?"

I sigh, opting to be honest with him. "The worst things." I pause briefly until I eventually get the courage to speak again. "What if your mom and stepdad hate me for making you marry me." I tap my fingers on my lap.

"First off you're not making me do anything." Dan places his hand on mine and shifts his steady gaze to me. "Secondly, they would never hate you. No one could ever hate you." He flicks his eyes to the road. "And if they did, they would have me to answer to. My mom already loves you. She told me on the phone just the other day."

"Really?"

He traces the pad of his thumb over my fingers. "Really. I told her everything about you. About what you were doing with Fix-Its. About how amazing you are. All of it."

"But that was before the whole marrying me thing."

"That won't change anything. She will understand. She will still love you. Believe me, you're hard not to love."

I squeeze his hand. "Thank you for always knowing what to say. For understanding me."

He rubs his thumb over my knuckles. "I normally don't have a clue what to say. But with you, it's different. A good different."

My face blushes as I shift my gaze to him. He's focused on the road, and he doesn't turn his head.

I can't believe I'm going to marry him.

"This is where I grew up," Dan says as he pulls his car into the driveway in front of his childhood home. It's a cozy, two-story brick house with black shutters.

He opens the passenger door for me. I smooth my dress down, and he takes my hand, guiding me to the porch. A dog barks, and the rumble of a train going over tracks fills my ears as we head toward the home. Dan rings the door bell and shifts his gaze to me. "You have nothing to worry about. Mom already loves you... like I said. And Jim loves everyone." He kisses me on the lips and strokes his thumb on my cheek.

I smile, silently thanking him for the reassurance. We've only been together a short amount of time, but Dan already knows me better than most people.

The door creaks open, and a woman with dark hair is yelling over her shoulder. She's wearing slippers and a set of flannel pajamas. "A three letter word meaning to cool off would be—Jim!" Her eyes widen when she sees us.

A deep voice, which I assume is his stepdad's, calls from another room. "What! Gym? You don't cool off at the gym! Wait—maybe you're right! You can cool off after a workout!"

"Jim, sweetheart! Screw the crossword puzzle! Dan's here!" she shouts back. Her voice softens. "Dan, honey, what in the world are you doing here?" She envelops him in a hug.

"I wanted to come to see you mom. And I brought someone to meet you." He chuckles.

She snaps back, letting go of Dan and turns toward me. "You're even more lovely than the picture Dan sent of you two. I'm just tickled pink to meet you, Marigold. Dan has told us so much about you." His mom pulls me into the next hug, squeezing me. My family didn't grow up as huggers, but I can see that Dan's entire family is made up of people who love to hug.

"It's nice to meet you, ma'am." I hug her back.

She releases me from the hug and says, "Call me Marlene."

"I'll be damned." Dan's stepdad stands at the threshold. A pair of glasses are on the tip of his nose, and a newspaper dangles in his hand. "Tinker Dan, it's not Christmas yet." He steps out the door, wearing his slippers and matching flannel pajamas.

Dan laughs lightly. "Thought we'd stop by a little early."

"Five months early. Whatever the reason, I'm glad to see you." He tucks the paper under his arm. "And Marigold, right?" I reach my hand out to shake his, but he gives me a one-armed hug instead. "We're huggers. You're practically family."

He doesn't even know the irony behind that sentence.

"Come on in. I'll make us a fresh pot of coffee," Dan's mom insists. Now, I see where Dan gets it from.

Marlene and Jim go to the kitchen to make some coffee. Once they're gone, Dan takes my hands and leans down, hovering his lips close to my ear. "See," he whispers. "You have nothing to worry about. By the way..." He trails off, moving his lips to mine for a soft kiss. Then he pulls away, and his breath fans over my ear. "You look beautiful in that dress."

"Thanks." My face warms.

Marlene and Jim do some sort of team handshake after scoring another point on Dan and I in the most intense game of table tennis I've ever played. They slap hands, fist bump, spin, and point at each other. Their handshake ends with a "Go team!"

I just look at Dan, and he rubs a palm over his face, hiding laughter. I bite my lip, failing to hold back a grin. I raise my hand. Dan gets the hint and gives me a hi-five. "Go team?" I ask.

"Go team. Or should I say go club? We're in a club and a team now," he says before kissing my cheek.

"We are." I laugh and return my focus to the game.

Jim lifts his paddle and holds the Ping-Pong ball, ready to serve. "Ready?"

"Ready," Dan and I say in unison.

"Jinx, you owe me a soda." I point to Dan.

His shoulders shake with laughter. "You beat me to it."

I shrug and look toward the competition.

Marlene motions her middle and pointer finger in a "V" over her eyes then points to Dan and I, in an I'm-watching-you gesture. Jim shuffles his feet, raises his paddle in the air, and bounces the ball off the table. He hits the ball. A loud *crack* echoes off the basement ceiling tiles. The ball shoots through the air, directly at Dan. I gulp, and Dan's eyes widen. "Oof," Dan grumbles when it lands smack-dab in the middle of his forehead. He leans forward, rubbing his forehead. "Hit it a little harder next time, why don't you?"

"Jim, honey, take it easy on them," Marlene scolds him.

"Sorry." Jim holds his hands up as Dan straightens his back, rubbing the pink spot on his forehead. "My bad. I got carried away."

I rest my hand on Dan's arm. "Are you alright?"

"All good." Dan nods his head. "I told you they get competitive," he whispers so that only I can hear him.

"I see that now," I mutter in reply.

Marlene serves next. The ball bounces on Dan's side of the table. He swings, misses, and it lands somewhere on the shag carpeting.

Dan wasn't kidding... Marlene and Jim are serious about their games. They don't go easy when they put their eye on the prize. *Winning.* Winning is the prize. I've noticed that from the multiple serves to Dan's side of the table. I scored a few points for Dan and I, but we are one point away from losing.

We lose moments later—no shocker there. It was fun anyway.

Although the games have left me no time to think, there's still this gnawing in the back of my mind. It's a reminder of what conversation is to come.

We head upstairs. Marlene and Jim set up a puzzle on the coffee table in their living room. They fill bowls with snacks, and we sit around the table on the floor, putting the puzzle pieces together.

Marlene breaks the quiet. "I'm so glad you came today, but you didn't drive all the way out here just to say hi and spend game day with us, did you?"

I swivel my necklace. *Here it is.*

Dan grasps my hand. "No, we came out here to tell you Marigold and I are getting married next week."

Jim and Marlene share a look. Then they both crawl over from their spots on the floor, giving Dan and me one giant group hug.

"Congrats!" Marlene cheers.

Jim's voice is chipper. "This is wonderful news!"

When they pull away, Marlene scrunches her brows, looking at Dan. "I'm excited. Please, don't take this the wrong way. I'm kinda curious. Why the rush?"

Dan scratches his head and takes my hand. "Well—"

"He is marrying me to help save my family's business." My voice comes out scratchy with the confession. *With the truth.*

We sit on the couch, and I explain the story from the beginning. Marlene and Jim listen intently. They don't seem upset at all, actually. They just listen.

"Well..." Marlene starts when I finish telling them everything. "I think what Dan is doing is a great thing. I think it all will work itself out for you two."

"We're proud of you, son," Jim says.

Dan wraps an arm around me, and I lean my head on his shoulder.

Marlene wipes a tear with a trembling hand. "And we're proud of you, Marigold, for doing everything you can to save your family's legacy. Your mom would be so proud of you. And I hope you don't hold any resentment against her for making marriage a condition. I think it was her way of doing what she could to ensure your happiness. In her own way."

"I don't." A tear trickles down my face and it drops on Dan's shoulder. I could never resent my mom. I could never for a moment be mad at her for doing what she thought was the only thing she had control of.

I miss her.

"Well then, we'll see you both on Friday for your wedding. This puzzle isn't going to put itself together," Marlene says, sliding the coffee table closer to the couch.

Dan's family supporting me means more than I can put into words.

Chapter 32

DAN

Marigold spins, outstretching her arms. "I love it here," she says. Her dress lifts at the bottom, floating through the air. She races barefoot through the sand toward the shoreline. I take off my shoes and jog, catching up to her in the water. She loosens the end of her braid and runs her fingers through her wavy blonde hair. The orange sky brings out a glimmer in her blue eyes that almost makes me fall to my knees, but I don't move as I study her awestruck expression. Her eyes track over the vastness of the ocean, and the waves crash against our legs.

I can't help but smile when I look at her. She's breathtaking. She's the *sun* to my morning, the *moon* to my night, and the *rainbow* after the storm. She's the missing *part* in my life.

Her lips curl upward, and she tilts her head slightly in a way that I wonder if she can hear my thoughts. "What is it?"

"I think I'm the happiest man in the world," I say. My chest physically aches with the certainty of it. *Because I am.* Marigold makes me incredibly happy. Just being in her presence is enough to lift my spirits. I wrap my arms around her waist, pulling her flush against me.

Marigold rests her hands around my neck. "And why are you so happy? Because of this place? The ocean?" She runs her hand through my hair, and her blue eyes search my face to find the answer.

I lift her, twirling her in the air. Her laughter is music to my ears. "That and mostly because I'm with you," I say as I spin her in a circle. Her legs dangle over the water, the ruffles of her dress glide through the air, and her hair blows in the wind. We laugh as the beach appears to spin around us.

Nothing in my life has ever compared to this. With her, I feel lighter. I feel like I've never fallen this hard. I feel like this could be *love.*

Love is terrifying and exhilarating. Being in love with her makes the prospect of getting married seem less intimidating. I've been down this road before, and that's what plants a seed of worry in my subconscious. *I could lose it again. Is the risk worth taking?* My mind is already made up, though: I will be marrying her.

My worries dissipate as I watch Marigold's gleeful expression. Everything that seems to be weighing us down washes away with the waves. She tips her head back and giggles. After another spin, I set her down. We're both uneasy on our feet, trying to steady each other. We stagger out of the water and fall into the sand instead. Laughter bubbles from her lips. I roll to my side, facing her. My fingers brush the hair away from her eyes.

"Why would you ever leave a place like this?" she asks.

I draw small circles on her arm. "I needed a fresh start to put space between myself and the memories. Don't get me wrong. They weren't all bad, but places have a way of holding onto them. Whether they're pleasant or not."

"I'm sorry for bringing it up." Her voice is merely a whisper.

"Don't be. You are the sole reason I have more good memories to cling to here." I brush sand from her cheek. "One good memory with you is all I need."

"Does right now count as your one good memory?" Her eyes sparkle in a way that looks hopeful.

I tap my chin, pretending to think it over. However, I already know now is the best memory. "Yes, I suppose it does, but earlier at my parents' counts too, especially when that Ping-Pong ball almost gave me a concussion. That was a great one."

Her shoulders shake with laughter but then her expression suddenly grows serious. "And what if I gave you two or three. Would that be enough?"

"I guess I could settle for four."

"Well, technically we already had two. One at your parents'. And another with you spinning me in the ocean. So, two more memories coming right up." She leans in and crashes her lips against mine. Her fingers thread through my hair. I run my hand over the goosebumps on her back. A small hum escapes her mouth as the kiss deepens. She pulls away, face blushed. "That's three," she says breathlessly. Her expression is hesitant as she softly asks, "Can we go somewhere more... private?"

"Are you sure?"

She nods. "Yes."

I lift her into my arms, carrying her through the sand. I bend over, grabbing our shoes. Marigold holds them for me as I carry her back to our hotel. We laugh as I walk up the stairs to the third floor, and she swings her legs. I push open the door to our room and lower Marigold onto the edge of the bed.

She smiles shakily as she reaches for the zipper on the back of her dress. "Can you help me out of this?"

"Sure." I step behind her and move the hair away from her back. Heat courses through my veins as I drag the zipper of her dress slowly. More goosebumps form on her skin as I continue downward. I stop moving the zipper when I reach her lower back.

My voice comes out grainy. "Can I confess something?"

"Anything." Marigold faces me, chest rising and falling. Her cheeks flush crimson, and her sun-tanned skin glistens in the dim lighting.

My heart thumps in my chest. "I've been thinking about taking this dress off you all day."

Marigold reaches a hand toward me, rests it on my arm, and dances her fingers over my slightly damp skin. "There's no time like the present, Danny."

"Are you sure?"

"Yes, Dan." Her brows furrow. "I want you. I want all of you. That is if you'll have me. I know I don't really know what I'm doing—"

"Hey." I run my thumb over her cheek. "It's not about that. I just want to be sure you are ready. That you want this. Because you deserve everything, Goldie. *Everything.*"

"I want you. Please," she begs, and that's all I need to hear.

I trace my fingers over her shoulders and take my time to carefully lower the straps of her floral dress. My fingers follow every curve of her body until it pools at her feet. She steps out of it and kicks it to the side. My knees wobble when I take in the sight of her. I lose all sense of reality as desire seems to radiate between us—almost tangible.

"Beautiful. You are absolutely breathtaking." My voice is thick.

She bunches the hem of my T-shirt in her hands, raising it up my chest. Heat spreads along my skin as her fingers move higher. I help her, pulling the shirt the rest of the way over my head.

I move closer to her and carefully work on unclasping her bra. It falls to the floor with our other clothes. Then she kicks her underwear to the side. I appreciate her for a moment, trailing my gaze over her, until my heart nearly stops when she removes my belt. Soon after, the rest of my clothes go with it, and she gasps, eyes raking over my features. She reaches out to touch my chest. My body tingles as her fingers dance over me. I rest a palm on her lower back, and she arches her feet to meet me for a kiss.

I lift her onto the mattress, and she giggles. My fingers drift along her collarbone. A delicate moan leaves her mouth. She moans once more when I glide my palms down the smooth skin of her curves and again when I kiss her neck, her lips, and her breasts. I pull back. "Are you okay?"

I want to do right by her and show her how much I care about her. I don't want to rush anything. I want her to feel comfortable, safe, and in control.

"Yes. Please, Dan. More." The look she gives me is gorgeous. The desire written on her face is enough to make my head fuzzy.

I kiss her mouth and hover over her, reaching for my bag on the floor to grab a condom.

When I enter her for the first time, careful to go slowly, my body tingles and sweat pools on my back. "Is this okay? Is it too much?"

"No." Her forehead glistens with sweat. "It's perfect."

My senses are in overdrive as she moans louder. Every whimper and pant that tumbles from her lips brings me closer. I kiss her again. Her lips taste salty like the sea. She bunches the covers in her hands and arches her back.

After another few beats, she comes undone. I follow quickly, unable to hold back any longer. I slump on the bed beside her, and she rests her head on my chest. I trace lines down her skin. She's so damn beautiful.

"How are you feeling?" I ask after a few minutes.

"Wonderful." She laughs.

I brush her hair from her face. "Are you in any pain?"

"A little bit." She smooths her fingers over my chest. "If the question is tired." She yawns. "Then yes—very."

I chuckle. "Let's get you cleaned up." I turn on the shower to let the water heat up and then carry her to the bathroom.

When she steps into the shower, she asks, "So, was this your fourth good memory?"

"Yes," I reply instantly, sure that nothing could be better. "And a damn good one."

She curls a finger, "Let's make it five." Her smile is contagious.

"If you insist."

We do just that while showering together and then clean off sand and sweat. After we move from the shower to the bed, I hold her in my arms. I whisper, "I love you." She's already fast asleep and doesn't hear my words. Even so, I know they are true. I love her.

I don't fret about our impending marriage. I don't worry about what is at stake. All I think about is her.

Chapter 33

MARIGOLD

Sunlight filters through the small gap in the curtains. I have no clue what time it is, but it's nice not knowing for once and not waking to the sound of my alarm. I pull the comforter over my shoulders and smell the subtle fresh linen that clings to the cotton. Dan faces me. Then he reaches out and wraps an arm around my waist, pulling me closer to him. I laugh, nuzzling my head into his chest. When I pull away to look at him, the dimples on his cheeks are prominent as he smiles. My stomach fills with butterflies.

"Good morning, Danny," I say.

"Good morning, Goldie," he replies in a gravelly tone. Then his lips make my skin tingle as he kisses my forehead.

Thinking about last night makes my face blush. It almost feels like I'm recalling a dream. It's a wonderful, life-altering one that I never want to forget. It was everything I'd hoped it would be and so much more. With Dan, I don't worry anymore. I don't feel self-conscious. He sees me for me, and I'm really falling for him.

"So we're off to Delaware?" I ask.

"I think I'm gonna call first. He might not even be there. Don't want to waste the trip." He kisses me, sits up, and grabs his phone from the nightstand. The faint ringing doesn't stop until the call goes to voicemail.

Dan's mood plummets, rightfully so. Disappointment washes over his face, but he tries calling again anyway.

I hope his dad answers. I really do. I can see how much it pains Dan even though he doesn't say it. I think he mentally prepares himself to be let down, and that breaks my heart.

He massages the back of his neck. "I'll try his work phone. If he doesn't pick up, we'll go home." Dan gets up and starts pacing beside the bed, but this time his dad answers on the fourth ring.

"This is Stone." His dad's voice comes through the phone speaker.

Dan stops pacing and scrubs his hand over the stubble on his face. "Hey, Dad."

"Dan, I'm at work right now. Can I call you back later?"

From what Dan has told me, I know that had to dampen his spirits. His dismissal upsets me, and I don't even know him. What if something were wrong? Life is unpredictable and short. Losing my mom taught me that. He should be glad his son wants to talk to him and still cares about him after everything. After every let down and never being there, he should want to try.

Dan's expression grows frustrated. "No, it can't wait. I was going to stop by your house later today, but it seems like you don't have time anyway. So, I'll quickly tell you right now. I'm getting married next week if you want to come. The wedding is on Friday."

"That's news. I'll have to see. I work on Friday, but maybe I can pull some strings."

News? He didn't say good news or great news—just news. I like to see the best in people. I like to give people grace. Although, I'm having a really hard time seeing something positive to cling to about his dad.

"Yeah?" Dan runs a hand through his hair.

"Yeah. I have to go. But we'll talk later."

"Okay, bye." The ping of the phone call ending is almost instantaneous.

Dan sits on the edge of the bed.

"Do you think he'll come?" I ask him softly after a few minutes go by.

I can't see his expression anymore, but I know he's clearly hurt. He slouches his back. "No, but, hey, at least it was a maybe this time. Not a flat out no."

I sit up and scoot my knees along the bed, enveloping him with my arms. I hug him from behind, and he relaxes into me.

He sighs, scrubbing a hand through his dark hair. "I'm sorry. He has a way of putting me in a mood."

"It's okay. I understand why. He wasn't very pleasant," I mumble against his back, tracing my hands over his chest. I change the subject in hopes of getting his mind off of that conversation. "Maybe some coffee would do the trick? And then we can drive to Texas to tell Carter, Eve, and Bella?"

He chuckles, making his body shake in my arms. "Coffee would be great. That might be a far trip. If we had more time, I would. How about we call them?"

"Sounds like a plan." I have a feeling this is going to be a much better phone call. At least I hope so.

I get dressed, and Dan makes the bed. He starts a pot of coffee and a cup of tea for me. We pack our bags, and then he calls his brother, putting the phone on speaker.

"Hey, brother," Carter answers almost instantly. Barking dogs and conversation fill the background. "Let me go to the break room for a minute."

A few seconds pass until we hear Eve's voice in the background. "Who is it?"

"It's Dan," Carter responds.

"Marigold's here too. I have you on speaker," Dan explains.

"And Marigold," Carter says. "I'll just put you guys on speaker too. There's no one else around just in case you don't want anyone listening when you tell us you're moving to another country or that you eloped or something."

Pretty close. Funny story...

"Hi, Marigold." Eve's voice is jovial.

I try my best to sound excited for the conversation we're about to have. "Hi, Eve!" I wipe my hands over my lap.

Dan clears his throat. "Marigold and I have some good news. We're getting married."

He really got that out of the way fast. Here I was working myself up trying to figure out a way to tell them.

Eve's the first to say something. "Oh, this is great news! Congrats!"

"I wasn't too far off with my eloping theory. But I'm happy for you two," Carter chimes in.

"How did you propose? Tell me everything," Eve says.

"The thing is, well, it's complicated," I say. Dan wraps an arm around my shoulder.

"How so?" Carter prods.

Dan looks at me and goes to answer, probably wanting to down play it, but I shake my head no. I tell them the truth like I told his mom and stepdad.

"Can we speak to Marigold alone for a minute?" Carter asks after I finish.

I should be nervous, but I'm not. They're probably worried. They only have Dan's best interests in mind.

"Anything you have to say, you can say in front of me too." Dan looks at me. His expression is full of compassion.

"It's okay, Dan," I reassure him. "I'm okay."

"I don't like this." Dan lowers his arm from my shoulders and stands. "But I'll give you a minute." Dan gives me a parting look full of worry before he steps outside onto our small, private balcony.

Carter waits a few beats and clears his throat. "I'm not trying to tell you not to marry him or anything. I know Dan was the one who offered to marry you in the first place. I also know that you need to save Fix-Its, but he's been hurt before. I just can't bear to see it happen again and not say anything."

"I would never hurt him," I say, knowing that to be the truth. "I know it may be hard for you to believe me since you've only met me once. But I would never hurt him intentionally."

"We believe you." Eve speaks for both of them. "You're good for him," she adds. "We want to see you two together. We're rooting for you. Dan has been happier lately."

Carter hums in agreement. "Yeah. He even calls more now. He shut himself off from everyone after Kate left him. I don't know what all he's told you, but she mailed him the divorce papers... She didn't even bother coming home to tell him. They were long distance for a while, and that's hard enough in the first place. They were young. But that doesn't mean it didn't hurt him. He turned to work as a coping mechanism. I hated seeing him like that.

Especially after our dad. It took him a long time to move on. Now, you're a big reason for his happiness."

"Do you love him?" Eve asks.

The question is *simple*. The answer is *simple*: yes or no. Still, I've never been in love before. What Dan and I have is special. There's a steady spark building between us. It feels like it could be love.

"I think I might," I admit.

"Well, then everything will work out." Eve sounds optimistic.

"All we can do is hope," Carter says.

"I'm sorry," I reply. I truly am sorry that we're in this predicament in the first place, but I can't do anything to change the past. I can't change my mom's mind. I can't lose Fix-Its without trying to save it first.

"There's nothing to be sorry about," Eve reassures. "We just worry about Dan. But we have faith that everything will work out. You give each other lovey-dovey eyes."

Carter laughs, and I giggle.

Eve is the second person to say that Dan and I look at each other with certain eyes. Wyatt was the first.

"Eve's right. Love-dovey eyes. Tell Dan we said goodbye, and we'll see you both this Friday."

Eve's tone softens. "And, Marigold, if you need anything... anything at all, please call."

"I will. Thank you." I hang up the phone and set it on the bed beside me.

I glance at the seashell-patterned wallpaper. I didn't know that Kate left Dan that way. If I'd known, I probably would've never agreed to him marrying me because I don't want to hurt him. He's been through enough. He deserves to do this for the right reasons—for happiness and love. My thoughts don't do much to quell my doubts, but in the meantime, I need to focus on the present. I can at least enjoy the rest of the day with Dan.

I head for the door to the balcony and open it.

Dan is leaning against the railing and turns as soon as he hears me. "Are you okay?" His hair is a mess, probably from running his fingers through it in worry.

"Yes, everything's fine. They're just looking out for you. That's all."

He walks toward me. "They weren't mean, were they?"

I laugh at the idea of Carter and Eve being mean. They are probably some of the nicest people I've met. "No, neither of them have a single mean bone in their body. They care about you. That's all."

"You promise?" He follows me into our hotel room and shuts the door, pulling me into a hug.

"I promise." I raise on my toes and kiss him.

He sighs, wraps me tighter in his arms, and rests his head on mine. "Did they tell you?" I don't have to see him to know he's worried. I also don't need to ask to understand the extent of his question.

"Yes, I'm sorry about what happened with Kate." I don't need to ask why he didn't tell me. I know what it feels like to want to be separated from things that happened in the past. It's in a different context, but I understand him.

"I'm not." His voice rumbles, chin bobbing over my head. "I would have never ended up with you. And that would be a damn shame. Because you, Goldie, are extraordinary."

"You're pretty great yourself." I smile against his chest.

We stand like this, wrapped around each other for a few minutes until he mutters, "Let's go home."

When we get in the car and onto the highway, I stare out the window. I swivel my necklace as I watch the beach grow further away. The sounds of the seagulls and the waves lapping the shore become a distant memory.

I think about the trip with my parents here and the happiness I felt in this place. I also can't help but wonder what is written in the letter that sits unopened on my kitchen island. *Is it the key to all my questions?*

"I miss her," I say, watching the beach disappear fully.

Dan rests a hand on my leg. "I know."

Chapter 34

DAN

"Can I please get all of your pink flowers?" I scan over the sea of flowers overflowing from every open space in the NSSG. There's plenty of pink.

Should be enough.

Violet's eyes bulge. "All of them? Like every single one..." She darts her eyes around the shop.

"Yes, please." I tuck my thumbs in my pockets. "Well, as many as you can find. Any shade of pink will do."

She flips open a calendar. "When do you need them by?"

I hope two days isn't too last minute. "Friday morning, please."

Violet gulps. "I can make that work. Where would you want them delivered or can you pick them up?"

"Either way works for me. But if you can deliver them to the pavilion that would be great."

"I can do it, and I'll arrange them too." Violet leans over the counter. She looks around and whispers, "Is it true? Is Constance actually telling the truth? Are you and Marigold getting married? Because I never know what to believe anymore. Constance can really turn a small thing into a far-fetched story. And I'm actually kind of excited if it's true. Plus, the flowers. What else would they be for? One heck of a grand gesture if you ask me."

"Yes." I laugh. It's not exactly a secret, but small town gossip travels fast.

"No way. I—sorry." She covers her mouth, holding back laughter. "I'm letting the gossip fiends get to me. It's making me crazy."

"That's okay. You and Dustin will be there, right?"

"Yes, we will be. And I'm sure Olive, Mason, Henry, and pretty much the whole town will be too. Even the chickens!"

"I figured." I laugh.

She moves to look at her laptop. "I wouldn't even know how to come up with a number for that many flowers. How about I bring over an invoice once I figure it out?"

"Perfect. Thanks, Violet. I'll see you Friday." I turn to leave.

I take a few steps, but she hollers, "See you then! Oh, and congrats on your engagement!"

I glance over my shoulder. "Thank you." I wave and head to Chloe's Closet.

I need plenty of things... starting with a suit, a cake, and a ring.

Marigold mentioned she dreamed of a grand wedding, and I'll be damned if I let her have anything less, even if it takes me up until Friday to get everything in place. Getting married may have started as a means to save Fix-Its, but I also want to show Marigold what she deserves and how much I care for her.

"I missed you too." I chuckle when Buttercup runs to me, pushing her snout against my hand while I walk into Fix-Its. Her tail wags back and forth until I pick her up.

"She really did miss you. She missed us both when we were gone," Marigold says. I tilt my head to the source of her voice. She leans in the doorway of the office.

"Hey, Fiancée." I grin.

Marigold's face flushes pink. "Hi, Fiancé."

Buttercup snorts, and I say, "They grow up so fast."

"Too fast." Marigold juts out her bottom lip. "She's already almost four pounds. I'm going to miss her being so little."

"Stop growing so fast," I say to Buttercup. She oinks as I set her on the ground and rolls onto her side. I rub her belly until she deems it enough and squeals as she takes off through the store.

I straighten my back and laugh. "Where's everyone? Where's Daisy and Harvey?"

"Daisy's on her lunch break. And my dad's on the road again." Marigold smirks and leaves the doorway. She holds my hands, leaning toward me. "He's on a quest to right a wrong."

I lean in a little and ask, "Where's he headed?"

Marigold smiles brightly. "Funnily enough, near where we just left, Assateague Island by Ocean City. He's going to ask Eleanor to be his date to the wedding. Our wedding." She pauses, scrunching her brows. "Does it feel weird for you too? This whole *us getting married thing*? I don't know what to think. A few days ago, we were dating, and now, we're planning to get married. This is all new to me. Being in a relationship. Falling for someone. We haven't even had our first fight yet. And now this weight hangs over my head. And yours. Are you sure you want this? Want to go through this again? It's not too late for you to say otherwise. I'll understand."

"I want this. I want you." I tilt her chin. "I want to help save this place. Look around. Everything holds a story. You've worked incredibly hard to restore everything. You can't let it go. Not if you can do something about it, and I can help. I want to help."

I would do anything for her if it meant she was happy. I will get married again. I'll do it for her because Marigold is special. She brings a lightness to my life. Marigold is the most beautiful person I've ever met, inside and out. Kate and I wanted different things in life. We were young and got married because we were high school sweethearts. We felt invincible, but the long distance was a wedge for us. It was too soon for us to be apart. She mailed me divorce papers with no explanation, and it broke me. For a long time, I believed the lie that I didn't want to find love again. I didn't think I'd want to be married again, but Marigold is showing me what real love feels like. It's exhilarating.

Chapter 35

MARIGOLD

Hummingbirds flutter their wings as they drink sugar water from the feeders on my front porch. I take the last sip of warm Irish Breakfast tea and set my empty mug on the end table. The wicker bench creaks as I cross my legs pretzel style.

I pick up the letter on the cushion beside me. It feels heavy in my hand, almost like lead. The letter itself weighs almost nothing, but what's written inside has plagued my mind for the past few days.

Is there an explanation? Is it a goodbye? Is it short or long? Will it break me? Will it ease my worries and solidify the decision to marry Dan?

I desperately want to know what's inside. I'm getting married today, so I can open it. However, I worry that once I know what's inside, there's nothing left to wonder about. It'll be the last words I read from her and that's what has kept me from opening it.

The front of the letter is inscribed in her beautiful calligraphy. The dots of her I's were always a heart, just like the I in my name on the front.

To Marigold. Open on your wedding day. Love, Mom.

My hands are shaky as I carefully peel the seal loose. A soft breeze blows past, striking the wind chimes as I pull the letter from the envelope. The folded piece of paper shakes between my trembling fingers. I shut my eyes, listening to the birds chirping and the water flowing from the stream.

I haven't unfolded the letter yet, but tears well in my eyes anyway. I'm sad because I miss her so much.

I'm scared to open it. After at least ten minutes, I work up the courage to unfold the letter. I finally read it.

My sweet Marigold,

If you're reading this, I'm sorry. I truly am. All I've ever wanted was for you to be happy. I wanted you to experience the adventures. Paint the strokes on your canvas of life with your own style and technique. Right now, you might feel like I'm contradicting that. I'll explain everything.

Do you remember when we'd run through the fields of flowers behind the paint studio? We were carefree. And you, my darling, would always bring that teddy bear of yours. We'd have pretend wedding ceremonies. I know you're close to twenty-six now and won't appreciate being reminded of Mr. Fluffy. But I saw how much your dreams meant to you. I know you wanted to be married some day.

It was never my intention to force you into anything. But it feels like this is the only choice I have control over at the moment. This trust. This marriage condition was my only way to guarantee your happiness. To ensure it. I'm sorry that I'm going to miss out on so much of your life. I'm living on borrowed time while writing this letter. I know you'll be okay. You and your dad have each other. My love for you is timeless. I am proud of you. I love you. And I wish that you get every single bit of happiness you dreamt of. Just know I'll always be looking out for you and cheering you on from Heaven.

P.S. There's a jewelry box in my paint studio. In the bedroom closet, there's an access panel to the attic. The box will be right on the edge. The necklace I gave to you on your sixteenth birthday is the key.

Love,

Mom

I wipe the tears from my eyes. I don't give myself a second to process. Instead, I rush inside, grab a stool from the kitchen, and beeline to my bedroom. Buttercup scurries across the floor, following me. I open my closet doors and set the stool under the square panel on the ceiling. Dust falls through the opening as I lift the panel to the side. I reach around until my hand connects with a box. I lower it from the attic and take it to the kitchen. Using a wet rag, I wipe away years of dust, revealing little painted flowers over dark wood. My fingers work to unclasp the necklace around my neck for the first time in forever. I slide the key into the keyhole, turning it until a click sounds.

The box creaks as I open it. A gold bracelet with blue opals sits at the center with a piece of paper tucked underneath it.

My sweet Marigold,

This is your something old and something blue. This was your grandmother's. And then mine. I wore it on my wedding day. I would love for you to have a piece of us both with you.

Love,

Mom

My heart fills with warmth as I hold the bracelet. It's beautiful. I trace the opals, and tears fall from my eyes, blurring my vision. Buttercup's snout pushes against my leg, and I smile at her. I place the bracelet back and lift Buttercup into my arms, hugging her to my chest.

"Just a few more," Daisy says as she fastens the buttons going up my back.

I watch myself in the full length mirror. The dress I'm wearing is breathtaking. The fabric is smooth. It's floor length and has puffy short sleeves. The champagne fabric has a hint of pink. Beth, the seamstress in town, made it for me. That was really sweet. I insisted on paying for it, but she wouldn't take anything for the dress. I thought it was because she felt bad for me. I thought the whole town knew the story of why I'm getting married. Instead, when I checked the article that was published two days prior, it wasn't there. There was only an announcement of our wedding. It listed when and where. It's unusual for details to be left out of an article. I, for one, am grateful that it was left out.

"You're all set." Daisy's voice wakes me from my thoughts.

"Thank you for everything." I hug my best friend.

"I have one more thing for you," she says, grabbing a bag from my bedroom floor. She hands me a shoebox. "Something new."

I gasp when I open the box. I pull out light pink converse with embroidered flowers. "Did you make these?"

"Yes." Daisy shrugs. "I didn't think heels were really your style, so I wanted to do something special. This way you can be comfortable. And they're your something new if you need it."

I hug her again. "You really are an amazing friend. Thank you for being here for me today. For always being there."

"You're welcome," Daisy says, pulling away. "Now, I need to get ready." She grabs her bag and heads for the door.

Knock. Knock.

"Can I let whoever is out there in?" Daisy asks.

"Yes." I nod.

Daisy leaves as Marlene, Eve, and Bella walk in, smiling.

"You look lovely," Marlene whispers, taking my hands and giving them a squeeze. She lets go and rifles through her purse.

"The understatement of the year." Eve gushes. "She looks ethereal."

"Pretty." Bella giggles, beaming a smile in my direction.

"And you are just beautiful," I tell her. She does a spin, and her pink dress swirls in the air. A butterfly clip fastens her hair in an updo. Two sections of curls fall from both sides, framing her face. I'm glad she's here. I'm glad they're all here.

"I have something for you," Marlene says, handing me a hair pin with pearls. "It can be your something borrowed if you'd like it to be." Warmness emanates from her.

"I would love it to be." I smile, holding the pin and flipping it over in my hands.

"Allow me," Eve says, taking the pin from me. She tucks it into my half-up braid. "There. You look ready to get married."

I wish I felt as ready on the inside as I look. My stomach is a ball of nerves. *You need to do this.*

Another knock sounds on the door. "Who is it?" I call out.

"I'm here to discuss your car's extended warranty." My dad's voice is instantly recognizable.

"That's too bad. I don't have a warranty. But the word on the town is that my next-door neighbor, Harvey, has a warranty he would love to discuss with you." I chuckle. "Come in Dad."

Marlene and Eve laugh, and then Bella asks, "What's a warranty?"

Eve's eyes crinkle as she explains it to Bella.

My dad introduces himself to everyone. Then Marlene, Eve, and Bella leave my room, sending me warm wishes.

My dad takes a seat in the rocking chair. "You look so much like your mother, kiddo."

"Thanks." I smile. It means a lot to me because I always thought she was the most beautiful woman in the world.

"Look at you. You're all grown up and independent. And I'm still having a hard time wrapping my mind around what you've done with the store. It's never been this profitable. The carts. They are a wonderful idea. I'm so proud of you." His voice cracks. "Are you sure you want to do this?"

I spin the bracelet on my wrist. "I think so. Yeah, I actually think I do."

"Well, I hope that you're doing this for you and no one else." He stands from the chair.

"I am. I want to save Fix-Its."

"Good." He nods, seeming content with my answer.

"How was your trip?" I raise a brow wondering if Eleanor is here, but I don't want to come right out and ask.

He pats my shoulder. "It went well…"

He doesn't say more, so I ask, "And by well, do you mean Eleanor is here?"

"Yeah, she is." He grins, looking at the floor. "Okay, well, I'll see you in the car, kiddo."

"Okay," I say. He leaves, shutting the door behind him. I smile, smoothing my hands over my dress as I look out the window.

I'm happy for him. I've wanted him to find someone again for years, and he finally has opened his heart again. He might not have said much, but I know he will when he's ready. The way he left the room just now was more than enough confirmation to me. He practically skipped with happiness.

Dark clouds float in the sky way in the distance. It's almost like a bad omen. However, I'm going to ignore it because I have enough worrying going on in my mind without a storm to add to that list.

I wish I could talk to Dan one last time. I can't, though. So, I mentally prepare myself to leave this room and head to town for *my wedding.*

Chapter 36

DAN

"Hey, son, how are you feeling?" my stepdad asks as he walks from the center aisle.

I grin, patting the fold-up chair beside me. "Ready. Anxious. Happy."

He sits down next to me. I stare at my hands in my lap. "Sounds about right," Jim says. "I remember my weddings. I had the same mix of emotions both times. But the second time I got it right."

I look up from my lap. "How did you know it was going to work out when you were married again?"

He scratches his head. "I didn't." He laughs. "I hope you weren't expecting some wise, all-knowing words of wisdom from me. It will work out if it's meant to. And taking the chance is scary. But it's worth it. For love."

I lift my chin. "Thanks. That helps." For love is exactly what I thought too. Love is what will make everything work out as long as it's reciprocated. I'm not sure if it is. I never spoke up. I never asked.

I brush my hands over my lap and slouch my back. I can't help but ask the question eating away at me. I don't want it to bother me. I don't want to care, but I do. "Did he show up yet?" I really don't need to be let down right now. A part of me wishes I was wrong about him and that, for once, my dad would actually be here.

"No, I'm sorry, son." Jim pats my shoulder. "There's still time. Don't come to any conclusions quite yet."

"Yeah," I say. I already know he's not coming, though. He never called like he said he would. He makes promises he can't keep, like usual. It shouldn't hurt me anymore. I'm grown. I expect it. However, it does hurt. Old wounds leave scars. Sometimes they're invisible to the eye because they're behind the walls I build, not letting anyone see. Marigold's the exception. She knows everything about me—even the secrets I've never shared with anyone else.

Maybe instead of letting my dad's absence wreak havoc on my thoughts, I should be grateful. My brother is here. My mom, Eve, and Bella are here. Jim is here, and he always calls me son. I like that he has considered me part of his family from the start. He never treated me differently even though he has kids from his previous marriage. He's been more of a dad to me than my biological dad has ever been. That's when it clicks in my mind. He is my family. Jim's my dad. Blood doesn't mean that I have to put up with the hurt any longer. My family is all here. The people that truly want to be are.

"Thanks for the advice, and thank you for being here," I tell Jim, hoping that he understands what I'm trying to convey. I appreciate him.

"I wouldn't want to be anywhere else. Watching you get married. And seeing how much you've changed in just a few months. I have an inkling that it'll all work out."

"That means a lot to me." I brush the lint from my dress slacks and check my watch. I have minutes before the wedding starts. "I'd better get ready."

We both stand, and Jim hugs me, clapping me on the back.

I take my spot under the wooden arch as the rest of the guests have a seat.

Constance comes out of nowhere, startling me. "Are you ready to get married?" she asks with a joyful lilt in her tone.

I nod, grinning. "I'm ready."

Her lips form into a line, and she clutches the papers in her hands to her chest. "Hey, Dan..."

"Yeah?"

Constance gives me a half-smile. "I know the real reason why you're getting married. And I left it out of the article. It felt wrong to share something like that."

I shake my head, shocked. "I appreciate that." For once, she kept something to herself. Do I know how she found out? No. One may never know. However, I appreciate her not broadcasting it. It was the right thing. "There's other reasons we're getting married, you know." Why am I telling her this? I don't know.

"Is there? What might that be?" She looks at everything in the pavilion besides me.

"I love her," I tell Constance, wanting to make sure that the truth is known. My intentions have shifted. I am marrying for love.

"Oh—well." She's speechless. and a glimmer in her eye lets me know that she's quite happy about this development. Maybe she already knew. "Well love is wonderful. Isn't it?" she whispers.

"Yes it is." I bob my head. That is something we can agree on.

The music starts. Constance and I take our places. She was the only officiant that I could find that would officiate our wedding this last minute. I look around at the sea of pink flowers, hoping that Marigold loves them.

The bridesmaids and groomsmen walk down the aisle in pairs, taking their places beside the wooden arch. Carter and Eve both wink at me. My mom and stepdad are seated in the front row. They share a look, wiping tears from their eyes. Daisy grins as she takes her spot. The flower girl, Bella, walks down the aisle next, dropping pink petals as she goes. Her smile is bright, and it makes me choke up. She gives me a thumbs up, and I grin.

The music shifts. Marigold and her dad start walking down the aisle. My breath catches in my throat. She's beautiful. She's stunning. There isn't a word strong enough to describe how incredible she is. Her flowy, light-pink dress looks as if it was made specifically for her. Her dad looks proud as he walks slowly, holding onto her arm.

I shift on my feet and grin at her, unable to pull my gaze away. Her cheeks turn pink to match the flowers, and she smiles shakily. I can tell she's nervous, and so am I. Well, I was.

Seeing her makes me feel at ease. There's not a doubt in my mind. I love her, and I want to spend the rest of my life with her, regardless of whether we're married or not.

Chapter 37

MARIGOLD

Constance, the officiant, says the normal string of words that I've heard many times in my favorite movies right before the couples get their happily ever after. She asks Dan if he'll take me as his wife as long as we shall live. My stomach churns.

"I do," Dan says with confidence immediately after Constance finishes. His smile is dashing. The dimples on this man make me weak in the knees. Dark hair curls around the tips of his ears. The pressure of his large palm against my clammy hand is comforting, but my fingers shake slightly. The movement is barely noticeable yet enough to make his brows draw together. I know that he knows I'm having doubts.

Husband.

Dan's going to be my husband. No. This is all wrong. I can't go through with this. I can't force him into getting married again, not after he got his heart broken. I can't hurt him like Kate did. I swore to his brother and sister-in-law that I'd never hurt him intentionally. So, what am I doing right now? I'm about to hurt this man who has been nothing but wonderful to me. This was a mistake, one I should have realized *before* I made it this far. I could've backed out this morning, on the drive here, or when I walked down the aisle. No, I had to wait until I stood at the wooden arch, moments after Dad gave me away. He looked so proud too. Well, he still does look proud when I turn my head to catch a glimpse of him sitting in the front row. His daughter is getting married... maybe. I don't know what I want to do yet. There were tears in his eyes. Legitimate tears were falling. My father has never cried in front of me before today.

I notice the flowers. They're everywhere. Pink flowers encompass the pavilion. I know it was Dan's doing. It melts my heart. It's literally the grandest gesture of them all.

But this is marriage, I remind myself.

I would do anything—almost anything—for the things and the ones I love. Yet, I can't go through with this. It's not right. It's not fair to Dan because...

I love him.

I love Dan. How did I not realize what this was? *Love.* I can't hurt the people I love.

Constance's voice is a reminder of what I'm about to commit to. "To be your lawfully wedded husband."

I missed the first part, but I know what was said. I'm fully aware of what I'm supposed to say in return.

I do.

Do I?

Do I take the man before me to be my husband? In sickness and health? For better or worse? I can't. It's not because I don't want to. It's because I love him. I can't make him marry me, not for a store, for a place that feels like home, or for a legacy.

"I do." My voice is thick with nerves. It felt like an out of body experience. Did I just say that?

I don't. I don't. *I don't. That's what you should've said.*

Why does my voice fail me when my mind is certain?

"Dan and Marigold will now exchange—" Constance's voice is another reminder.

"Not! I do not!" I interrupt her sentence. Any other day, you couldn't catch me interrupting anyone, but this is a dire situation.

Gasps filter through the pavilion. Thunder erupts around us. *Thank you, weather.*

I give my sweet Dan a shaky smile of apology and whisper, "I'm really sorry." He looks to understand, but he also looks hurt by my words. I don't know if I'm making the right decision, but before I can contemplate it, I find myself running down the aisle. I follow the path of the park to nowhere and somewhere at the same time.

Thunder erupts from the sky again. Raindrops coat my skin, a stark contrast to the hot summer air. The material of my dress is soft in my hand, and my bracelet brushes my wrist. Knowing what the bracelet means to me, what Dan means to me, and what Fix-Its mean to me, it makes this all the more harder to do. I might lose everything.

"Wait!" Dan shouts, but I don't turn. I keep running through town, desperate to escape my problems—to fix this somehow. The drizzling rain turns into a torrential downpour. The rain pounds in my ears. The sheer force of it blurs my vision.

If I don't go back there, I could lose everything. However, I'm doing this for Dan. I will try to save Fix-Its another way. I have worked so hard to find my own way for once in my life. I can do this.

"Marigold, please wait!" Dan's voice is breathy as he almost catches up to me. I stop in front of Fix-Its, unable to see from the rain. I turn to find him standing a few feet away. His chest rises and falls, trying to catch his breath. "Please, hear me out." His voice sounds broken, and it breaks my heart more.

"I can't make you marry me, Danny! I can't force you to be my husband! This is all wrong!" I have to shout over the pouring rain. I need to stand by the decision I made.

He takes a few steps toward me.

"You're not forcing me to do anything." He brushes back his shaggy, rain-drenched hair from his forehead. Worry lines form on his face as he keeps the small distance between us.

"You didn't want to get married again unless you were sure that someone was your soulmate. Then you threw it all away… for me!" My voice cracks as tears mix with the rain. He steps closer to me until we're only inches apart. I shake my head. Tears continue to spill from my eyes. "I can't force you into this. It isn't right. You're supposed to marry someone you love. Especially after your parents divorce. After your divorce. You didn't want to settle down again unless you knew it was right. This is wrong. I can't do this to you. I'll have to fight for Fix-Its but not like this. It's just a store. *This is your life.* I will always hold the memories of my mom and my grandparents right here." I place my hand over my loudly thumping heart. "And there are other ways I can fight this. I can get a lawyer and contest the will in court, or I can get a loan to buy Fix-Its when it's on the market."

His deep mahogany gaze is full of determination. His eyes don't waver from mine even for a second. "I *want* to marry you. It's that simple."

The rain continues to pour. The sky crashes with a loud boom of thunder that sends a shiver down my spine. "I know you want to. To help me. But this is bigger than a place," I say loudly, hoping he hears me over the rain.

The heat wave that's lasted for weeks is gone. My whole body feels cool from the water pelting my arms. My heart is racing so fast in my chest; I feel like it might burst. If he comes any closer, I might change my mind, but I don't want to.

"Yes it is." He walks closer to me. Pressing a palm against my cheek. He caresses the side of my face with his thumb. His touch is comforting, warm, and everything to me at the same time. "Because I love you, Goldie. I want *you*. I wouldn't have agreed to marry you if I didn't feel anything. I want to be your husband. I want to see your smile every single day for the rest of my life. Actually, I need it. This isn't a want, Marigold. It's a damn need. I need you in my life. I long to call you *my wife*. My *love*. My *everything*. I won't settle for less. But only if that's what you want too."

Butterflies fill my stomach with his words.

I laugh hysterically as the rain pelts my face. I must look ridiculous, but Dan doesn't seem to mind. He laughs along with me. He holds my head in his hands. Our faces are inches apart as his lips hover over mine. I bite my lip while my eyes trace the dimple indents at the edges of his smile.

He kisses me, pressing his lips against mine slowly. It's soft and full of meaning. His lips move in tandem with mine, and I feel the kiss all the way to my toes. The rain mixes with tears, love, and hope. Then my mind clears. The rain seems to slow almost instantaneously.

"I love you too," I say as I pull back. "And I want that. Everything you said. I do."

Dan pokes my nose. "Let's get married before you lose everything you worked for. Fix-Its is thriving right now because of you."

A thought pops into my mind. "So, is this considered our first fight?" I ask, flashing a lopsided grin.

"I don't really consider this fighting. More like having a conversation and working through things together. But if you want to consider it a fight, it is one."

"Well, then I like fighting with you, Danny." I bite my lip.

"Me too." He grins, and then gets on one knee.

I look around, unsure of what's going on. "What are you doing?"

He chuckles and looks up at me. "Asking you the right way. Like I should've the first time." My heart skips a beat as he says, "I love you. You are the most wonderful woman I've ever met. Your smile is the best thing in the world. I don't know how I spent so many years working with you and never said more than a few words. I missed out. And I don't want to miss out on another day without you. So, Marigold Evans, will you marry me?"

"Yes." I laugh as I wrap my arms around his shoulders and kiss him.

Dan spins me through the air just like he did at the beach. "Then what are we waiting for? Let's get married," he declares.

This time I know in my heart that I want him. I want everything. I want a life with Dan.

Chapter 38

MARIGOLD

Later that day

"I do." I smile at Dan with hearts in my eyes. Obviously, there aren't actual hearts in my eyes, but I feel it: the love. I don't add a *not* this time. I don't feel a pit in my stomach. I do feel butterflies. I touch my bracelet, knowing my mom would be incredibly proud. I look heavenward, smiling there as if to tell her thanks in a way.

"Dan and Marigold will now exchange rings as a symbol of their love and commitment." Constance's voice is bright.

I let the happiness wash over me, and I look at my almost husband, Dan, seeing the same grin painted on his face. I hear an oink and little grunts. I turn to look down the aisle, pulling my eyes from Dan's. Buttercup comes rushing to her favorite person, Dan. It's almost like he trained her or something.

"Thank you." Dan pats Buttercup's head and unfastens the rings tied to her collar. I could melt right here, right now, with how sweet this is.

Dan hands me his ring while holding mine out too.

His voice cracks as he starts. "I know that you've always dreamt of exchanging vows. The kind that are completely unprepared. And now, I intend to make it a reality. I'm going to try my best." He pauses, looking into my eyes. "Marigold, I love you more than I could ever begin to express with words. You have brought me immeasurable happiness. I constantly think of you when we're not together. And I vow to always show you that you deserve the world. I vow to make sure that your gummy worm stash is never ending." The pavilion erupts in laughter, and he swipes a hand over his face, eyes glossy. "I vow to bring you pink marigolds because they remind you of your mom. I vow to always find a table in the corner so we can hide out from people together. I vow to be your forever Ping-Pong teammate. And that comes with a lot of losing because of me. And maybe a few more Ping-Pongs vaulting at my face. But you'll be there by my side to make sure I'm okay." Dan chuckles, and I laugh with tears in my eyes. Marlene and Jim also cackle from the front row. "I vow to do everything in my power to bring a smile to your face. Just like the one you have now. I vow to always have coffee as soon as I wake up so that

I'm never moody. I vow to make you my famous pancakes. And I'll continue to give you my hats because they look better on you." His words make my face warm. "You are the reason I've learned to live again. To stop working my life away. To embrace every moment. And I vow to love you forever." His hand trembles as he slides the ring onto my finger. "I vow to spend the rest of my life with you."

Tears trickle down my face, and my lip trembles. His words render me speechless. I wipe away my tears. I gasp when I realize the ring is my moms. I look at my dad seated in the front row. I shift my eyes to the woman with a radiant smile sitting next to him. I'm assuming this is Eleanor. I glance back at my dad again. He nods in a way that reassures me of his happiness. Everything feels right in the world.

I squeeze his hands. "Dan, Danny, Tinker Dan." I hide my blushing face for a few seconds before uncovering it. "You made it almost impossible to go after that." More laughter surrounds us. "I normally avoid this kind of thing. Events." I don't take my gaze from Dan's as I continue my vows. "But with you, the crowd of people is the furthest thought from my mind. You manage to calm my nerves when we're together. You make me feel comfortable. At ease. I can be myself when I'm with you." My smile grows. "You've shown me what love feels like. You've ruined my favorite movies for me, honestly. Because none of them compare to our story. Our love. You're patient. You're kind. You listen to me. You remember everything. I mean, look at all the pink flowers. This is seriously

Max coded. I know you don't watch *Gilmore Girls*, but we'll have to remedy that. And I vow to talk your ear off. I vow to always be there for you. I vow to go on road trips with you because even if we're sitting in comfortable silence, there's no one else I'd rather be with. And we can sing *Wannabe* together. I vow to always run across the road to save chickens. I vow to always love you too. And I'm so ready to be your wife." I slide the ring onto his finger, and we both swipe tears from our eyes. "Thank you for making my dreams come true. These vows that came from the heart, well, they weren't a silly wish after all."

Following a few beats of the guests clapping and cheering, Constance speaks up, raising her voice an octave. "I now pronounce you husband and wife. You may kiss the bride."

When I kiss Dan, he sweeps me off my feet. I'm so in love.

This whole time, I've been trying to save a place. Fix-Its felt like home to me for my entire life. Now, I realize home is not a place or a pin on a map. Home is a person. Home is a state of mind. Home is a feeling. Dan, my dad, my mom, Daisy, Dan's family, Buttercup, this town, the people, and even the chickens are all my home. Home is love, and I've never loved anything more than my *home*.

Epilogue

DAN

One month later

"Can you please hold the ladder for me. I need to reach a little higher," Marigold calls from the top of the A-frame ladder.

I set down my paint pail and brush. "Anything for *my wife*." I grab the ladder. My grip is unwavering as Marigold steps two rungs higher.

"Thank you, *Husband*!" She waves her paint roller and drops some paint on my hat, making me chuckle. We wouldn't be painting if we weren't covered in some of it.

"What's so funny?" she asks as she rolls the paint on the exterior of Fix-Its.

"Just got some paint on me. That's all."

"Sorry." she mumbles.

I know she's probably biting her lip. She's always doing that when she feels bad.

"Don't be. It's my new favorite hat. Every time I wear it, I'll think of you," I say, reassuring her.

She laughs. "Okay, I'm done with this section. I'm coming down." She steps down the ladder, and I take the paint supplies from her.

"Can we go for a ride in your car after this is finished?"

"Yes." I kiss her lips, feeling as breathless as the first time I kissed her.

The front door to Fix-Its opens, and out comes Eleanor and Harvey, holding hands.

"Wow, you kiddos are doing great. The place looks brand new." Harvey shields his eyes and traces his gaze over the painted brick.

"Thanks, Dad."

"We're headed for a walk." Eleanor smiles at Marigold.

"Sounds romantic," Marigold says, adjusting her hat.

Harvey grins at Eleanor. "We're going on a romantic walk."

"That sounds nice," Eleanor replies to him. They wave and head toward the park.

I'm glad to see Harvey and Eleanor happy. It seems that their happiness has only brought more joy to Marigold. I know she worries about her dad. Now that he isn't alone anymore, I think she worries less. Harvey's still working part time but plans to stay with Eleanor in Maryland for half the year.

"They give each other the *I-really-like-you* eyes," Marigold whispers as they walk away, headed down the sidewalk.

"They do. I have the *I-really-love-my-wife* eyes," I say, wiping my finger along a wet streak of paint on her cheek.

She blushes, covering her face. "Well, I have the *I-love-my-husband* eyes."

"No really in there?" I tease her.

"Trust me. There are plenty of them in there." She bites her lip.

Marigold bends down and picks through her tool bag. "I need my cutting brush to get around the windows. Where is it?" she mumbles, pulling different tools from the bag. "Oh! This is yours. You left it that day we were fixing the golf cart. I completely forgot to give it back to you. Oops. Sorry, I hope you weren't missing it." She holds out an adjustable wrench to me.

"That's not mine." I shake my head. I'd know if I were missing a wrench. They're all hung in order above my work bench. There's not one missing... that I know of.

"What do you mean that's not yours?" She waves the wrench. "It's not mine."

"As a mechanic, I'm very particular about my wrenches." I lean down to look at it. "Are you positive it's not yours? I normally know the size wrench I need just by looking at the bolt. After working on cars so long, it's become second nature."

"That's news to me." She shrugs. "My tools have pink handles, Dan. It's not mine."

"Then whose would it be? Oh…" It clicks in my brain. Only two other people were there that day. One was busy fishing. The other is a master matchmaker.

"Yeah." Marigold nods, covering her face with a palm. "If it's neither of ours, I know now. It all makes sense." Realization dawns over her face.

Beep. Beep. The horn of The Chicken Coop golf cart honks as Constance comes driving down the street. *Speaking of the culprit.* She stops in front of Fix-Its. Blanche, the chicken, rides with her, sitting on the passenger seat. I've truly seen it all.

Constance runs her fingers through her gray hair. "Hey, lovelies. The place looks wonderful. I wanted to stop by to see if you have any thoughts on prospects for Daisy. The gossip mill and I are working on some matchmaking."

Matchmaking. That seems about right.

Marigold giggles. "Nope, I've got nothing. Good luck."

"What about her ex, Clay? Have you heard anything about him lately?"

Marigold shakes her head and does a zippering motion over her lips.

"Would you, by any chance, know where this came from?" I point to the wrench Marigold holds up, changing the subject.

Constance's eyes bulge. "Umm... Nope. Got to go." Blanche just perches on the edge of the seat as if she's hanging out with her.

Constance takes off in the golf cart as fast as it goes—a whopping fifteen miles an hour. So, it's less of a dramatic exit and more of a slow-moving turtle.

"That was the quickest mystery ever solved." I chuckle, crouching to my knees beside Marigold.

Marigold laughs, setting the wrench into her toolbox. "You're telling me."

THE END

Acknowledgements

To you, reader. Thank you for reading my words. I wouldn't be able to do this author thing without your support. I hope you fell in love with Marigold and Dan. And I hope the ending left a big smile on your face.

To my beta readers: Andrea, Jimena, Dara, Tiffany, Scott, and Sarah. Thank you for being AMAZING! Thank you for taking the time to read, give feedback, and suggest things that made this story even better. I was so excited when reading your reactions; there were plenty that made me laugh. I appreciate every single one of you. Thank you again.

To my editor, Haley. You are AWESOME. Thank you for catching everything and making this book flow so much better. I'm glad to have you as a friend.

To my ARC readers. Thank you for everything. For shouting into the void. For reading. For sending me messages. I don't have the words to express how much your support means to me. Thank you.

To my grandparents and my husband. Thank you for always encouraging me and supporting my dreams.

About the author

Sarah Madeline lives for small town romances and swoon worthy, tension filled moments. She fills her pages with laughter and happily ever afters. She resides in small town Pennsylvania with her husband, miniature dachshund, cat, and eighteen chickens. Hopefully adding some goats to her family soon. When she's not writing, you can find her reading in front of a warm fire, fishing, baking, or gardening.

Email: sarahmadelineauthor@gmail.com

Instagram: @sarahmadelineauthor

TikTok: @sarahmadelineauthor

Goodreads: goodreads.com/author/show/54572302.Sarah_Ma
deline

A Fowl Match is
the first book in
the Thornwood Valley
Series.

A Merry Pair is
the second book in
the Thornwood Valley
Series.